The
Calvin Coolidge
Home for
Dead Comedians

To Heather —

Live well!

Bradley Denton

10/2/10

THE CALVIN COOLIDGE HOME FOR DEAD COMEDIANS

BRADLEY DENTON

ILLUSTRATED BY

DOUG POTTER

THE WILDSIDE PRESS
NEWARK, NJ ◆ 1993

THE CALVIN COOLIDGE HOME FOR DEAD COMEDIANS

This one is for Barb, too.

"Skidmore" originally appeared in *The Magazine of Fantasy & Science Fiction*, May 1991. "The Calvin Coolidge Home for Dead Comedians" originally appeared in *The Magazine of Fantasy & Science Fiction*, June 1988. "The Sin-Eater of the Kaw" originally appeared in *The Magazine of Fantasy & Science Fiction*, June 1989. "The Hero of the Night" originally appeared in *The Magazine of Fantasy & Science Fiction*, January 1988. "The Territory" originally appeared in *The Magazine of Fantasy & Science Fiction*, July 1992.

Printed in the USA by Baker-Johnson Printing

ISBN: 1-880448-36-X (26-copy lettered hardcover edition)
ISBN: 1-880448-37-8 (100-copy numbered hardcover edition)
ISBN: 1-880448-38-6 (300-copy trade hardcover edition)
ISBN 1-880448-89-0
FIRST EDITION: NOVEMBER 1993

CONTENTS

INTRODUCTION
BY HOWARD WALDROP

Long 'bout grandfather time, say mebbe Plenty Many-Less Many-86, I was at the opening ceremonies at an SF convention in Kansas City MO.

A woman walked in the room. I immediately wanted to fall down and have *all* her children.

She was about 4'6" and cute as a button. There was some geek with her, obviously as smitten as I was, walking along behind her all sappy-eyed, afraid to make any sudden movements lest he startle her like a fawn.

"Come with me to the Cash Bar," I said, offering her my arm, "and ditch the bozo." I nodded my head toward the boy-toy.

The guy looked at me. He had the kind of haircut they give you a free car wash with, and these Pepsi-Cola bottle-bottom glasses on. He must have known I was staring at them, because he took them off. Gah! It was worse. His eyes looked like Moon Pies! Gah!

"I mean, cut the sea-anchor, Baby," I said.

"My name is Barbara," she said, in her most charming Miss Manners voice, and turned me toward the ginzo. "Have you met my husband, Bradley?"

Well, friendships have been built on a lot less.

They lived somewhere out in the scenic flint hills of Kansas, Baldwin City to be exact, about a bazooka shot from Lawrence.

Once I warmed up to him, really made an effort, I found

7

that Brad could be fairly okay company.

Suddenly, six months later, I found myself showing them around Austin; they were moving here so Barb could get her M.L.S. at UT. Well, good, I thought, at least I'll get to look at Barb occasionally. So then they and their dog Watson and the two catlike creatures they tolerate moved down here, where they've been ever since, thanks to Barb's consummate library skills. (If we could only get them to move south of the river to Bubbatown, everything would be hunky-dory.)

Oh yeah, it turns out Brad writes a little, too.

Enough of this sarcastic humorous stuff.

As a general rule, great novel-writers are not great short story-writers. It's two entirely different types of work, folks.

Well, Brad breaks the old general rule.

I want to say right now in what total awe I am of Brad's novels and short stories.

Sure, you've read Wrack and Roll, his alternate history novel, which he wrote even before he met me. And what are you doing listening to me yammer if you haven't read his Buddy Holly Is Alive and Well on Ganymede, which is just out? and which is merely great?

What I've done that you haven't is to read his next novel, Blackburn, which is, in the old record business phrase, a True Monster, like, you know, "96 Tears" was the first time you heard it.

Well, good as they are they're, you know, novels. What you have in your hands is one of Brad's first two short story collections, here only six or seven years into his career, which should tell you something right there.

This volume is as wonderful (and sometimes as chilling) a reconnoiter into that field of SF and fantasy as it could and should be that you can find between covers. (This isn't hype talking. This is Howard.)

I don't want to talk about the individual stories; they speak fluently, as Errol Flynn said in another context. What I want to tell you about is what you will find in this book.

You will find what true salvation is all about in a couple of these stories; and it shows what a writer Brad is because sometimes it's pulling a trigger, and sometimes it's not. Sometimes, again, it's just standing there while whatever makes you you takes the beating and the killing.

Sometimes it's eating your Beanie Weenies under the strangest circumstances.

You will meet, in these five stories, the truly prosaic weird, and the truly weird weird. It is a dark (and funny) and a chilling (and wonderful) trip into our past (the one not found in any history book), our present (the news that never makes the bottom of page 32B or even CNN at 3 a.m.) and our future (is this really what those Greek-speaking Syrian goatherds had in mind for all of us 2000 years ago?).

There are a couple of scenes in this book that will stay with me the rest of my life; soon it will be your turn.

I can't describe what Brad's writing does to me; you'll have to experience it for yourself, and you'll know exactly what I'm not saying.

(And you couldn't have read "The Territory" before; as in the manner of all great short story writers, Brad's done it as an original for the collection.)

So come on in. The theatre's about to open. Get your Milk Duds and take a chair (fifth row, third seat in). Make yourself — well, comfortable . . .

I wish I could have written any of these stories less than five years on in my career. Yow!

And, since he moved to Austin, Brad's hair is better. Now his haircut looks like it came with a free set of steak knives.

YOUR PAL,
HOWARD WALDROP
OCTOBER 7, 1991

SKIDMORE

For a long time I wanted to kill a certain man of my acquaintance. He was the sort of man who professed peace, love, and liberal viewpoints, but treated people like shit. If my conscience had been that of an infant, I could have blown him away and suffered not an hour of guilt.

And I wouldn't be caught. I've never owned weapons, but it's an easy thing to steal a firearm and replace it without detection. I'm a good shot, too, but few know it. Certainly no one would suspect me. This is because I have the reputation of being a good boy. And so, by upbringing and training, I am.

But upbringing and training can be overcome.

Let me tell you about Skidmore.

Skidmore, Missouri. Population 447.

In Nodaway County, in the northwestern corner of the state. Farm country.

On Friday, July 10, 1981, a 47-year-old coon-dog breeder named Ken Rex McElroy climbed into his pickup truck in front of the D & G Tavern in Skidmore, on Missouri Highway 113. His wife, half his age, sat beside him.

More than thirty people, the moral heart of the community, stood nearby. They had all been part of a meeting at the American Legion hall that morning. The topic had been What to Do About McElroy.

McElroy, five foot eight, two hundred and sixty pounds.

McElroy, said to have cut off one of his wife's breasts.

McElroy, thief, arsonist, and rapist.

McElroy, convicted of second-degree assault for shooting the grocer.

McElroy, free on bond, with 25 days to file a motion for a new trial.

But the new trial had been held.

As McElroy sat in his pickup, a .30-30 steel-jacketed bullet shattered the rear window and caught him under his right ear. Then a .22 Magnum slug took off the back of his skull. More bullets followed, but they weren't needed. Somebody pulled McElroy's wife from the truck and took her into the bank. She was unhurt. Outside, the truck's engine raced. McElroy's foot was jammed down on the accelerator.

No killer was ever named. No one was arrested.

Justice.

I thought about Skidmore every day for the next six years, drawn there by an urge that was like an instinct. The parallel between McElroy and the man I wanted to kill was inescapable. Their methods of abuse differed, but they were of the same mold and spirit.

Nevertheless, when discussing McElroy's execution, as everyone in my part of the country did for a while, I expressed the horror of vigilantism that I believed was proper. This was a result of my upbringing and training.

I had always been a good boy.

Let me tell you what that means.

I have never been in a fight. As a child I was often beaten up, but that isn't the same thing. It is, in fact, the furthest thing from it. I took the blows, believing what my parents and church had taught me. When my lips bled and eyes swelled, I told myself that I would, as Jesus might say, inherit the earth.

I also told myself that I would behave no differently if I were stocky and tough instead of skinny and weak. My size had nothing to do with my values. Violence was wrong. Violence solved nothing. I knew this because I watched the TV news. I grew up during the war that was scored by body counts. I swore that I would never strike another person.

For several months during grade school, an older kid pounded me and my brother after we got off the bus to walk home. He threw us down in the ditch, then kicked us. Running did no good; he was fast. Fighting back did no good; he was stronger. Once, I gave in to my brother's insistence that we defend ourselves, and this taught me the price of betraying my convictions. We were beaten and trampled as we had never been beaten and trampled before.

Some weeks later, a friend invited me to spend a Friday night at his house. My parents said it was all right, and for the first time, I didn't get on the bus after school. I sent my brother off alone.

My friend lived near school, so we walked. On the way, we encountered a kid who didn't care for my friend. He shoved my friend; my friend shoved back. The kid then knocked my friend to the ground and punched him until blood ran from his nose. Then he punched him some more.

I stood by.

I was a good boy.

On the morning of Friday, July 10, 1987, I kissed my wife goodbye and watched her drive away down the gravel road. We were living in a crumbling farmhouse in the hills south of a Kansas college town, and she had to make the long trip in every day. I worried about her.

She worried about me, too. Things had not happened for me the way they had been supposed to, and this had made me bitter. Worse, I had been lied to, used, and ridiculed. The man I wanted to kill had been instrumental in these events.

My back ached. I slept little, and awoke scowling. I shouted at my wife. I refused to speak to friends when they telephoned. Worst of all, I couldn't work. In my profession, being unable to work is the same as being dead.

And so it was that as the profitless days stretched to weeks, my desire to kill that man of my acquaintance intensified. At the same time, my other instinct urged me toward Skidmore with increasing insistence.

On July 10, as I watched my wife drive away, I knew that I could resist no longer. I would have to answer one call or the other before the day was out. After a few minutes of indecision, I made the choice that I believed would be the easier to reconcile with my upbringing and training. I made sure that my dog had food and water, and then I climbed onto my motorcycle and left. The dog chased me down the road, and I had to stop and yell at him. He slunk back to the yard.

The trip would be one hundred and fifty miles, give or take ten. I had checked the atlas and memorized the roads. The day was hot and bright.

I took the most direct route: North on U.S. 59, then northeast across the Missouri River into St. Joe. North again on U.S. 71 to Maryville. West eleven miles on Missouri 46.

South four miles on 113.

Skidmore.

It was a few minutes before noon. The trip had taken four hours. My back hurt worse than ever, and I was hungry.

Skidmore: Two service stations, a grain elevator, church, post office, bank, cafe, and tavern. A few parked pickup trucks. Peeled paint and a rusty stop sign. No human being in sight.

The instinct that had brought me there was gone. Skidmore had been revealed as nothing more than a podunk town after the pattern of all the other podunk towns I had ridden through on the way. If anything, it was even less alive. It was worn down, decayed. Silent. The only thing Skidmore had to distinguish it was the killing of McElroy, and that had happened six years ago.

I ate a greasy cheeseburger at the cafe. The air-conditioning was weak, and my hair stayed sweaty. When the burger was gone, I nursed a Coke until my back felt better. A couple of stoop-shouldered farmers came in, and one asked if that was my bike out front. I said it was, and he said it looked sharp. Then they sat down across the room and ignored me. I left three quarters on the table, used the restroom, and went out. The waitress nodded. Her mouth was a dry pink line. She looked a hundred years old.

What had I expected?

I put on my helmet, got on the bike, and headed south. I would take a less direct way home, cutting west through the southeastern corner of Nebraska. Unfamiliar territory. I hoped it would be distracting. Since the urge that had brought me to Skidmore was gone, there was only one thing I wanted to do.

I was less than a mile out of town when the motorcycle died. I let it roll to a stop on the dirt shoulder of 113 before realizing that it was out of gas. I glanced down and switched the fuel valve to the reserve so I could return to Skidmore and fill the tank. As I looked up again, I glimpsed something to my right. I turned to see it.

In the ditch, Ken Rex McElroy was waiting.

A ragged, gaping hole took up most of the left side of his face. He climbed up from the ditch, and I saw that the back of his skull was gone.

"Welcome," he said.

Some of his teeth had been shot away. He was bloody.

"Welcome to Skidmore."

McElroy was big. Redneck big. His tattooed arms were like tree trunks.

I knew men like this. I had grown up with men like this. Men like this had beaten me up for practice when they were kids. He stood on the highway shoulder, staring at me with his dead eyes, and I was afraid of him. But even more, I hated him. I hated him as much as the man I wanted to kill.

"Get away from me," I said.

McElroy didn't move. "Ready to go?" he asked. His voice was flat. Stark.

I knew then that he wouldn't leave. "I have to get gas," I said.

He returned to the ditch. "I'll wait."

I was shaking, but I managed to start the bike and ride back to Skidmore. I bought gas from an old man who wanted to talk. The weather, the crops, the goddamned politicians and courts, all in a dull monotone. I left as soon as I had my change.

I would go home the way I had come. I would ride fast.

Just north of the Skidmore city limits, a right turn took 113 between two soybean fields. As I came out of the turn, I saw McElroy standing in the road ahead.

I stopped. McElroy waited. After a while, I let the bike idle up to him. He got on behind me.

The ride home was hard. McElroy was heavy, and I wasn't used to riding with extra weight. Once I lost control on a curve, and the bike veered into the left lane in front of a semi. I went off onto the shoulder, and the semi rushed past, blaring.

I was still more than seventy miles from home. I didn't think I would make it.

Then the mirror showed me a flash of silver in McElroy's eyes, and I didn't think I wanted to.

Let me tell you about a flash of silver.

One day during my eleventh summer, my grandfather, my father, my uncle, three of my male cousins, and my brother and I went tramping in my grandfather's pasture. The day was hot and bright. The adults had beer. Once in a while we kids were given a sip. My uncle carried a new .30-06 bolt-action rifle with a scope. It was a heavy weapon with a kick.

We gathered on one side of a pond that was maybe seventy yards across. On the far side, near the top of the dam, my uncle had placed a flattened beer can. It shone like a mirror. If I looked straight at it, my eyes hurt.

The others took shots at the can, and the dust that flew up showed where the bullets struck. The men each shot within two feet of the target. My cousins and brother did less well. No one hit it. I hung back, hoping they would forget to give me a turn. I had a terror of guns.

When everyone but me had fired, they started to walk around the pond. I hurried to join them, and my uncle saw me. He made them all stop, then handed me the rifle and grinned. The men and boys shaded their eyes and gazed across the water.

The weapon was even heavier than I had imagined. The barrel wavered as I brought the stock to my shoulder. My arms were white twigs.

But when the rifle was in place and I was squinting through the scope, everything felt different.

I let out my breath. The stock was smooth and warm against my cheek. The trigger nestled within my curled finger. My vision was sharp. I had become a thing of metal and wood, of crystalline sight. A thing of power.

The stock crunched against my shoulder. A crack of thunder numbed my ear. My power was gone, and I strained to see.

There was no puff of dust. I had fired over the dam.

"Pretty big gun for a little guy," my grandfather said. My father said nothing. I handed the rifle back to my uncle, and he winked at me. It was a consolation wink.

We walked around the pond and started across the dam. Then my uncle stopped above the beer can, and we all stared at it. A round hole had been punched through the middle. My uncle winked at me again.

One of my cousins said that it must have been his shot. But his bullet had sprayed dust, as had everyone's but mine. He had to know, as my uncle knew, that it was the runt, the white-armed bookworm, who had hit the target. Dead center.

My uncle gave me the can, and we headed back toward the house. I was proud. I put my thumb through the hole. Then I felt sick, and I dropped the can in the dirt.

As I had put my thumb through the hole, the beer can had changed. It had become the face of a kid who had taunted me throughout the preceding school year. It had become the face that had called me "Muskrat."

It had become the face that I had seen through the rifle scope, in the flash of silver across the pond.

It was after five when I made it back from Skidmore. McElroy was with me. My wife would be home soon.

My dog came running at the sound of the motorcycle, then saw McElroy and stopped. The hair on his back rose, and he growled.

McElroy stood in the driveway. "I liked dogs," he said.

I took off my helmet. "Well, this dog doesn't like you."

McElroy looked at me then, and I was scared.

"You don't have to be afraid," he said. "I don't get mad now. I don't feel nothing. I don't need nothing."

Hate suppressed fear. "Then why did you want to come here?"

"You're the one wants something."

McElroy walked toward the house. He moved stiffly. Wet stains smeared his brown shirt and pants. His suede cowboy boots were speckled with dark spots.

"What in hell would I want from a corpse?" I yelled. My voice echoed from the barn.

He stopped on the porch. Something dripped from his face and spattered on the cement.

I could hear my wife's car coming up the road, so I went

around McElroy and unlocked the door. He went inside.

I put him in the basement. It was mud-floored, dank, and cluttered with piles of junk that a previous tenant, long since deceased, had left there years ago. These were infested with mice. I had also seen a five-foot blacksnake down there once. I doubted that McElroy would mind.

He stayed in the basement whenever my wife was home. If we needed frozen food brought up, I made sure I was the one to go down and get it. He always stood in the corner beside the freezer. Spiders built webs on him. He didn't speak unless I did.

In August, I went to a week-long conference on the west coast. I knew that I should skip it, but I had bought my plane ticket before McElroy came home with me, and it was nonrefundable. So I talked my wife into staying with a friend in town, and I asked a neighbor to stop by and feed my dog. My wife would have known something was wrong if I'd spent money on a kennel. The poor dog would be scared the whole time, but McElroy wouldn't hurt him. I didn't think.

As it turned out, McElroy came with me.

I didn't know it until the plane was in the air. There had been two empty seats beside me, but when I returned from a trip to the lavatory, McElroy was in one of them. I had to squeeze past, sucking in my breath so as not to touch him. His wounds never dried.

I sat down. "Go back," I said. "People will be watching me this week."

McElroy gave me his stare. "You want me here."

A flight attendant came by and asked if I would like something to drink. She didn't ask McElroy. Her eyes avoided him. Blood smeared her sleeve when she reached across him to hand me a beer, and she didn't even notice.

A few days into the conference, I discovered that one of the attendees was very much like the man I wanted to kill. He was a master of ridicule, and he made it clear that he didn't consider me worthy of anything but contempt. During his most scathing comments, I had to suppress a laugh. What would he consider me worthy of, I wondered, if he knew what

waited in my room?

I thought then of what McElroy had done to the people of Skidmore, and of how they had reached a point beyond which they could take no more. I wondered how much I would be able to take before I reached that same point.

More, I believed. Much more. My upbringing and training had steeled me. I accepted my colleague's contempt and gave back a smile. I had higher limits than he could reach.

I was, after all, a good boy.

Let me tell you what that doesn't mean.

I've already said that I've never been in a fight, and that's true. But that doesn't mean I've never hurt anyone.

After the day that I saw a classmate's face as a rifle target, I had an even greater terror of guns than before. I knew now what they could do to me. What I didn't know was that a gun wasn't the only weapon that could do it. I didn't learn better until my nineteenth summer.

I had graduated from high school and was working for wheat cutters to earn money for college. One of my duties was to drive truckloads of grain to an enormous elevator on the east side of Wichita. This is what I was doing when I committed my first true act of violence.

The day was hot and bright. I had been working hard, and my shirt was stuck to my back with sweat and dirt. Grain dust grated under my eyelids. The truck cab was hot enough to bake biscuits. A single narrow alley led to the elevator's scales, and it was marked ONE WAY.

I drove to the scales, transacted my business, and helped the elevator employees auger the grain from the truck bed. My swollen eyes itched, and my chest ached from inhaling dust. As soon as the truck was empty, I jumped into the cab and continued down the alley. When I was thirty yards short of the street, a loaded truck turned in. In front of me. Going the wrong way.

I hit the brakes and blared the horn. The other truck slammed to a halt and spilled part of its load. The red-faced driver leaned from his window. "Get out the way, asshole!" he yelled.

And I could have. I could have put the truck into reverse and backed up an eighth of a mile to the entrance. I could have let him come in the wrong way. I was supposed to be a good boy.

But I was tired and hurting, and I forgot. I yelled back at him, using the same word he had used against me. I added that he was going the wrong goddamn way.

I had never done anything like that before.

He yelled something again, but I didn't hear what it was. I was revving my truck's engine. I popped the clutch and lurched forward.

He backed out fast. Even so, I nicked the corner of his bumper. My truck rumbled onto the street at ten miles an hour, and the other guy jumped from his truck and ran after me. I saw him coming in my side mirror.

I couldn't believe it. He had left a loaded truck on the street to chase me on foot. He was screaming obscenities, demanding that I stop and let him kick the shit out of me. I leaned out the window and told him to go fuck himself. Another first. I was almost as mad as he was.

But I wasn't as stupid.

He was running behind the left rear wheel of my truck. His face was at the level of the bed. The bed was metal-edged hardwood. I sped up a little, and he kept coming. I let him gain on me until he was about four feet from the tail of the bed.

He screamed, "Stop, you little cocksucker!"

So I stopped. Hard. I heard the *whunk*.

I waited a few seconds, then shut off the engine. The street was quiet.

I got out and went to the rear of the truck. The guy was lying on the pavement with his hands over his face. He rocked from side to side. When he heard my boots scuff beside him, he uncovered his face. It seemed to swell as I watched. There was only a little blood, but it was from both nose and mouth. I saw the result of rage.

"Muffa*fucchhah*," he said. He had bitten his tongue.

I pointed at the alley. "The entrance," I said, "is at the other end."

I got back into the truck and left. In the mirror, I saw the guy stand and stagger back toward his load. I felt better than I had all day. At the first red light, I adjusted the mirror so I could see myself laugh. My face looked familiar, but not like me.

That night, I dreamed that I was the one running after the truck, that I was the one struck down. After I fell, the truck backed over me. I awoke clutching the sheet, choking. I stumbled to the bathroom and retched up phlegm and grain dust. When I was finished, I avoided looking at the medicine-cabinet mirror. I swore that I would never again retaliate against one who had attacked me.

I still have that dream. Sometimes, after I've been run over, it's as if I'm looking down at my own dead face.

Ever since going to Skidmore, I look like McElroy.

On Thursday, July 7, 1988, my wife came home crying. Hours passed before she would say what was wrong. As I held her, waiting for the words to come, I heard thumps from the basement. McElroy was doing something, but I couldn't go down to find out what. My wife needed me.

At last, she told me what had happened. It involved the man I wanted to kill. His words and actions had been cruel and insidious. He was always careful to camouflage his behavior to everyone except his victims. I knew. I had been one of those victims. But while I had sworn to endure attacks upon myself, I had not sworn to endure any upon the one person I loved. I didn't tell my wife, but at the moment she revealed what he had done, I knew that I would finally do it.

After my wife had fallen asleep, I went down to the basement. My fear and hatred of McElroy were still strong, but I had to tell him what I was going to do. Who better to consult about death than one already dead?

McElroy stood in his usual corner, shadowed. The basement's single bulb wasn't bright enough. I could see his eyes and part of his ruined face, but the rest was hidden. Hideous as he was, I preferred seeing his entire form, as I had in the sunshine outside Skidmore.

I stopped under the bulb. "I understand now why those people had to kill you," I said. "And I think I know why you said I wanted something. Since you came here, I've become less afraid of death. So now I can use it against someone who deserves it. What do you think of that?"

McElroy stepped into the light. A long, plastic-wrapped bundle was cradled in his arms. He held it out to me. I took it, careful not to touch him. The plastic, speckled with mouse droppings, was secured with duct tape.

I set the bundle on the floor to unwrap it. Beneath the plastic was a layer of canvas, and beneath that was a zippered leather case. Inside I found a .30-06 bolt-action rifle with a scope. It was in perfect condition. Someone had cleaned and oiled it before wrapping it up. A box of cartridges nestled in a pocket of the case.

McElroy pointed toward a pile of junk against the wall. "I found it under there."

That pile had been undisturbed for years, and I was certain that neither my landlord nor any other living soul knew the rifle had been there. I could use the weapon the one time I would need it, rewrap it, and replace it under the pile. Unless I was caught in the act of pulling the trigger, many more years would pass before anyone else even knew of its existence.

I sighted down the rifle and checked its action. The sensation was just as it had been on that day at my grandfather's pond. I would hit my target on the first shot.

"This," I said to McElroy, "is what I wanted from you." I held up the gun. "*This*."

It would happen tomorrow. I would have to ride my motorcycle, but transporting the weapon wouldn't be a problem. McElroy would carry it.

I knew he would be joining me.

We left for town at 11:00 A.M. on Friday, July 8. The day was hot and bright. My dog didn't follow us. McElroy rode behind me, holding the rifle across his chest. No one would see it because no one would see him.

Earlier, after my wife had driven away, I had tested the rifle behind the barn. I had shot at a sheet of typing paper fixed to a bale of hay. From seventy yards I had hit dead center. From eighty I had blown off a corner. Close enough.

As the bike accelerated, I shuddered with the knowledge that I was about to do something wonderful. The man I wanted to kill had crushed my upbringing and training to scar tissue. I had entered a higher plane of morality. This act would be easier than hitting the brakes on the truck had been, and would do more good. Even knowing that McElroy sat behind me gave me no qualms. Death was nothing to me now but a tool to be used to improve existence. I had to struggle to keep my speed below sixty.

In town, I left the motorcycle on a side street and walked to the college. McElroy followed with the rifle. Several people passed us on the sidewalk when we reached campus, but none acknowledged me or noticed McElroy. We proceeded to the grove of maples below the campanile. A few students were picnicking, but they didn't look up. We entered a clump of bushes beside the street, and I crouched. McElroy did likewise. A bicyclist went by without giving us a glance. We were hidden.

The man I wanted to kill had his office on the third floor of the building across the street. He ate his lunch there, alone, every day. His desk and chair were beside the window, which was open. He wasn't there yet, but I knew he would be soon. I took the rifle from McElroy, then settled onto my knees and peered through the scope. I estimated the range to be about seventy-five yards. The gun barrel protruded only a few inches from the bushes. I loaded the rifle and then laid it across my thighs to wait.

The dirt under the bushes was damp, but I'd expected that. I would launder my jeans as soon as I got home, and I was wearing old sneakers that I would burn. Hate doesn't make one stupid. Rage does, but I had been careful to avoid rage. I checked my watch. It was three minutes to noon. I looked at McElroy. He stared back.

Up in his office, the man I wanted to kill sat down and opened his briefcase. I had a clear view of both chest and head.

He unwrapped a sandwich and started to eat. I wondered if they would find some of it still in his mouth. I brought up the rifle. The stock was smooth and warm against my cheek. The barrel quivered, and then was steady. In the scope, the man smiled as he chewed. He was reading something. Probably a story of pain or humiliation. The spiderweb-thin crosshairs intersected below his left eye.

The campanile chimed to announce the hour. I flinched at the sound, and the rifle twitched. I brought it back true and waited for the big bell to begin tolling. I would remain still through the first two knells to get the rhythm. On the third I would fire, blending the noise of my shot with the rumble that filled the grove.

The ground vibrated with the first deep tone, and my teeth hummed. I let out my breath. At the second tone, the man above laughed.

My finger tightened.

At the third tone, the man I wanted to kill became a bleeding wound. The rifle stock hit my cheekbone. I dropped the weapon and sat on my heels.

Before me stood McElroy, a new hole bubbling under his throat.

"Take me back," he said.

The bell tolled a fourth time, and a fifth. Blood crept down the front of McElroy's shirt like syrup.

I lunged sideways to see around him, branches scratching my face. In his office, the man I wanted to kill was still chewing and chuckling. My bullet had stayed inside McElroy. I picked up the rifle and reloaded, then saw that the barrel was clogged with dirt. I tried to clean it out with my shirttail. The bell tolled a sixth time, and a seventh.

On the eighth I raised the rifle and sighted. Again, McElroy stepped into the way. I shouted, asking him why. My voice was swallowed by the ninth toll.

"You don't want me here anymore," McElroy said.

At the tenth knell I scrambled around him, crashing through the bushes, and aimed my weapon. At the eleventh the crosshairs centered on my target's grinning mouth. I saw a flash of silver.

The twelfth knell sounded.

The man I wanted to kill went on eating. I lowered the rifle and looked back at McElroy.

"Home?" I asked.

He stared down at me.

"Skidmore," he said.

It wasn't the town we had left the year before.

The buildings had been painted. The windows gleamed. Old men in denim overalls sat outside the gas stations and chewed tobacco. Women in polyester pants gathered in front of the grocery store while their toddlers sucked on popsicles. A banner announcing a community barbecue hung over the entrance to the American Legion hall. Children rode bicycles up and down the side streets. A young farmer sauntered into the tavern, whistling.

I parked the motorcycle in front of the cafe and killed the engine. McElroy and I got off.

Silence.

I pulled off my helmet and looked around. The old men were staring down the street at us. The women stared too, then gathered up their babies and hurried away. The barbecue banner came loose in a gust of wind and blew onto Missouri 113. A child stopped his bicycle, let it fall, and ran. The door to the tavern opened and the farmer peered out, his lips still pursed.

McElroy handed me the rifle, then walked to the center of the street. The banner tumbled past him. He stopped and raised his hands as if in benediction.

People began disappearing into buildings.

McElroy stood there until I was the only one left outside. Then he continued down the street, his hands still raised. He left a red trail on the asphalt.

The cafe door opened, and the waitress ran out and grasped my arm.

"Please," she said. Her eyes begged. "Don't leave him here."

McElroy turned a corner and vanished. His blood remained.

I looked at the waitress. "I'm sorry," I said.

I leaned the rifle against the wall beside the cafe door, then went inside with the waitress and bought another cheeseburger. It was all I could do. Afterward, I rode up the street and filled the bike's tank at the same station as before. This time, the old man didn't want to talk. He just gazed off down the highway.

I called my wife from the pay phone there, catching her before she left work, and told her I'd be home late. Then I got on the bike and headed south. When I passed the cafe, I saw my rifle leaning against the wall. I slowed, then went on past.

South of Skidmore, the ditches were empty. I left the dead town behind.

The man I wanted to kill is still alive, though my upbringing and training have nothing to do with it. Someone will kill him someday . . . but it won't be me.

Let me tell you why.

I won't live with a hated man forever, as the people of that small Missouri town must live with Ken Rex McElroy. A year was enough. I've seen the price of justice, and it's a higher price than I can pay.

So I've again sworn that I will, as Jesus might say, inherit the earth. It isn't an easy vow to keep. After all, there are always those who treat people like shit, and there are always weapons available. But whenever I find myself filled with hate, I repeat these words:

"Welcome.

Welcome to Skidmore."

As a result, I have not killed anyone.

Yet.

Which is the most, I think, that any good boy can say.

THE CALVIN COOLIDGE HOME FOR DEAD COMEDIANS

"The what-should-be never did exist. . . .
There is only what is."

1

The author of *How To Talk Dirty and Influence People* couldn't remember his own name, so he decided to ask the driver of the pickup truck in which he was riding.

Red stitching over the right breast pocket of the driver's blue overalls spelled out "Ol' Pete."

"Excuse me, ah, Pete," the author said hesitantly. "Who am I?"

Ol' Pete, an elderly man with a creased, suntanned face and a white beard, adjusted his blue baseball cap and scratched his scalp.

"Yuh," he said. "That's typical."

"Typical of *what*?" the author asked.

Ol' Pete grimaced. "Take a look at yourself, sonny."

"Sonny" looked down at himself and saw that he was dressed in a brown jacket, tie, and slacks; brown shoes; and a white shirt. The belly threatening to pop the shirt buttons was too big for the rest of his body.

Gotta get on a diet, he thought.

Then he saw the thin copper band encircling his left wrist. LEONARD was stamped into the bracelet in capital letters.

"That's me?" he asked.

"Yuh, unless somebody made a mistake."

Leonard rubbed at the bracelet with his right thumb.

"It doesn't feel right," he said. "Is it my first name or my last?"

"Yuh, that's typical, too."

Leonard wanted to ask "Typical of *what?*" again, but Ol' Pete began whistling "Camptown Races," and Leonard decided it would be a shame to interrupt.

Instead he looked out the open window on his right. The pickup truck — a dusty, battered red International Harvester — was chugging along a narrow dirt road that wound through a forest of thick-trunked trees. Leonard guessed that most of the trees were cottonwoods, but he wasn't sure.

He made a mental note: He was not a botanist. Or at least not a botanist who specialized in trees.

What kind of botanist would write a book called *How To Talk Dirty And Influence People*, anyway?

He took a deep breath. The warm air smelled wonderful, like sunshine on mown grass. The season was spring, he guessed, but late spring, because the trees were fully-leaved. The gently swaying branches created an ever-changing pattern of sun dapples on the road.

"Nice area," Leonard said. His voice, at least, was familiar. "Where are we going?"

Ol' Pete stopped whistling long enough to say, "Ain't there a one of you willing to think for yourself?"

Leonard wanted to say something sarcastic but didn't know what, so he searched his mind for a memory that would help him.

In brief flashes, he remembered —

— *crowds, laughter, drugs, sex, cops* —

— but he couldn't imagine what any of that had to do with being in an International pickup with a man he had never seen before.

He twisted the mirror attached to the outside of his door and looked at his reflection.

The pale, smooth-shaven face had brown, wavy hair; blue eyes surrounded by dark, slightly puffy circles; and an ordinary, medium-sized nose. Although he thought the face would look better with a beard, it was definitely his — a good face, a face practiced in attracting women. But it didn't look like the kind of face that would go with the name "Leonard."

Without trying to recall the information, he remembered that he was forty years old.

He turned back toward Ol' Pete. "Hey, do I look forty to you?"

Ol' Pete shrugged his shoulders. "Y'all look alike to me."

Leonard began to feel irritated.

"Look, pops," he said, "I don't know where I came from or how I got here. I'm one-hundred-percent confused, and you're not helping, which is making me one-hundred-percent pi — pi — pi —"

Leonard frowned. There was a word he wanted to use, but he couldn't think of more than its first two letters.

"You mean 'angry,' right?" Ol' Pete said, the corners of his eyes crinkling in amusement.

"Yeah," Leonard said, looking first at his hands, then at the cracked leather seat, and then at the dashboard, as if he might have misplaced the unknown word. "Yeah, I'm angry, but . . . that isn't the way I was going to say it."

Ol' Pete adjusted his baseball cap and chuckled. "Well, I can see why you've been assigned to Mrs. Vonus."

Leonard stopped trying to think of the word. "Mrs. Vonus?" he said.

"She'll be your Housemother."

"Housemother?"

Ol' Pete clicked his tongue. "You got yourself a bad case of echolalia, boy."

Leonard wanted to punch Ol' Pete in the nose, but restrained himself. He had enough trouble with the cops without adding battery to the list.

He made a mental note of that, too.

"How about some compassion, pops?" he said. "Something weird's happened to me, and all I'm getting from you is 'that's typical' and enough whistling to make Jiminy Cricket toss his cookies. I didn't ask for this, you know."

Ol' Pete laughed and beat on the button in the center of the

steering wheel. The horn blared out derisive honks, and panicked birds flew up on both sides of the road.

Leonard glared. "Just what's so funny, you smug coc —
coc —"

Again, he knew there was a word he wanted, but was
unable to remember it.

Ol' Pete raised an eyebrow. "Got in trouble for that one,
I'll bet."

Leonard experienced another flash of memory, like a hot
rush of blood, and the force of it suppressed his anger.

"Yeah," he said. "Yeah, I did. I don't know why, but the
cops took me in for it."

Ol' Pete patted him on the shoulder. "Don't worry, sonny.
It'll come clear in a bit. We're almost there." He pointed.

A few hundred yards ahead, a three-story red-brick mansion sat in a fenced clearing at the base of a huge hill. Half-hidden golden buildings shimmered at the top of the hill, but it
was the brick mansion toward which Ol' Pete pointed.

"That's the Calvin Coolidge Home," Ol' Pete said.

Leonard rubbed his forehead, which was starting to hurt.
"I thought you said I was assigned to a Mrs. Vopis."

"Mrs. Vonus, boy. She runs the Coolidge Home. And it
ain't Calvin Coolidge's; that's just what she calls it."

"Don't call me boy," Leonard said. "I'm forty god — go —
forty years old."

The old man pounded the horn again. "A babe in the
woods!" he chortled.

Leonard was beginning to think that Ol' Pete was more
than a little crazy. He was glad the ride was almost over.

Even though he had no idea where it had taken him.

2

Leonard had to cross a narrow plank over a deep ditch to
get to the brick walk that led to the mansion's front door. He
was halfway across when the International's horn blared behind him, and he windmilled his arms to keep his balance.

"So long, sonnyboy!" Ol' Pete bellowed. "Hope to see you

on the Hill one o' these days!"

Leonard didn't look back to acknowledge the farewell. He was too busy trying to avoid falling into the ditch, which was half-full of murky water.

He did turn around when he'd finally made it to the other side. The truck was gone, without even a puff of dust to mark its passage.

He hadn't heard it drive away. He couldn't even remember when he'd stopped hearing the engine noise.

"Holy sh — sh —," he said, and began to see a connection between the words he couldn't remember.

He walked slowly up the path, staring down at the chipped bricks. He tried to mutter obscenities as he went.

"Sh — sh — Excrement," he said. "Fuh — fuh — Sexual intercourse. Genitalia. Scion of a golden retriever. Immoral congress with a chimpanzee. Guano cranium."

It was the best he could do.

He was so preoccupied that he stumbled over the step at the end of the walk. His palms came up just in time to keep his face from impacting on the wall to the right of the door.

His eyes were five inches from a bronze plaque bolted to the bricks:

THE CALVIN COOLIDGE MEMORIAL
REHABILITATION FACILITY
VISITORS WELCOME
THANK YOU FOR NOT SMOKING

"What the coitus," Leonard muttered, and pushed away from the wall to face the dark wooden door, which was intricately carved with depictions of bored-looking cherubim.

A black iron knocker shaped like a microphone dominated the center of the door. The flat piece of metal the knocker was to strike had been forged in the shape of a laughing face, but Leonard only knew this because of the open mouth. The rest of the face had been beaten smooth.He didn't want to knock, so he kicked at a loose brick in the step for several minutes, waiting for something to happen. A bluejay landed in a mimosa tree and scolded him.

What am I afraid of? he thought. *Any place named after Calvin Coolidge, for crying out loud, can't be too horrible. Besides, they might have something to eat.*

The knocker felt hot in his hand. He brought it up quickly and let it fall.

The sound was like a thunderclap.

Startled, Leonard jumped backward off the step and fell, landing on his buttocks on the sidewalk.

"Fornication with one's maternal parent," he said. It was distinctly unsatisfying.

The massive door swung inward. Leonard wanted to run into the woods, but before he could stand, he saw the woman in the doorway. She was a blue-haired little old lady in a dark gray dress.

It would be hard, he thought, to imagine a more unthreatening figure. Yet he was frightened, and he thought he knew why when he noticed that the woman's right hand was curled into a veined, bony fist.

If there's a balled-up handkerchief in there, he thought, *I'm at the mercy of somebody's Jewish mother.*

Not his, though. His mother had been larger . . .

Another mental note. Sooner or later, he'd have enough clues to know who he was.

The woman in the doorway looked down at him and pursed her lips in displeasure.

"So much for first impressions," Leonard mumbled, and stood. His legs felt rubbery.

The woman gave a short sigh and said, "I am Mrs. Vonus. You must be Leonard. We've been expecting you." Her voice was high, thin, and dry.

"Who's 'we'?" Leonard asked.

Mrs. Vonus stepped back and gestured with her left hand. "Come in, come in. We might as well get started."

"Get started on *what?*"

Mrs. Vonus sighed again. "Rule Number One, Leonard, is that it's rude to question your Housemother in such a belligerent tone. Please come inside now, or I'll be forced to give you a minus for your first day."

Leonard walked, a little shakily, up the step and into the dark, cool mustiness of the Calvin Coolidge Home. The worn, wine-colored carpeting in the foyer felt spongy under his shoes.

Mrs. Vonus shut the door, and the dim foyer became even dimmer.

"Saving on electricity?" Leonard asked, trying to keep his voice from quavering.

The woman appeared out of the dimness and looked up at him. She sighed a third time.

"You sure krechtz a lot," Leonard said.

The Housemother shook her head. "We have our work cut out for us."

Leonard backed away a few steps. "Speaking of cutting," he said, "I'm cutting out if somebody doesn't give me a good reason to stay. For one thing, it's too dark in here, and for another, it smells like moldy bread."

Mrs. Vonus placed her right hand on his forearm.

No handkerchief, he thought. *Must've stuffed it down her dress when I wasn't looking.*

"Your eyes will adjust to the light," Mrs. Vonus said, "and you will become accustomed to the scent of age. As for your questions — This is your Orientation Day, and I shall answer those questions that are appropriate."

Leonard tried to pull away from her grip and found that he couldn't, even though she wasn't holding him tightly. He began to suspect that he was dreaming.

"You are not dreaming," the Housemother said.

"Which is exactly what I'd expect a dream-character to say," Leonard said quickly, before he had a chance to panic. "On the count of three, I'm going to wake up." He closed his eyes. "One, two, three."

When he reopened his eyes, he could see a little better. But he was still in the foyer of the Calvin Coolidge Home, and still in the grip of Mrs. Vonus.

"Three and a half," he said.

"Come into the Front Parlor," Mrs. Vonus said, and pulled him to the left. His feet shuffled along against his will.

They passed through a wide, arched entranceway into a large room with the same wine-colored carpeting as the foyer.

Tall windows with gauzy drapes let in just enough sunlight for Leonard to see clearly. Ornate sofas and chairs were arranged neatly throughout the room, and huge bookcases loaded with black-spined volumes hulked against the walls. The wallspace between the bookcases was covered with blue paisley paper.

Leonard shuddered. It was hideous stuff.

It wasn't quite as awful, though, as the massive mantel around the fireplace. It was carved from the same dark wood as the front door, and more bored cherubim flapped morosely across it in suspended animation.

Over the mantel, illuminated by two kerosene lamps in wall brackets, was the painted portrait of a clean-cut, Presbyterian-looking man.

Mrs. Vonus pulled Leonard close enough for him to read the brass plate at the bottom of the painting's frame. The words engraved into it were JOHN CALVIN COOLIDGE.

"Who's that?" Leonard asked. "I've heard of Calvin Coolidge, but —"

"John was his first name," the Housemother said reverently.

Leonard forced himself to smile, pretending to love the painting. Maybe if he was nice, she'd let go of his arm and he could split.

"You shan't go anywhere," Mrs. Vonus said.

She released his arm, and he found that his feet were stuck to the carpet.

Giving in to panic at last, he twisted his body painfully in an effort to escape. "Lord curse this mightily!" he yelled, and realized that he sounded ridiculous.

"You're heading for a minus," Mrs. Vonus said.

Leonard stopped flailing and tried to calm himself. He didn't know what a "minus" was, but the Housemother obviously had some sort of arcane power, and it wouldn't do to upset her. A "minus" might involve his liver escaping via his belly button.

He wondered why the idea that this little old lady had supernatural powers didn't strike him as meshugge.

The answer came floating up from his brain's lower layers:

Man, I've been dragged before people whose only power came from the word "Judge" in front of their names. What I'm dealing with here doesn't make any less sense than that.

"You must learn how to behave toward those who have been placed over you," Mrs. Vonus said.

"Yes, ma'am," Leonard said, trying to sound meek.

The Housemother pursed her lips. "You don't fool me. You're telegraphing a great deal of unhealthy defiance. Sooner or later, though, you must accept the order of the universe if you want to exist in a state of spiritual peace."

Leonard, to keep himself from responding sardonically, looked up at the portrait again and asked, "Is this the same Calvin Coolidge who was President during Prohibition?"

Mrs. Vonus reached up and buffed the brass plate with a wrinkled lace handkerchief.

Aha! Leonard thought, and was immediately afraid. But the Housemother didn't seem to have "heard" him.

"Yes, this is he," she said. "The finest man to have ever served in public office. I find it ironic that you, one of the least fine men to have ever existed, were born during his administration."

Leonard made yet another mental note. If he had been born during Prohibition and was now forty years old, then this must be nineteen-sixty-something-or-other . . .

"Time has no meaning here," Mrs. Vonus said. "We have days and nights, but only for convenience. A day is as a thousand years, a thousand years as a day."

Leonard couldn't stand it anymore. "Where the he — he — heck *am* I, then? You keep giving me this mystical shtick, but you're not telling me anything."

Mrs. Vonus sighed for what Leonard was sure must be the hundredth time since he'd entered the building. "Very well," she said in a tone of voice that clearly said *You'll be sorry.* "I prefer to give new residents more adjustment time before their screenings, but if you're impatient, we'll do it now. Come along." She began walking back toward the foyer.

Leonard found that he could move again, but before he followed the Housemother, he took a last look at the portrait.

"What a goyisher face," he muttered, and then remembered not only who Calvin Coolidge had been but who John Calvin had been:

Predestination. Purity. Punishment of sinners. Burnings-at-the-stake. No sense of humor.

Leonard turned away from the mantel. He didn't think he was going to enjoy working this dump, but there didn't seem to be anything he could do about it.

3

Mrs. Vonus led him through the foyer, past a staircase that she said went up to "the dormitory," and down a wide hallway lined with glass cases. She walked like an overfed duck.

Some of the glass cases were in shadows so dark that Leonard couldn't make out the contents, but every thirty feet or so, a skylight let in diffused sunshine that revealed dusty medals and trophies. One case was full of china dinnerplates painted with portraits of Presidents and Biblical figures.

"I never saw so much dre — dre — natural fertilizer in my life," Leonard said.

Mrs. Vonus sighed.

She paused under one of the skylights and gestured at the wall. Leonard stopped beside her and looked where she pointed.

Here, instead of a glass case, was a white plastic-coated board, ten feet high and eight wide, marked off in a grid of perpendicular black lines forming sixty rows of two-inch squares. Many of the squares, particularly on the right half of the board, were blank, but each of the others held one of three black symbols: +, =, or -. Hanging on a long string to the right of the board was what looked like a capped felt-tipped marker.

To the left of each row of squares was a single name. Leonard found his and saw that every square in that row was blank.

"This is the Progress Board," Mrs. Vonus said. "Each day, I shall evaluate your attitude, composure, manners, posture, and language. A plus-sign means that you are making great progress, and you shall receive a silver dollar. Since there are only forty spaces in each row, the Board cannot display a record of a resident's entire stay — however, all that matters is the total number of pluses. Each resident's total appears at the end of his row. When the total reaches two hundred, the resident may ascend to the top of the Hill."

"What's at the top of the Hill?" Leonard asked.

Mrs. Vonus gave him a severe look. "You'll know when you have two hundred pluses."

Leonard looked at the column of numbers and saw that only three of the sixty residents had more than a hundred pluses.

"An equals-sign," Mrs. Vonus continued, "indicates that you are equivocal. You are not rewarded, but neither are you penalized. For each minus, however, you must pay a dollar to the Dessert Fund. If you have no dollars at the time, you must pay double when you do."

Leonard cleared his throat. "What's the Dessert Fund?"

For the first time, the hint of a smile flickered at the corners of the Housemother's mouth. "Every day at dinner, those residents who have received plus-signs are given a special dessert at the expense of those who have received minuses."

Leonard kept his eyes riveted on the Progress Board. *The old bat has power*, he thought, *but she's as crazy as an eighty-year-old stripper.*

"You'll soon know better," Mrs. Vonus said.

Leonard gritted his teeth. "If you don't mind," he said, "I'd appreciate a little privacy in my own brain."

"If you think dessert is crazy, Leonard, that's fine. From the looks of you, though, you take dessert quite seriously."

Leonard glared at her. "I've been planning to go on a diet, you rotten old set of external sexual characteristics!" he yelled. He didn't know what it was that he really wanted to call her, but he hoped she did.

Mrs. Vonus stepped closer to the Progress Board, uncapped the marker, and put a minus-sign in the first box to the right of Leonard's name. Then she recapped the marker, dropped it so that it bounced on its string, and began waddling down the hall again.

"Please follow me," she said.

Leonard looked at the Progress Board and grinned. A

quick vertical stroke could change a minus into a plus . . .

He grabbed the marker, and a jolt of white-hot pain stabbed up his arm into his head.

When he could see again, he was on his back on the worn carpet. His arm and head throbbed. Mrs. Vonus stood over him, her helmet of bluish hair framed by the rectangular halo of the skylight.

"Come along, Leonard," she said. "You said you wanted answers. It's time for you to get them."

4

The hallway ended in a movie-theater lobby, complete with a popcorn machine and candy counter. The wine-colored carpet of the hall gave way to thick, plush scarlet, and velvet ropes strung between brass posts defined a path leading to a pair of wide doors on spring hinges.

Leonard ached, but he almost forgot about the pain when he saw where he was. His first thought was that the place had to be an illusion, but there was no way to fake the smell of hot buttered popcorn.

What was a movie theater doing in an old mansion?

"It serves a purpose," Mrs. Vonus said.

Leonard was about to yell at her again — he already had a minus, so what could it hurt? — but then he spotted the two young women behind the U-shaped glass candy counter.

Both were wearing red-and-white striped blouses and short blue skirts. One was tall, blue-eyed, and blonde, with hair so long that its end was hidden behind the display of Milk Duds. The other, a brunette, had dark eyes and the most sensual mouth Leonard had ever seen. So far as he remembered, anyway.

He felt that there ought to be a redhead, but two out of three wasn't bad.

"Excuse me," he said to Mrs. Vonus without looking at her, and hopped over a velvet rope.

It was only when he leaned far forward over the counter that he noticed that the women, although extraordinarily beautiful, looked as if they never smiled.

"Hey, why so depressed?" Leonard asked. They didn't look depressed, exactly, but it was the closest word he could come up with on short notice. "It's a beautiful day outside. Lots of sunshine, birdies singing, green leaves all over the place. When do you two get off work, anyway? We could go for a picnic."

The blonde looked at him with a complete lack of interest. "May I help you, sir?" she said flatly.

"You bet, babe," he said, grinning. "You can tell me how much a smile costs."

The brunette said, "We have Goobers, Snocaps, JuJus, Milk Duds, Junior Mints, Licorice Whips, red or black, Hershey bars, and Jordan Almonds. We also have popcorn, with or without butter, and Royal Crown Cola. What will you have, sir?"

"A phone number," Leonard said. "A look, a smile, a touch, a wink."

"We don't have any of those, sir," the blonde said.

So that was the way they wanted to play it. Okay, fine — he knew the game as well as they did.

He straightened and shook his head in exaggerated dejection. "Some Goobers and Milk Duds, then. And your biggest tub of popcorn. Better give me a soda, too."

The brunette reached for the candy.

"Five dollars," the blonde said, moving toward the cash register.

Leonard's mouth fell open. "Five bucks? I've been places where I could've bought *you* for that!"

Something touched his right elbow, and he jumped. Then he looked down and saw Mrs. Vonus standing beside him.

"This isn't World War Two," she said, "and you aren't in a French brothel. These ladies are my employees, and they do not fraternize with residents."

Leonard leaned down and whispered, "I don't wanna fraternize. I wanna boink their brains out." He was pleased to discover that he remembered the word "boink," and wondered if the reason he was able to remember it was that it wasn't really a word at all.

The Housemother grasped his arm again. "You will be

going to bed without dinner tonight, and there will have to be a considerable improvement in your demeanor before I will consider allowing you to come to dinner tomorrow."

Leonard tried to pry her fingers loose. "Hey, who d'you think you are, my mother? I don't have to stick around, y'know —"

"Yes, you do," Mrs. Vonus said, and yanked him away from the counter so hard that he thought his shoulder had dislocated.

"Hey, what about — ow! — what about my Milk Duds?" he cried.

"You don't have any silver dollars with which to buy them. At the rate you're going, it will be some time before you do."

The Housemother stopped before the double doors and released Leonard's arm.

"I'll bet your kids hate you," he said, rubbing his shoulder. "I'll bet you've never gotten a Mother's Day card in your life."

Mrs. Vonus pulled open the left-hand door, revealing darkness. Cool air rushed out and made Leonard shiver.

"Go in," the Housemother said. "Take any seat you like."

Leonard tried to step forward, but a tingling sensation in his spine stopped him.

Whatsa matter, schmu — schm —

Yet another word he couldn't remember. What kind of stupid dream was it where a man couldn't even call himself an obscene name in Yiddish?

He compromised:

Whatsa matter, schnook? Movie theaters are always dark inside. Otherwise you can't see the film. So go on in, because if you don't, Grandma Goering is gonna break your arm.

"You're going to be awfully hungry in a day or two," the Housemother said grimly.

Leonard wanted to beat his head against the wall. "Are you gonna spy on me when I go to the john, lady?"

Mrs. Vonus gestured toward the darkness with her free hand. "Please, Leonard. I'm tired of holding the door."

He took a step toward the darkness and then paused. "Are you coming?"

"No, thank you," she said. "I must turn on the projector."

Leonard looked back at the unsmiling goddesses behind the candy counter.

"If I'm not back in two hours," he called, "better come revive me. Nude massages with baby oil often seem to be effective."

Then, before Mrs. Vonus could admonish him, he walked into the theater.

5

The door swung shut behind him, and he paused at the top of the aisle to let his eyes adjust. A dim yellow light burned at the end of each row of seats, and the screen on the wall ahead glowed a dull gray. Leonard estimated that there were two hundred seats, all of them empty.

He was amazed at how clean the place was. "What's a movie house without trash?" he said aloud, then walked down to the fifth row and sat in the third seat left of the aisle.

The screen brightened and the face of Mrs. Vonus appeared, ten feet tall and in ludicrously overtinted color.

Leonard wished he had a popcorn box to throw. He had to content himself with booing and hissing, and the sounds echoed eerily.

"Welcome to the Calvin Coolidge Memorial Rehabilitation Facility," the amplified voice of Mrs. Vonus said from the ceiling and walls. "This facility specializes in the purification of those who have spent their lives trying to gain earthly rewards through the practice of so-called 'humor,' which, rather than evoking the laughter of joy, instead appeals to the listeners' prurient interest —"

"What's wrong with that?" Leonard yelled.

" — thus leading to the deterioration of the moral fabric of society."

"Moral fabric?" Leonard shouted. "One-hundred-percent cotton denim, maybe? Rayon? Dacron? The weak, frayed elastic in most of my shorts?"

"Our therapy," Mrs. Vonus said, "consists of teaching our

residents those things their parents and peers failed to teach them — patience, politeness, obedience, reverence, decorum, piety, and chastity."

Leonard jumped up and waved his right index finger at the screen. "Oh, no, you don't! The Constitution says I don't have to be obedient, reverent, or chaste — especially chaste — as long as I don't abridge the rights of others, which I've never done! Furthermore, you wear too much makeup! I've spent decades in burlesque palaces, and I never saw so much rouge in my whole life!"

His last three words reverberated in his skull:

My whole life.

His legs felt rubbery again, and he collapsed into his seat. He was beginning to feel uncomfortably warm despite the theater's coolness.

What was the last thing he could remember before the ride in the red International pickup truck?

. . . something hot and delicious coursing through my body . . .

Orgasm?

No; it had been hotter, faster, more like falling into a volcano —

"And now," Mrs. Vonus was saying, "a short feature to clarify the meaning of your presence here, after which you shall meet our other residents and enjoy a heartwarming and spiritually uplifting cinematic masterpiece. You shall return to this theater every day when you feel you must, which is the only way we have of telling time here. You shall come to the theater, eat dinner, and gather for housemeetings . . . according to when you feel you must."

"Whenever Nature calls, huh?" Leonard mumbled.

The giant Mrs. Vonus disappeared and was replaced by the black-and-white image of a toilet.

"A toilet," Leonard whispered. His head felt as if it had been soaked in gasoline and lit with a match. "The villainous source of all those 'dirty toilet jokes' . . ."

An overweight, pale man with dark hair and a beard appeared on the screen and sat on the toilet. He was nude.

Leonard tried to stand again, but his seat held him with the same irresistible force with which Mrs. Vonus had held his arm.

The two-dimensional phantom tightened a strap above an elbow.

Leonard tried to turn away from the screen, but his head wouldn't move. Nor would his eyelids close. His eyes began to sting.

The man on the screen held a syringe. With the tip of his tongue touching his upper lip, he slid the needle into the bulging vein on the inside of his elbow. He loosened the strap.

After a moment, he looked happy.

Then something happened to his eyes, and he fell off the toilet. He lay awkwardly on the tiled floor, as if frozen in the act of rolling from his back to his side. His bearded cheek was against the tiles. His eyelids closed.

Leonard wanted to scream, but his throat and tongue were paralyzed.

The cops came into the bathroom.

They looked at the naked man on the floor and talked. Through the roar of his fever, Leonard could only hear a fraction of what they said, but that was more than he wanted to hear.

"What'd I tell you?" one of the cops said.

A second cop said something else. A third laughed.

You sons of bit – bit – Leonard thought. But the word, the right word, the only word, wouldn't come.

Then, two by two, like animals trooping into Noah's Ark, the photographers and television cameramen came in. They shone bright lamps onto the body and popped flashbulbs at it as if to purify it with white light.

The tightness in Leonard's throat broke.

"Vultures!" he cried. "Can't I have some peace in my own bathroom?"

Two by two, they came and went.

"Bound to happen sooner or later," one of them said.

Leonard wanted to run to the screen and rip it with his fingernails and teeth.

"You drove me to it!" he shouted. "You and the cops who wouldn't have gotten out of their cars to keep a black man from getting beaten up but were ecstatic to come after me for telling the truth! I had to do something to get away! Sickest of the

sick, huh? You bet I am! Sick of you self-righteous coc —
coc — genital lickers!"

The last photographer finished shooting, then said "Bye-
bye, junkie," and walked out of the bathroom. Other people
came in, but the picture was fading.

Leonard slumped, staring at the fading image of his own
body.

"I'm not a junkie," he said weakly. "I just needed to get
away from the tapes and papers for a while. I just needed . . ."

The screen went black.

Leonard wanted to cry, but his tear ducts wouldn't work.
All he could do was dry-sob.

This is what I get for getting a tattoo, he thought bitterly.

But when the lights brightened and he rolled his shirt and
jacket sleeves up from his left forearm, he saw that the tattoo
was gone.

For a moment, he had been sure of who he was, but now
he knew that he could never again be sure of anything.

6

As Leonard's fever began to break, the double doors
opened. Leonard turned and saw dozens of men, all dressed
in brown slacks and jackets with white shirts, coming down
the aisle. Some were barely out of their teens, and some were
painfully old; yet they all looked alike. All were Caucasian,
and all walked as if they were afraid of the floor. None of them
were smiling.

Leonard used them as an excuse to try to forget the film he
had just seen.

*These guys told jokes for a living? So why do they look so . . .
unfunny?*

A shrunken, ancient man took the aisle seat on Leonard's
right. Tremulously, he reached into a jacket pocket and with-
drew a box of JuJus.

"Hey, pops," Leonard said, leaning to the right and trying
to keep his voice steady. "What's going on here?"

The old man looked at Leonard with a puzzled expression.

"It's —" he began uncertainly, as if trying to remember something he was always forgetting. "It's the afternoon movie," he said finally.

"Yeah? You know what it is?"

The old man stared with grayish, red-rimmed eyes. "Same as always, I suppose," he said, as if Leonard had been foolish to ask the question, and then opened his box of JuJus.

Leonard's stomach rumbled.

Dead or not, he was hungry.

"Mind if I have a few?" he said, leaning closer.

The grayish eyes regarded him curiously in the fading light.

"You're new, aren't you?" the old man asked.

"Yeah, yeah," Leonard said, becoming impatient as the screen lit up and music rang from the speakers. "C'mon, can I have some?"

"Up to you," the old man said, extending the box.

Leonard held out his hand, and several JuJus slid into his palm.

"Thanks, man," he said, and turned to look at the screen. He had already missed the title, but he recognized the credits, which were flipping past on what looked like Christmas cards.

JAMES STEWART, he read, and then DONNA REED.

He popped one of the candies into his mouth, and it crawled across his tongue.

He choked and spat it out, then felt the JuJus in his hand crawling too. He could just make out their shapes in the flickering light from the movie screen.

Cockroaches.

Leonard yelped and shook his hand violently, scattering the roaches in all directions. One landed in his hair, and he began to hyperventilate as he frantically brushed it out.

"Real —" he began, shuddering and gasping. "Real — real funny, pops."

"Not to me," the old man's voice answered from the darkness.

Leonard felt cold. Why was the air conditioning in a movie theater always strong enough to freeze meat?

Shivering, he drew up his knees and hugged them to his chest.

He had seen his own death.

He had put a cockroach into his mouth.

On the movie screen, Jimmy Stewart, as good old George Bailey, was about to discover that *It's A Wonderful Life*.

Leonard leaned to his left and threw up into the adjacent seat.

7

Seventeen "days" later, Leonard lay on his hard, narrow mattress and stared at the gray ceiling of his room. The cubicle had no window, so the only thing to look at besides the ceiling was the framed print on the wall above the foot of the bed. He refused to do that, because he hated it.

The print was a reproduction of a painting depicting a female saint being sliced to death by a huge wooden wheel studded with knives.

Earlier that day, Leonard had decided he couldn't stand the thing anymore, and he had tried to take it down. It hadn't budged, so he had tried to break the glass with his shoe. That had also failed, and he had received yet another minus for his efforts.

He didn't think he'd mind the print so much if the saint hadn't looked overjoyed about her impending filleting.

"It's perverse," he had told Mrs. Vonus after she'd called him down to the Progress Board to answer for his attempted vandalism. "Nobody should be happy about something like that. Talk about sick — *that's* sick!"

The Housemother had sighed, then pursed her lips.

"Why is it so difficult for you to understand, Leonard," she had said while uncapping the felt-tipped marker, "that sacrificing oneself for something greater is the highest achievement of spirituality?"

"Oh, I understand, all right," Leonard had said. "I just don't think she should be so pleased with the method. I mean, she looks like she thinks she's about to make it with Omar Sharif, for crying out loud."

Mrs. Vonus had dutifully marked the minus in the seventeenth box after his name.

As Leonard stared at the ceiling, he thought he understood what the Housemother had said about the nature of time here.

The sun had set only sixteen times since his arrival, but he felt as if he'd been in the Home at least five years.

He had considered trying to escape, but even when the house let him go outside, the ditch bounding the front yard and the high wooden wall bounding the grounds on the other three sides kept him trapped. He hadn't been able to find the footbridge he'd crossed the first day.

He had also tried to befriend some of the other residents, hoping that together they might find a way out, but none of them would even talk to him. It was as if they were too preoccupied with trying to earn pluses to think about what might lie beyond the mansion's seven acres.

Leonard, though, was curious about the world outside the grounds, particularly the golden buildings on top of the Hill. He could just see them from the yard, glimmering between the trees high above like the sun peeking through gaps in green clouds.

Mrs. Vonus had told him that he might someday be allowed to go up the Hill, but that he had a great deal of work to do first. Living on the Hill was a reward, she said, a privilege to be bestowed only upon those who proved themselves worthy.

"Who wants to live there?" Leonard had said. "I just want to check it out for chicks."

That had been his fifth minus.

Let's see, he thought, still staring at the ceiling. *Seventeen days with a total of fourteen minuses, three equals-signs, and no pluses. That means I need twenty-eight straight pluses just to pay off what I owe the Dessert Fund. Then still more pluses if I want to buy anything for the movies . . . that is, The Movie.*

Seventeen days at the Coolidge Home meant that he had seen *It's A Wonderful Life* seventeen times. He didn't think he could bear to sit through it more than three or four more times if he didn't at least have something to eat to take his mind off it.

The fingers of his right hand plucked at the loose fabric of his shirt where his belly had tightened it two weeks earlier. Seventeen days without sweets — six of them without anything to eat at all — had helped him begin to lose the weight he'd been wanting to take off for months before his death. He supposed he ought to thank the Housemother for that, at least.

Maybe that would get him a plus. Unless, of course, she caught him thinking that it would. Mrs. Vonus wasn't an easy woman to please. He thought he'd go nuts trying to figure out how to get along with her, or at least how to avoid her.

He also thought he'd go nuts if he didn't get into the pants of at least one of the candy-counter women, which was one of the reasons why he couldn't get along with Mrs. Vonus.

"Desires of the flesh," she had told him over and over, "must be overcome if you are to reach the goal of spiritual purification."

"I agree," he had said on Day #9. "However, to overcome desires, they must be eliminated, and the only way to eliminate them is to supply what is desired. Ergo, the only way for me to reach spiritual purification is to spend several weeks bouncing up and down on each of those young lovelies."

He had missed dinner two days in a row for that.

Then he had behaved himself relatively well, he thought, until this afternoon's campaign against the masochistic saint.

Now he lay with his stomach growling, mourning his lack of tact and wishing he could curse Ol' Pete for schlepping him to this dive in the first place.

No one he had known in all his forty years had tsooris like he did now, because the Calvin Coolidge Memorial Rehabilitation Facility was Hell. It was the place where Jewish boys who got tattoos, slept with shiksas, and told dirty toilet jokes went. Not all of the residents had been Jewish boys in life, but they had all become Jewish boys in death because they had a Housemother who expected nothing less than perfection.

The fact that Mrs. Vonus seemed more Methodist, Presbyterian, and/or Baptist than anything else was irrelevant. Leonard had met so many Jewish mothers who acted Presbyterian, and so many Baptist mothers who acted Jewish, that he'd come to the conclusion that they were all interchangeable.

"The only mothers that out-Jewish-mother the Methodists, Baptists, and Presbyterians," he said to the ceiling, "are those Catholic Jewish-mothers, who on top of everything else get to complain about their swollen knees. And the only ones who out-Jewish-mother *them* are the Sisters, who remain chaste out of shame that they were born to the goyim."

The disapproving face of Mrs. Vonus appeared above him, and he choked on his own breath. He couldn't get used to her habit of materializing without warning. It might be that she was simply good at sneaking up on him, but he preferred to think that she had the ability to transform herself into a gnat.

"One of your most serious problems," Mrs. Vonus said, "is your apparent inability to comprehend the meaning of the word 'respect.' "

You should talk, Leonard thought before he could stop himself. *I could've been naked in here, doing who knows what vile and perverted things in the absence of female companionship.*

Mrs. Vonus regarded him severely. "I have been placed over you as your teacher and guardian, and I shall do whatever is necessary to further your spiritual development. That includes confronting you when you do not expect it, which will train you to behave properly at all times."

"Oh, I see," Leonard said sarcastically. "Then I can wind up like Saint Whosis there and behave properly to the bitter end, huh?"

The corners of the Housemother's mouth twitched upward for only the second time since Leonard had come to the Home. "You have already had your 'bitter end,' Leonard. That you met it as you did is one of the reasons you are here."

Leonard turned onto his right side to face the wall. *I've already got a minus for today,* he thought miserably. *What more can she do to me?*

"What I am going to do," Mrs. Vonus said, "is allow you to do something you love."

All Leonard could think of were the two unsmiling candy-counter women and the various methods he wanted to use to teach them to laugh out loud.

"Don't be ridiculous," Mrs. Vonus said. "The non-fraternization rule shall never be broken."

Leonard turned back toward the Housemother and gave her a murderous look. "Then just what are you going to allow me to do, O Great Giver of Just Desserts?"

Mrs. Vonus's eyes narrowed. "Be in the Front Parlor in two minutes, or I shall do something I've never done before."

Have an orgasm? Leonard thought, and was immediately horrified at his stupidity.

He was dead now. He was definitely dead now.

Of course you are, schnook. That's the whole problem.

He expected something far worse than a minus for this transgression. He expected the Housemother to wave her hands and start his insides boiling like so much stew.

But what happened was that, for the first time, Mrs. Vonus looked upset. Her face flushed, and she averted her eyes. Her hands fumbled with the handkerchief she always carried.

Oh-ho, Leonard thought, feeling a bright bit of glee. *Methinks I've struck a nerve in this old yenta.*

The Housemother's discomfort, however, came and went in an instant.

"Be in the Parlor in two minutes," she said, "or I shall assign a minus a day in advance — something I have never considered doing to any other resident. How does it feel to be unique, Leonard?"

She turned and waddled out of the room.

If God placed her over me, Leonard thought, *why'd He build her to walk so funny?*

8

The furniture in the Front Parlor had been arranged in a circle and was occupied by thirty dour men and women, all dressed in stiff black clothing.

"What's this?" Leonard asked as Mrs. Vonus took his arm and pulled him into the center of the circle. "The Inquisition?"

The Housemother handed him a cordless microphone and then sat on a sofa with three unsmiling, horse-faced men.

Instinctively, Leonard spoke into the mike. "Hey, what's the scam?" he said, and was startled when his amplified voice emanated from the walls.

Mrs. Vonus waved a bony hand. "This is what you lived for. A performance."

Leonard's skin began to itch. His body was telling him to get out of there, but he knew better than to try. The carpet would hold him as it always did whenever the Housemother wanted him in a certain place.

He looked at the men and women in black. Their faces seemed to have been molded into perpetual frowns.

"Who are these people?" he asked. "Ex-lawyers?"

Mrs. Vonus gave him her almost-smile. "You spent a large part of your life claiming that you knew what your country stood for and that your judges did not. These are the founders of your nation. Perform for them, and see if they approve."

Leonard scanned the audience. "So where's George Washington? Ben Franklin? Tom Jefferson?"

"Those men came after," Mrs. Vonus said with a strong note of satisfaction in her voice. "These people came to escape persecution . . ."

Realization hit Leonard like a splash of icewater.

Oh, terrific. She expects me to do my gig for a slavering pack of Puritans.

"Please begin," Mrs. Vonus said.

"Why? So they can tie me up and toss me into the pond out back to see if I float?"

"If you want to eat tomorrow," Mrs. Vonus said, "begin. I am curious to see just how funny they think you are."

Leonard wanted to fling himself onto the Housemother and beat on her head with the microphone, but instead he took a deep breath and let himself free-associate.

"Puritans, huh?" he began, pacing around the circle and shaking his head. "I hear you were really strict. 'If you don't work, you don't eat.' That was yours, wasn't it? Funny, I knew a rabbi who said it originated with Moses. 'Those crummy Pilgrims!' the rabbi used to say. 'They stole all our best stuff!' But, hey, I believe you, it's yours —you want the Ten Commandments, you can have those too.

"Don't get me wrong — it was a fine rule, although it might've been more effective if you'd made it 'If you don't work, you don't shtu — sht —"

Leonard stopped pacing and glared at Mrs. Vonus. "How am I supposed to do my act if I've got half of my vocabulary blocked?"

"Do you think these people would find that portion

funny?'' the Housemother asked. "For that matter, would any decent person? If you feel you must be obscene to be funny, then you must not be too intelligent, must you? Shouldn't an intelligent person have better tools at his command?''

Leonard began pacing again, faster than before. "Y'know, I really don't get it with this obscenity hangup," he said, the words starting to come rapid-fire. "I mean, obscenity is in the eye of the beholder, isn't it? You take this schlepper here —" He stopped pacing and pointed at an especially grim-looking Puritan. "What's a dirty word to you, Jim — how about 'toilet'? Now, of course that's not dirty to you, because you don't have the faintest idea what a toilet *is*, do you? I could stand here and tell you dirty toilet jokes all night long, and you wouldn't be offended because you wouldn't know what I was talking about. But suppose I started talking about witches —"

The Puritan stiffened in his seat.

"Ha, that got you, didn't it?" Leonard half-yelled. "Now *there's* a dirty word. Hey, I've got one — when is a witch not a witch? When the broomstick she's riding belongs to Ye Revered Pastor, Leader of the Flock. 'Cometh ye here, naughty witch,' he sayeth righteously. 'I'll put the fear of the Lord into you. Well, I'll put something into you, anyway, yea verily.' "

Leonard waited for a reaction, but it didn't come.

"Didn't quite catch that one, eh? You guys never were much for subtlety, except when it came to killing off the Indians. What you did was, you drowned, burned, or hung your witches, but only if they didn't have any social diseases. If they *did* have social diseases, you sent 'em to be social with the Mohicans, sort of your basic cultural exchange program . . ."

The Puritans sat stone-faced.

Leonard zeroed in on a matronly woman.

"Excuse me, ma'am, but I'm conducting a survey. Have you ever, you know, had, um, *relations* with a Mohican? No, I thought not; you look unhappy. You don't follow the logic? Well, look at it this way — who has more stamina, a fat old preacher whose only exercise comes from turning pages in the Good Book —" He gestured at the man sitting next to the woman. " — or a copper-skinned nature boy who wears a loincloth and wrestles bears for a living? 'Ugh, that tenth bear me wrestled today. Bring on fourteen white squaws; me got a few weeks vacation coming.'

"And speaking of Indians — or did you folks call them 'savages' or 'heathens'? — how about that Manhattan Island deal? Bunch of goyim similar to yourselves shelled out twenty-four bucks in beads for a prime chunk of real estate. The kicker, though, is that the savage who sold the island had bought it from God the week before for a sack of rocks, so he went away chuckling because he'd done so well on the deal . . . 'Those white-eyed schlemiels with the funny hats! What a bunch of suckers!'

"Later on, of course, the white folks felt guilty for taking advantage of the poor ignorant redskins, so they threw in some good used blankets. Who knew the previous owners had died of smallpox?

"Speaking of disease, though, the Indians had the last laugh. They gave us tobacco in exchange for the blankets, and sooner or later all our lips are going to fall off. We're going to be up to our tuchuses in lips, which, ultimately, is what we all want anyway, right? Who says white people are stupid?"

The Puritans were still unsmiling. They clearly understood no more than every fifth word, and that word invariably made their expressions even grimmer.

Leonard was getting no laughs. Ultimately, when he wound down, that would hurt. He would finally run out of things to say, and then he would stand in the center of the circle, drained and defeated.

For now, though, he wouldn't think of that. For now, he was high on his own patter, his own stream of consciousness.

For now, he was on a roll.

". . . and after you boys and girls came over, you discovered that this nation-building business was a real pain, so you imported black men and women to do it for you. You were awfully smart to do that, but not as smart as us Jews. *We* waited until the country was built, and *then* we came over. Meantime, of course, we were getting slaughtered wherever else we happened to be living, but we didn't mind, because we knew that eventually we'd get to go to the Promised Land — Brooklyn.

"Oh, I see what you're thinking, sir. You reacted when I

identified myself as Jewish, and I know what you want to ask. The answer is Yes, we killed Him. Why? Because He refused to go to med school, that's why . . ."

Calvin Coolidge looked down disapprovingly.

9

During his time in the pillory, Leonard began to think that he finally understood the true horror of the Home: It was exactly like being alive again.

It wasn't that being in the pillory was so bad — at least he was in the back yard beside the pond, which was the best place on the grounds to be if you were trapped in a pillory. Since the pond was near the "northeast" corner of the wooden wall that defined the "eastern," "western," and "northern" boundaries of the mansion's grounds, he not only had a good view of what Mrs. Vonus called "the east yard and arbor," but could see all the way to the road beyond the front yard.

What bothered him wasn't the punishment itself but the fact that he had been forced to perform for people who couldn't possibly understand him, and that the Puritans had been allowed to put him into the pillory simply because they hadn't liked him.

"Well, of course you don't like me, you idiots!" he'd yelled as they had carried him out through the East Doorway. "A cave-man wouldn't have liked *you*, either! For that matter, neither do I!"

"I'm terribly sorry, Leonard," Mrs. Vonus had said as the Puritans had latched the pillory. "But you see, they wouldn't have agreed to hear you if I hadn't promised them the opportunity to punish you for your blasphemies. Rest assured that this is the worst I'll let them do. I'll release you in a few hours, after they've gone."

"Gone *where*?" Leonard had wanted to know, but the House-mother had already turned to waddle back to the mansion.

Then, as the sun had gone down, the Puritans had thrown overripe vegetables.

"Now, tell me, you bozos," Leonard had cried. "Would

Christ have approved of this? Would Jesus have thrown the first cabbage?"

A moldy turnip had hit him in the eye.

Now, as he watched a pair of white geese paddle across the pond, it occurred to him that Mrs. Vonus had wanted to pillory him herself, but had let the Puritans do her dirty work. The black-clad fanatics had disappeared at sunrise, but it was midday now and the Housemother still hadn't appeared to release him.

None of the residents walking nervously about the grounds would offer any help. A few of them shrugged their shoulders as if to say, "Tough luck, but I've got my own tsooris, you know?" but most of them simply ignored him.

So Leonard waited as the sun rose higher, watching the geese and smelling the vegetable stuff baking on his face and hands. At least there weren't any flies.

After what felt like several more hours, he raised his eyes and looked past the mansion toward the road. If it were only possible to make a move without Mrs. Vonus knowing about it, someday he would cut a branch and try to pole-vault the ditch so he could run down the dirt road in the direction from which he had come. He wouldn't care where the road went, not even if it led back to the toilet he'd been sitting on when he'd died. He wouldn't even care if he died all over again, as long as it meant that he would ruin the Housemother's plans.

It was an impossible hope. Mrs. Vonus always knew what he was doing, and she always appeared whenever he was about to do something "against the Rules of the Home."

His crotch began to itch.

"Wonderful," he muttered, and rubbed his thighs together. It didn't help.

A flash of red appeared down the road, and then Leonard heard the sound of the International's chugging engine. After a few minutes the pickup truck emerged from behind the trees and stopped.

The passenger door opened, and a stocky, overweight man stepped out. He was wearing the standard brown suit.

"Go back!" Leonard yelled hoarsely. "Throw Ol' Pete in the ditch, hijack the truck, and go back before she's got you!"

The stranger peered in Leonard's direction, but didn't follow the instructions. He began to cross the narrow footbridge that had reappeared with the arrival of the International.

The pickup's horn blared, and the stranger flailed, nearly falling into the ditch.

Engager in filthy activity with sows, Leonard thought, wishing he could remember the words that really expressed what he thought of Ol' Pete.

He watched the newcomer totter across the footbridge and then look back, just as he had done. The truck had vanished.

Shaking his head, the stocky man stepped onto the walk that led to the front door.

"Hey!" Leonard yelled, trying to force his voice to overcome its hoarseness. "Don't go that way! Come on back here! Back here, schnook!"

The stranger paused.

"Yeah, I'm talking to you!" Leonard shouted. "C'mere and get me out of this thing!"

The stranger came toward the pond, and as he drew near, the puzzled expression on his broad, doughy face became more evident.

"I'm Leonard," Leonard said when the stranger was close enough to hear unshouted words.

"Uh, pleased to meet you," the newcomer said uncertainly. "I'm —" He peered at the copper band on his wrist. " — John, I guess." His voice sounded like a combination of a baby's gurgle and an old man's cough.

"Well, that might be in your favor," Leonard said. "You're named after the Housemother's hero, sort of. Is 'John' all it says?"

John looked at his bracelet more closely. "Why? Should it say something else?"

Leonard tried to shrug, but the pillory wouldn't let him. "I've been trying to figure out if 'Leonard' is my first name or my last, and nobody else will let me look at their bracelets. But if yours just says 'John,' it's got to be a first name."

"Who says? What about Elton John?"

"Is that who you are?"

John looked surprised. "Do I look like Elton John?"

Leonard tried to shrug again. "How should I know? I never heard of the guy."

"Where have you been the last fifteen years?" John asked, incredulous.

"Dead," Leonard said. "Get me out of this thing, will you? I got an itch. Find something to break the lock."

John squinted. "There isn't a lock. Just a latch, like on a toolbox, you know?"

Leonard was finding it difficult to be patient. His crotch felt as if a thousand crabs had settled down to lunch.

"So quit kibbitzing and unlatch it already!" he yelled.

John reached for the latch, then paused and eyed Leonard suspiciously. "Am I going to get in trouble for this?"

"No!" Leonard shouted, not caring that he might be lying. "Now either get me outta here or scratch me where my pants are binding me!"

John raised an eyebrow in a way that Leonard supposed meant, "Hmmmm . . . interesting proposition," and then unlatched the pillory.

Leonard flung off the upper board, jammed his hands into his pants pockets, and scratched vigorously.

"That's disgusting," John said, and began to scratch himself in a similar fashion.

Leonard's first impulse was to snarl at the newcomer for mocking him, but then he realized that John's exaggerated mugging and scratching were *funny*.

"You should talk about disgusting," Leonard said. "You look like a sex-starved gorilla."

"I *am* a sex-starved gorilla," John said emphatically, and began lurching around the pond, waving his arms and screeching like a chimpanzee.

Leonard had a feeling that he was going to like this guy.

10

"I'll thank you not to bother our new resident," a thin, high-pitched voice said behind him.

Leonard's heart seemed to drop into his stomach and jump back up. Mrs. Vonus had sneaked up on him again.

He turned and glared at her. "I was merely making his acquaintance," he said. "He was kind enough to let me out of that Pilgrim peep show, which you promised you'd do a long time ago."

"I promised no such thing," Mrs. Vonus said.

"Bullsh — Bull —" Leonard began, then gave up and fumed.

Mrs. Vonus waddled a few steps closer to the pond.

"Please come with me, John," she called. "We must begin your orientation. My name is Mrs. Vonus."

John, still an ape, screeched in happy mock-recognition and scampered to the Housemother.

Leonard grinned.

"That will be enough of that, John," Mrs. Vonus said.

John made ooh-oohing noises and began to probe Mrs. Vonus's blue-gray helmet of hair with his thick fingers.

Leonard laughed. It would probably earn him a minus, but he didn't care. He was getting to the point where he didn't miss dessert that much, anyway.

"Stop this instant, John," Mrs. Vonus said.l

Her voice was so deadly cold that Leonard's laughter died. John continued to search for lice.

"You have two seconds," Mrs. Vonus said.

Leonard started toward John, intending to pull him away, but he was too late.

John stiffened convulsively, and his eyes rolled back. Then he crumpled to the grass, landing on his side with a faint "whuff."

Leonard knelt beside him and gently slapped his cheeks. He had to do something, because if he didn't, he would go for the Housemother's throat.

"He is quite all right," Mrs. Vonus said. "In any case, it is none of your affair."

I hate you, Leonard thought in a red heat. *I hate your scrawny guts, you miserable old yenta. You exist only to dictate rules, just like those self-righteous religion pimps back home.*

"Unless you wish to feel what John has just felt," Mrs. Vonus said, "I suggest you redirect your thoughts. I also suggest that you take a stroll about the grounds. Now."

Leonard stood stiffly and walked toward the back wall.

"Stand up, John," he heard the Housemother say. "There is a film I think you should see."

"A movie?" John's slurred voice said. "I love movies. I think I've been in some . . ."

You can bet you'll be in this one, Jim, Leonard thought as he forced his eyes to stay focused on the wall that was too high to scale. *You'll goddamn sure be in this one.*

He stopped short.

He had just thought one of the forgotten, forbidden words.

He waited for the lightning to strike, but it didn't come. Then he tried to think of the word again, but it was gone.

No matter. The chink in the armor had been tiny, but it had been there. All he had to do was make it bigger.

To discover how to do that, he would need an ally.

The way to start, he decided, was to do something he knew was against the Rules of the Home.

He would wait until Mrs. Vonus and John were inside the mansion. Then he would follow and hide until the Housemother had finished showing the newcomer the portrait and the Progress Board. He would watch for his chance to sneak into the theater, and then —

He would watch the screening of John's death. Maybe he could find some way to use the film against Mrs. Vonus before she had a chance to use it against John.

I'm already dead, Leonard thought as he pretended to wander aimlessly about the back yard, *so what have I got to lose?*

When Mrs. Vonus and John were almost to the East Door, Leonard went to the pond and washed the dried vegetable stuff from his face and hair. It was time to prepare for battle.

11

Leonard waited in a shadow in the hall a few yards away from the entrance to the lobby. He saw Mrs. Vonus open one of the double doors and usher John into the theater, then watched as she went behind the candy counter.

For a moment he was afraid that he wouldn't be able to get in without her seeing him, but then she opened a panel in the wall and disappeared up a flight of steps. Apparently, her powers didn't include turning on the projector by telekinesis.

The two women behind the candy counter would be a problem, but Leonard decided to take his chances. He stepped into the lobby and strode across to the double doors.

"Excuse me, sir," the blonde said. "The main feature does not begin for thirty minutes."

Leonard didn't slow down. "Yes, I know I'm late, sorry," he said, then opened the right-hand door and stepped into the darkness. He sat in the back row, not wanting to find John until he had some idea of how to approach him.

After a half-minute, the screen brightened and the House-mother's introductory spiel began. Leonard fidgeted in his seat, wanting desperately to shout an insult at the giant Mrs. Vonus-image to see whether he could remember that word again.

When the death film began, Leonard experienced such a strong sense of deja vu that he wondered whether he had known John in life. But as the film progressed, he realized that the feeling came from the fact that John's death was remarkably like his own.

In the same grainy black-and-white, John overdosed and died.

There were differences, of course: The camera-eye didn't remain stationary, but roamed from room to room, following John as he blundered through his final minutes. And there was a woman who gave him the injection, but she left before the end.

Finally, John lay on a bed, alone and still. Someone came into the frame and tried to revive him, then shouted angrily.

The final shot was a closeup of John's puffy face, the swollen tongue pushing out between dark lips.

The screen went black, and Leonard heard soft moaning noises.

Give the guy a few minutes of privacy, he thought. *Everybody ought to have a little time alone when they die.*

"I coulda," John moaned.

Leonard tried not to listen, but John's voice became louder with each syllable.

"I coulda," John said again. "I coulda gone back to New York. I coulda saved my stupid fat . . ."

There was a long pause, and then an explosive bellow:

"But NOOOOOOOOOOOOO. NOOOOOOOOO, I had to stay in HOL-LY-WOOOD so I could get off on a speedball and be COOOOL."

Leonard was impressed. Better to rail than to whimper and slide farther down in your seat.

The double doors opened, throwing a slanted shaft of yellow light down the aisle, and Leonard stood quickly so he could sit beside John before any of the others did. He didn't want the newcomer to meet anyone with JuJus before he had a chance to warn him.

12

Leonard found John in the same seat he had chosen on his own first day.

"Mind if I sit here?" Leonard asked, indicating the seat on John's right.

John looked at him through slitted eyes for a moment and then turned to face the screen again, shrugging his substantial shoulders.

Leonard sat down. "Whatever you do," he said, "don't take candy from these schmoes. It turns into bugs in the mouth of anyone except the guy who bought it."

John glanced at him. "Uh-huh."

"I'm serious," Leonard said. "The Housemother would rather you found out on your own, because she enjoys torturing schlimazels like you and me. I'm telling you in advance to save you the grief."

"Thanks," John said. "Now shut up. The movie's starting."

The screen was brightening, and Leonard closed his eyes even though he knew he wouldn't be able to keep them shut. He smelled popcorn somewhere behind him and hated whoever had been "good" enough to get the money to buy it.

"All right!" John yelped. "Jimmy Stewart!"

Leonard opened his eyes and shuddered. "You won't be so pleased after a while," he said.

"Are you kidding? *It's A Wonderful Life* is great!"

"Once, maybe, or even ten times if they're spread out over a few years. But not every afternoon for all eternity."

John shifted his bulk, jostling Leonard's elbow off the armrest. "What're you talking about?"

"Haven't you figured it out? Didn't Mrs. Vonus show you the Progress Board before she hustled you in here?"

"Yeah, but she's senile, isn't she? Hey — no more talk, okay?"

On the screen, the absurd nebulae-angels began discussing the poor soul who was about to take his own life.

Just once, Leonard thought, *I wish they'd let George croak himself. Let him leap into the ice-cold river. That's all, folks, thanks for coming. Frank Capra has suckered you, man.*

But it happened the way it always did — the ice-sledding accident, the distraught druggist, the swimming-pool-under-the-gym-floor, the evil banker, the war-hero brother, the insufferably cute children, the bumbling, wingless angel named Clarence —

Leonard wanted to scream, but he didn't. He had, once, on Day #6, and had been served burnt gristle for dinner. He also knew better than to try to walk out. His seat wouldn't let him up until the last frame had whisked through the projector.

So he resigned himself to sitting through it again, miserable and thoroughly angry at John, who, despite his outburst after seeing his death, didn't seem to care that he was stuck here.

What was wrong with him, anyway?

For that matter, what was wrong with *all* of these schmendricks? Hadn't they ever considered the possibility that where one failed, many could succeed?

Or did Mrs. Vonus see to it that new residents arrived at long intervals, so she'd be able to break the spirit of each one before Ol' Pete brought the next?

It made sense, considering the nature of time at the Home. A hundred comedians might die in the same hour, but they'd arrive singly, one every fifteen or twenty "days," if that was the interval chosen by the Housemother.

Or by someone else?

If Mrs. Vonus chose the length of the interval, how could her failure to tame Leonard before John's arrival be explained?

Now that he thought about it, it seemed to Leonard that the previous night's performance for the Puritans and his subsequent imprisonment in the pillory had been the House-mother's last-ditch attempts to bring him into line before she had to concentrate on breaking in a newcomer.

That would explain how he had managed to remember that word: Mrs. Vonus had been preoccupied with John.

She was not omnipotent.

Leonard grinned. If he could enlist John's help before she sank her claws into him too deeply, they could bounce her back and forth between them like a ping-pong ball.

For what purpose? he wondered. *What good will that do me? Will it get me out of here?*

He brushed the questions out of his mind. Maybe running the Housemother ragged wouldn't accomplish anything; maybe he was bound here by forces beyond those she commanded. It didn't matter.

To rebel was to be doing something because *he* wanted to do it. That was enough.

13

"Punch him out, Jimmy!" John yelled, startling Leonard out of his thoughts. "Give the old fu — fu —"

John paused, and in the dim reflected light, Leonard could see an expression of confusion on the pudgy face.

" — the old fuddy-duddy a clop in the chops!" John concluded.

Leonard laughed.

"Sshhhhhh!" someone several rows behind them hissed. "Quiet, or I'll report you to the Housemother."

Leonard looked back over his shoulder.

"Dracula had his human henchmen, too," he said loudly. "Eat your flies and leave us alone."

"Fuddy-duddy?" John said, obviously bewildered by his own description of Lionel Barrymore. "*Fuddy-duddy?*"

Leonard leaned closer to him. "You beginning to get the drift? I had to deal with censorship in my life, and maybe you did in yours, but at least it was censorship you could see, censorship you could fight. Here they censor your *mind* so that you can't even think of what you want to say in the first place."

"How . . . how can they do that?" John seemed torn between listening to Leonard and watching the movie.

" 'How' I don't know," Leonard said, "but 'why' is no problem. Because this is Hell, or maybe Purgatory, where they punish you for your sins. And it's a rigged wheel, because they also decide what constitutes 'sin' in the first place."

"Who are 'they,' anyhow?"

"I don't know for sure, but they're represented by Mrs. Vonus. She's not known for excessive kindness to the recently deceased."

John made a derisive noise through his nostrils. "That little old lady? She's about as dangerous as a lobotomized gerbil."

"You forgetting what she did to you out back?"

"Sshhhhh!" the resident behind them hissed again.

"Somebody back there spring a leak?" John yelled.

"Pay no attention," Leonard said. "They're whining lackeys. Besides, they'll see this again tomorrow. That's the power of a lobotomized gerbil — whether you want to or not, you'll be here again tomorrow afternoon. She'll hook that invisible claw of hers into your brain and drag you here. If you try to resist, she'll send you to bed without dinner for a day or two."

John drummed his thick fingers on the armrest. "Let me get this straight. I have to come back here at the same time tomorrow. And I'm going to see the same movie?"

"Bingo, bubee."

"Well, he — he — heck, then, I don't need to see the rest of it now. I've already missed too much listening to you, so I might as well go find something to eat."

John struggled to stand. When he finally gave up, he slumped like a chubby wrestler who had just lost a long, painful bout. Sweat glistened on his cheeks and forehead.

"See what I mean?" Leonard said. "If this doesn't qualify

as Hell, I don't know what does."

"Certain portions of Utah," John said, panting heavily.

Leonard smiled. Mrs. Vonus would probably crush them both eventually, but he had a feeling that they were going to give her a run for her money.

That feeling grew stronger when John, having recovered from his struggle, straightened in his seat and began heckling the characters on the screen.

"Come on, you jerk!" John yelled. "Take an axe to the piano if it bugs you! Whop the kid up side the head!"

And later: "G'wan, jump! The water's dee-lightful!"

And still later: "You talk like a sissy, Clarence!"

Toward the end of the film, Leonard decided to get into the act.

"Merry Christmas, Main Street!" he cried. "Merry Christmas, old building and loan! Merry Christmas, old movie theater! Merry Christmas, old five-and-dime! Merry Christmas, old cathouse!"

John guffawed and then bellowed, "Merry Christmas, old chuckhole! Merry Christmas, old dirty bookstore! Merry Christmas, old dog-frozen-to-the-fire-hydrant!"

"Merry Christmas, old social disease clinic!" Leonard shouted.

By now, the scene of Stewart-as-George-Bailey running down Main Street was over, but Leonard and John didn't care. They were on a roll.

"Merry Christmas, old drunk in the alley!" John yelled.

"Merry Christmas, old bird-do on the sidewalk!" Leonard cried.

Something strange happened then, something Leonard never would have expected.

A few other dead comedians joined them in their heckling, and then a few more.

"Merry Christmas, old mashed cat in the gutter!"

"Merry Christmas, old rats in the sewer!"

"Merry Christmas, old tires at the gas station!"

Before long, the soundtrack was drowned out by the shouts. Leonard thought he even heard the voice of whoever had tried to quiet him earlier.

"Merry Christmas, old jokes on the john wall!"
"Merry Christmas, old strippers on the stage!"
"Merry Christmas, old scotch-and-soda!"
"Merry Christmas, and a Happy New Rear!"
"Merry Men, save Robin Hood!"
"Marry me, darling!"
"Mary, Mary, quite contrary . . ."

It degenerated into lunacy, and Leonard felt happier than he had at any moment since dying.

The movie ended as it always did, with the bell on the Christmas tree ringing and the little girl in Jimmy Stewart's arms expressing the opinion that some angel was getting his wings. This time, though, when Stewart said, "That's right," John shouted "That's ridiculous!"

Leonard decided that was the perfect response, so he added his own, "Yeah, that's ridiculous!"

Before the credits came on, the whole audience was chanting, "That's ridiculous! That's ridiculous! That's ridiculous!"

"Merely silly!" someone cried between chants.

Joy thrilled up in Leonard, giving him a greater rush than he'd ever gotten from horse. The Revolution, he was sure, had begun at last.

14

But the joy was more like the transitory ecstasy of a narcotic than Leonard had thought. As soon as the lights came up, the chanting stopped, and the other residents hurried out of the theater like frightened mice.

John stood up and yelled, "Any of you guys play the blues?"

A few of the residents glanced back, but none answered.

"Forget it, man," Leonard said sullenly. "I thought we might've put a spark into them, but they were just having flashbacks to when they had some guts, to when they were alive. She's got them under her thumb."

The last of the others disappeared beyond the double doors, leaving Leonard and John alone.

John's stomach growled so loudly that the sound echoed

off the walls.

"This is the first movie I've ever sat through without at least a box of popcorn," he said. "Where can I get something to eat around here?"

"You can't," Leonard said.

"Whaddaya mean, I can't? I'm hungry, aren't I? I've gotta eat if I'm hungry, don't I?"

Leonard stood and moved toward the aisle. "The dinner bell rings a few hours or a few days after the movie, depending on your time sense. You get to the dining room by going through the Front Parlor. You know, Calvin's room."

John walked beside him toward the double doors. "Hey, I can't wait. I'm hungry *now.*"

"Me too. But I doubt that the Housemother'll let me eat today. I've been a bad boy."

"I didn't figure you were wearing a wooden collar to be stylish. But I'll get to eat, won't I?"

"That's up to her," Leonard said, pushing open the doors. "In all fairness, though — hanging out with me won't do you much good in that department. I'm on her excrement list."

"Don't you mean sh — sh —" John said as they stepped into the lobby. He stopped and frowned.

Leonard paused and studied John's face. The heavy eyebrows were angled and pushed together so that the frown seemed almost a parody of the expression.

"Weren't you listening to what I said about censorship?" Leonard asked. "Haven't you caught on yet?"

John seemed about to answer, but then his eyes shifted to the candy counter. His expression changed abruptly, and he nudged Leonard in the ribs.

"Women and junk food," he said eagerly. "I noticed 'em before, but the gerbil was with me." He headed toward the counter.

"You're wasting your time," Leonard said.

John looked back over his shoulder, raising an eyebrow. "I've got nothing *but* time, Jack." He turned toward the counter again.

Leonard considered heading for his room to avoid seeing John's coming humiliation, but there was nothing waiting for him there except the picture of the saint-about-to-become-chopped-liver.

He reached the counter at the same time as John. Together, they leaned with their elbows on the glass countertop and leered at the women.

John waggled his eyebrows lasciviously. "Helloooo," he said. "I couldn't help but notice that there are two of you ladies and two of us gentlemen. A convenient coincidence, wouldn't you say?"

The women stared blankly.

"Arithmetic seems to be beyond them," Leonard said.

"I don't care if they can count," John said. "I don't even care if they can talk. I'll take the blonde, you take the brunette. Deal?"

"Sure. Just out of curiosity, though, how do you plan to convince them of the reasonableness of the arrangement?"

"Sheer animal charm," John said, and vaulted over the counter with far more ease than Leonard would have thought possible for a man of his bulk.

"Which animal?" Leonard asked. "An orangutan, maybe?"

"Maybe," John said, and grabbed the blonde around the waist, dipping her backward as if he were Rhett Butler and she were Scarlett O'Hara.

Leonard winked at the brunette and started clambering over the counter.

"Baby," John was saying in a bad imitation of Clark Gable, "you're for me."

"I suggest you release me immediately," the blonde said.

"Better turn up the animal charm a notch or two," Leonard said, swiveling on his belly on the countertop.

"I cannot release you, *mon cher*," John said, his lips less than an inch from the woman's. "We're bound together by invisible diamond chains of hot volcanic love."

Leonard landed heavily on the tiled floor inside the U of the counter, slipping a little on a slick of spilled popcorn butter. " 'Invisible diamond chains of hot volcanic love?' " he asked.

"Shut up," John said. "Can't you see I'm seducing this woman?"

"Release me now," the blonde said.

John planted his lips on hers in what appeared to Leonard to be the sloppiest kiss in history.

Leonard grinned at the brunette. "I'd hate to feel left out, wouldn't you?"

"You might find it preferable," she said.

Leonard moved a step closer. "Oh, I don't think —"

The rest of his sentence was cut off by John's scream.

Leonard whirled and saw his friend locked in an embrace with a catfish-woman.

She had arms and legs, but they were sickly-gray, *slimy* arms and legs. Her head, although still covered with blonde hair, had transformed into that of a scaleless fish, complete with whisker-like barbels.

John was writhing in the creature's embrace, spitting frantically.

"For the love of — pahhh!" he cried. "She tastes like rancid cat food!"

Leonard glanced back at the brunette woman, who still looked delectably human, and said, "Maybe some other time."

"I doubt it," she said.

John tore away from the catfish-woman, shoving her to the floor in the process, and lunged for the candy counter.

"Gotta get that taste outta my mouth!" he yelled, and grabbed several boxes of Junior Mints.

"That will be six dollars," the brunette said.

"Don't," Leonard said, grabbing John's arm. "They'll start crawling in your mouth."

John twisted away and ripped open the boxes, dumping their contents onto the countertop. Dozens of chocolate-coated mint-buttons rolled and slid across the glass.

"They don't look alive to me, bud!" John yelled.

Leonard stared at them. Maybe the thing with the cockroaches only happened if you ate candy that someone else had bought. No one had bought this stuff yet, so —

"Junior Mints, prepare to meet thy doom!" John roared, and squatted so that his mouth was at the edge of the counter.

The catfish-woman flopped on the floor and made a gurgling noise.

Leonard gave her a sidelong look. "No offense, sweetheart, but you've got an odor problem."

John began scooping the candies into his mouth with both hands, making small noises of pleasure as he chewed.

The scents of chocolate and mint overpowered the fish-stink and filled Leonard's head, making him dizzy. He resisted for several seconds, but when he saw that nothing was happening to John, he decided to grab some candy before it was all gone.

He knelt beside his friend.

"I feel like a Catholic who just hit the Host jackpot," he said, and shoved a handful of mints into his mouth.

"You must stop immediately," the brunette woman's voice said behind him. The warning was accompanied by the sounds of the blonde's flopping and gurgling.

Leonard ignored them and concentrated on his feast. Even when Mrs. Vonus let him eat, the food was relentlessly bland, but this — this was smooth, creamy, minty, and luxuriously chocolatey. He reveled in it, filling his mouth with a huge blob of sweetness.

For a second, he thought he was no longer in Hell, but Heaven.

Then something squirmed out of the blob and tried to slither down his throat.

He gagged, and as he spun away from the counter he heard John give a strangled cry.

I knew better, Leonard thought as he saw the writhing mass he had spit onto the white tile.

Worms and slugs.

I knew better, and I did it anyway.

He felt nausea, but no regret.

15

"Yes, you did know better, Leonard," Mrs. Vonus said. "Why are you so self-destructive?"

He looked up and saw her standing over him. He wasn't surprised to see her.

John was crawling across the floor like an overweight dog.

"Oh, mother," he moaned. "Bad acid. Bad, bad acid. I knew I'd get flashbacks, I *knew* it, but NOOOOOOOOO, I had to have three tabs, and six years later, here they are again."

Leonard stood and wiped his mouth on his jacket sleeve. "You're not flashing back. This is what's happening. And this —" He nodded toward Mrs. Vonus. " — is who's doing it to you. She claims she's trying to mold us into perfection, but she really means to crush our spirits, not build them up."

"You're confusing 'spirit' and 'will,' " the Housemother said. " 'Will' is the evil part of man and has always been his downfall. Only by denying the will can you be saved."

Leonard tugged on John's left arm, trying to pull him to his feet. To his surprise, the brunette woman grasped John's right arm and helped.

"That isn't necessary, Melody," Mrs. Vonus said sharply.

"Nice name," Leonard told the brunette as they brought John to a standing position. "Thanks."

Melody looked down. Leonard's eyes followed, and he saw that the blonde had flopped across the floor and was gulping the worms and slugs.

John was swaying back and forth and beginning to babble nonsense.

" — ponies jump sniff good hot mother don't needle ah yes Baskin-Robbins —"

Leonard couldn't tell whether it was an act or not.

"Come on, friend," he said. "Let's get out of here." He tugged John toward the narrow gap between the end of the candy counter and the wall.

"Another resident will show John to his room," Mrs. Vonus said. "I would rather you didn't have any further contact with him."

Leonard was maneuvering the chunky man through the gap with some difficulty; John's belly had folded over the countertop and didn't want to move.

" — tutti-frutti all over the redeye Louie Louie —"

"What are you gonna do?" Leonard asked the House-mother. "Babysit him constantly so he doesn't meet me in the hall or the back yard? Well, that's fine with me, because if you're with him, you can't be nudzhing me. Here, he's all yours."

Leonard left John stuck in the gap and clambered over the counter again, kicking a few stray Junior Mints across the lobby.

It was only when one of the mints bounced off a resident's forehead that Leonard noticed eight other comedians standing in the mouth of the hallway.

"What are you guys doing here?" he asked. He had never seen anyone loiter in or near the lobby after the movie. "Enjoying the floor show? What'd you think of the amazing fish-faced bimbo?" He glanced back and saw that the blonde was in human form again.

"These gentlemen are my most advanced residents, and they aren't here for amusement," Mrs. Vonus said. "Four of them are being assigned as companions to John, and four are being assigned as companions to you. At least one will be near you at all times and will report any problems."

Leonard stopped in the center of the lobby and stared at the eight men facing him. They seemed so incredibly dull — as if they were all from Buffalo, New York — that he found it hard to believe that any of them had ever made it in comedy.

But they had, or they wouldn't have been brought to the Home in the first place.

Realizing that, he studied their placid faces and saw what Mrs. Vonus wanted to turn him into. He saw the truth of the Afterlife:

The way to move up the Hill, to get to a Better Place, was to resign oneself to an Eternity of white-bread complacency and ordinariness. To become a thing of flesh-colored clay.

To become a golem.

He backed away from them. "Oh no, you don't. You don't transform four of these schmendricks into my shadows, lady. Where this Jewish boy walks, he walks alone. Or if not alone, then in the company of a good-looking chick."

"You have no choice in the matter," the Housemother said. "Frederick, you shall take the first shift with Leonard. Albert, you shall take the first shift with John."

Two of the white-bread golems stepped forward.

Leonard held up a fist. "Who wants to be the first to sing soprano?"

"If you touch your companion," Mrs. Vonus said, "you will experience pain three times as intense as what you experienced for trying to alter the Progress Board."

John, who had been babbling quietly since getting stuck between the wall and counter, now shouted, "You useless weenies!"

Leonard turned and saw the fat man squeeze himself out of the gap like a cork out of a bottleneck.

"What are you, men or mothballs?" John yelled, pointing at the golems.

"'Mothballs?'" Leonard said.

"Whatsa mattayou pimple-brains?" John bellowed, gesticulating so vigorously that his paunch shook like gelatin. "Don'tcha know when you're being walked all over? Are you just going to sit back and take it? Did Custer sit back and take it when the Japanese attacked? Did Joan of Arc let her religion stop her from eating her enemies raw without salt? Did Dagwood cower like a whipped dog when Mister Dithers hit him with a typewriter? You bet he didn't, boy! He went ahead and asked for a raise anyway, and when Mister Dithers hit him with another typewriter, he asked *again*! And here you are, standing like doofs with your elbows up your noses, afraid to —"

John turned toward Leonard and whispered, "What are they afraid to do?"

"Anything," Leonard said. "Everything."

John's face took on an expression of exaggerated disgust. "What a bunch of wimps," he said.

"Enough nonsense," Mrs. Vonus said. "Frederick, Albert — please take these gentlemen to their rooms. If they are reluctant, touch them lightly. Neither of them will be allowed to eat this evening. Lock them in their rooms until you've finished your own meals, then allow them the freedom of the grounds as long as they do not meet. You will be relieved in the morning."

The brown-haired, Presbyterian-looking golem named Frederick gestured to Leonard, and the brown-haired, Presbyterian-looking golem named Albert gestured to John.

"Sorry, friend," Leonard said to John. "Looks like I got you into trouble after all."

John went into a Sumo wrestler's stance. "Trouble? Ha! I'll show these guys trouble. Trouble is my middle name. I'm John T. Something-Or-Other. Let 'em at me. I'll eat their gall bladders. I'll stomp their toes. I'll move their kneecaps to their ankles. I'll put black dots on their teeth and play dominoes. I'll —"

The golem called Albert walked up to John and brushed his wrist with a fingertip. John sat down on the scarlet carpet.

" — do whatever you say," he mumbled.

Leonard charged at Albert. Before he could get there, a spear of heat stabbed from the top of his head to the soles of his feet.

He found himself kneeling before Frederick. He looked up at the white-bread face through a red-and-black checkerboard of pain and said, "I wish you were an enemy plane and I were on the U.S.S. *Brooklyn* so I could do horrible things to you with a five-inch deck gun."

The golem gestured for Leonard to stand. Leonard did so, after three tries, and was about to help John up, but stopped when Frederick shook his head.

"He won't make it without me," Leonard said.

Mrs. Vonus came around the candy counter and waddled toward the hallway.

"That's where you're wrong," she said. "He'll 'make it' perfectly well without you, and you without him. If you meet again, it will be because I have decided that there will be some benefit to both of you as a result. I do not expect that day to arrive for quite some time."

The Housemother entered the hall and was gone.

The brunette woman, Melody, came around the counter and helped John to his feet. The blonde frowned at her but said nothing.

John looked pale and disoriented. As his eyes refocused, he stared at Melody as if seeing her for the first time. "Are you one of my groupies?" he asked, slurring the words.

Leonard noticed that Melody flushed slightly. He managed to smile at her, although it made his teeth hurt. "How'd a nice chick like you wind up working for the Gestapo Queen? I'd've thought you'd have gone to the Florence Nightingale

Home For Knockout Angels Of Mercy."

Melody returned to the other side of the counter. "I was given the opportunity to volunteer," she said. "How about you . . . sir?"

Leonard shrugged, even though that hurt too. "I was drafted."

Frederick gestured at him again.

"Gotta go now," Leonard said, waving to both John and Melody. "Command performance in my room. There's this saint about to be made into bratwurst who wants to laugh before she dies."

"A challenge!" John cried, a little weakly. "Did Magellan give up getting to the South Pole just because it was a challenge? Did Alexander Graham Bell throw out the penicillin just because it was a little moldy? Did Abe Lincoln stop being President just because he got shot?"

"Yes," Leonard said, and headed for the hallway. Each step sent a red rush of pain boiling into his head.

"Oh," he heard John say behind him. "Darn that Abe Lincoln, anyway."

Yeah, Leonard thought. *Darn it all to heck.*

16

Within five sunrises, Leonard was spending all of his free time in his room, coming downstairs only for mandatory activities — sing-alongs (endless repetitions of the Doxology), meals (one out of every three dinners he was allowed to eat consisted of broiled liver and Brussels sprouts), and the daily movie (after a while, he was so bored that he even stopped wishing Jimmy Stewart would jump into the bush after the possibly-nude Donna Reed).

At least one of his four guards, his golem for the day, was always with him. When he lay on his bed, the golem sat on a hard-backed chair beside the door. When he awoke in the morning, the golem accompanied him down the hall to the communal bathroom. When he went to the afternoon movie, the golem sat beside him.

None of the four would talk to him or do anything besides

watch him. Leonard began calling them all 'Fred,' knowing he would be right at least twenty-five percent of the time.

"Hey, Fred," he said on the seventh evening, lying on his bed after eating a dinner that thankfully, blessedly, had not been liver and Brussels sprouts, "tell me a story."

Frederick sat on his chair, looking like an embalmed corpse in the weak yellow light given off by the kerosene lamp on the nightstand.

"Don't feel like it, huh?" Leonard said. "Okay, then, explain things to me. Explain why this place has electricity — you've gotta have electricity to run a movie projector, right? — but every lamp has a wick instead of a light bulb."

Fred didn't even blink.

Leonard sat up. "You don't seem to understand," he said, the muscles in his throat becoming as taut as stretched steel cables. "I have to have a conversation. You won't let me near the candy counter, so I can't even say hello to Melody or the amphibious bimbo. I only see John at distances of twenty yards or more. And talking to Mrs. Vonus is like trying to chum up to my executioner. So here's the deal: I'm going to talk to you, and you're going to talk to me, or I'm going to take off your head, Fred."

Leonard searched the golem's face for some evidence that he was getting through — a muscle twitch, an eye movement, anything — and found nothing.

"All right," he said slowly, "if you're shy, I'll go first. The topic we'll begin with is Early Trauma: When I was in seventh grade, I stole money from my school's Red Cross drive so I could buy a pair of sneakers for gym class. I was caught, and my father, in addition to beating me up, never forgave me for the shame I had brought upon him. Your turn."

Frederick remained still and silent.

"C'mon, Fred," Leonard said, "surely you can remember something of your life before death, of life before servitude to an ancient and vindictive Daisy Duck."

A muscle in Frederick's left cheek twitched, but that was all.

"I'm going to count to five," Leonard said, pressing the balls of his feet against the hardwood floor and tensing on the edge of the bed, "and then I'm tearing out your esophagus. One, two, three, four —"

He paused, waiting for Frederick to do something, or at least to warn him again of the penalty Mrs. Vonus had imposed for touching a golem. But Frederick did nothing.

Leonard had no desire to feel the pain he knew he would feel when his fingers touched his guard's skin, but he had committed himself. He had told the golem he would attack, and to fail to do so would be to demonstrate that the Housemother had frightened him into obedience, that she had won.

"Five!" he yelled, and launched himself across the room.

In the instant before his hands closed on Frederick's throat, he saw the golem smile.

Then he fell into an inferno of blue-tinged pain.

When it faded, he found himself lying on his side looking up at the ecstatic saint. His shoulders throbbed violently, and his arms felt as if they had almost been torn off.

Groaning, he turned onto his back and saw Frederick sitting like God on Judgment Day, looking down on him with an expression similar to that of the *Mona Lisa*.

The throbbing subsided to a painful tingle, and Leonard pushed himself up to a sitting position.

"That made you happy, didn't it, Fred?" he asked.

Fred's expression didn't change.

"I'm glad," Leonard said. "If you're taking pleasure in my pain, that means I've broken your spirituality a little. They don't want sadists on the Hill, do they?"

Frederick's half-smile faded, and Leonard was pleased to see that the golem actually looked distressed.

He hadn't been able to strangle the jerk, but he had accomplished something anyway.

With that realization, Leonard knew what he would do next.

What was the saying? *That which does not kill us makes us stronger*, wasn't it? And who had said it? Plato? Nietzsche? Teddy Roosevelt? John Wayne? The coyote from the Road Runner cartoons?

Doesn't matter, Leonard thought. *The point is, nothing can kill me, on account of I'm already dead. So pain can only make me stronger . . . in theory, anyhow.*

He struggled up to his feet. "Don't worry, Freddy boy. I'm going to give you another chance to turn the other cheek."

He took a deep breath and fell on the golem before he could change his mind. His hands closed around Frederick's throat, and a razor of pain slit his arms, shoulders, and head.

He felt his eyeballs boiling, his teeth shattering.

But he held on.

A second razor followed the first, and he thought he screamed. He wasn't sure, because he couldn't hear anything except a thundering rush of white noise.

But he held on.

Then came the third razor, and the red-and-black checkerboard pattern flooded in.

But, until the last half-second of consciousness, he held on.

When he came to, Leonard knew that he had not been out long. He was on his knees beside Frederick's chair, and the golem was looking down at him with something in his eyes that might be fear.

Forcing a grin, Leonard stood shakily, staggered to the bed, and sat down.

"I'm going to rest a few minutes, Fred ol' buddy ol' pal," he said, surprised at the strength of his voice, "and then we'll try it again."

"I will report," the golem said. The three words were the first that any of the guards had spoken.

"So go ahead," Leonard said. "Let's see what she comes up with this time. Variety is the spice of life." He chuckled, and winced at the pain in his chest. "Or, in this case, death."

When the pain subsided, he walked across the room and jabbed his right index finger into Frederick's shoulder. The jolt sent him stumbling backward, but he didn't fall.

He jabbed the golem again. And again.

It hurt horribly, but after several more jabs he began to think that he might be able to get used to pain, just as he had gotten used to the tattoo he'd had in life.

"You can hit me back if you like," he said as he continued to jab.

Frederick didn't answer, but now Leonard was sure that

the look in his guard's eyes was fear.

When he finally lay on his bed again, exhausted and half-paralyzed with pain, Leonard winked at the saint on his wall.

17

Mrs. Vonus called him down to the foyer two nights later, and he had to restrain himself from laughing when he saw that John, without his guard, was there too.

He had to restrain himself because laughing was extremely painful.

"Frederick, you may leave until I call for you," Mrs. Vonus said as Leonard and his guard left the stairway.

The golem turned to go back upstairs.

"See you later, eh, Freddy?" Leonard said, punching the golem in the shoulder. His arm felt as if the skin were being flayed off, but he only grinned and tried to keep his mind blank. He wanted the Housemother to think he didn't feel a thing.

Frederick, looking distraught, retreated.

John whistled admiringly. "How'd you do that? I tried to get Prince Albert in a half-Nelson once and thought I was gonna split open like Humpty Dumpty."

Leonard shrugged, barely keeping himself from wincing, and said, "Looks like you've lost some weight."

John's expression switched from admiration to unhappiness. "That'll happen when you're only allowed to eat every other day."

Leonard glared at Mrs. Vonus. "You starving this kid?"

The Housemother seemed perturbed. "He is overweight, so I have put him on a diet."

"Diet, schmyet," Leonard said. "He's dead, isn't he? You've got powers, don't you? Why don't you just hocus-pocus the excess baggage away?"

Mrs. Vonus sighed. "I've told you before: Here you must learn the things you did not learn in life. John was a glutton in life, so he must learn to avoid that sin before being allowed to —"

"Yeah, yeah, yeah," Leonard interrupted. "Before he goes skipping up the Hill like a good little angel, tra-la-la, whoop-te-do. Bullsh — Bull — Nonsense." The word was far too weak. "The truth is that you still want to punish him for the trouble he got into on his first day. You made up this 'diet' scam as an excuse to hurt him."

John's eyebrows shot up, and he spun to face Mrs. Vonus. "Is that true? I've been good except for the half-Nelson, haven't I? I paid for that mistake as soon as I made it, didn't I?"

The Housemother pursed her lips. "You mustn't listen to Leonard. I'm afraid he hasn't progressed beyond the point where he'll say anything to cause difficulty for me."

"Hey, John," Leonard said, "am I the one who gave you a two-legged electric eel for a playmate?"

John opened his mouth to answer, but Mrs. Vonus spoke before he had a chance.

"Enough of this," she said. "Leonard, you are dangerously close to losing dinner privileges for three days in a row. Kindly be quiet and come with me, both of you." She turned and waddled into the Front Parlor.

Leonard leaned close to John and whispered, "She's scared, man. Why else would she crack enough to let us get together again?"

John edged away and followed the Housemother.

Leonard hurried to catch up. "What's wrong? I got a disease or something?"

John paused at the entrance to the Parlor. "Nothing personal," he said softly. "It's just that I'm dying from lack of food, and I don't want to tick her off. You've only been downstairs two minutes, and you've already made me gripe at her."

Leonard felt dazed for a moment, then angry. "You're a coward."

"No," John said, "I'm hungry." He followed Mrs. Vonus into the Front Parlor.

Leonard stood in the entranceway, debating whether to finally try to escape.

"The front door won't let you out," Mrs. Vonus called. "And if you hesitate any longer, the floor of the foyer will become hot enough to burn the flesh off your feet."

Leonard went into the Front Parlor and saw that the furniture was arranged in a circle again.

This time, the audience consisted of forty Orthodox rabbis wearing phylacteries, tallithim, and yarmulkes.

John and Mrs. Vonus waited in the center of the circle. The Housemother was holding two cordless microphones.

"You're slipping," Leonard said as he walked sideways between two chairs to enter the circle. "These guys aren't going to slap me into a pillory."

"Perhaps not," Mrs. Vonus said, handing him one of the microphones. "But can you make them laugh?"

Leonard considered that.

With the Puritans, he had known what to expect. But with this audience . . . How could he predict how they would react to him? It would depend on where they were from, who they knew, in which decade they had died . . .

"Sure I can," he said, hoping that the Housemother wasn't reading his mind.

Mrs. Vonus turned toward John. "And you? Can you make these good men laugh?"

John looked nervous. "I, uh . . . what am I supposed to do?"

"Why, what you did in life," the Housemother said. "Be funny." She handed John the second microphone and went to sit beside one of the rabbis.

"You want to go first?" Leonard asked John.

John's face looked waxy. "I —" he began, whispering hoarsely, and swallowed. "I can't do standup. I'm a sketch player. Besides, I need some . . . some stuff."

Leonard nodded. "Sometimes I needed a little taste, too. But no matter what I did to get ready, I always needed to throw up before going onstage. Three good upchucks, and I was fine."

"I heard that about you," John said.

Leonard was taken aback. "You know who I am?"

John licked his lips. "I think so, but I can't remember your name. It's as if it's one of those words we can't say here."

Leonard grinned. "Sounds right." He looked around the room at the rabbis, most of whom were stroking their beards in an irritated fashion. "Tell you what. I'll start, and if you think of something, jump in."

John swallowed again, his Adam's apple jerking as if it were trying to escape his throat. "Don't count on me. I feel like barfing."

"There'd be something wrong with you if you didn't," Leonard said, and brought his microphone up to his lips.

18

"*Sholem alecheim*, gentlemen," Leonard said, his voice booming from the walls, and waited for the rabbis' response.

They said nothing.

"What's this?" Leonard said in mock surprise. "Rabbis unwilling to wish a fellow Jew peace? Have you been hanging out with Baptists or what? Oh, not that I blame you — you probably don't consider me a proper Jew. I was foul-mouthed, disrespectful, unobservant, and irreverent. Besides which, I had a tattoo and consorted with so many shiksas that you'd all drop dead if I told you the number — if you weren't already dead, that is."

"Shame," one of the rabbis said severely.

"This is funny?" said another.

"*Oy, Gottenyu!*" moaned a third.

Leonard turned to gesture at the portrait of Calvin Coolidge. John was standing to one side of the fireplace, looking pale and sick.

"Now there," Leonard said, indicating Coolidge, "was a good Jewish boy for you. He was clean, reverent, chaste, temperate, and so polite that he often seemed to be in a coma. Not to mention that he grew up to be President. Why is it, rabbis, that all of the really good Jewish boys turn out to be goyim?"

As he asked the question, he brought his gaze down from the portrait and saw that John's eyes were wide with terror.

Leonard turned quickly and saw that all of the rabbis had become smooth-shaven Catholic priests.

They've been waiting for this chance ever since Chicago, ever since I started doing the Religions, Incorporated bit, he thought. *Now they can keep me in a hostile courtroom until the universe disintegrates and each of them puts a spot of the ash on his forehead —*

He saw that Mrs. Vonus was smiling more broadly than she had at any time since he'd come to the Home.

— *and Miss Self-Righteous Daisy Duck gave me to them.*

"Are you going to tell us your confession or aren't you?" one of the priests asked sternly.

"Confession?" Leonard asked. "That's only for the faithful, isn't it? Do I look faithful? Let's try a test: 'Hail, Mary, full of grapes —' What the heck, you didn't wanna hear my confession anyhow, pops, er, Father. It's pretty messy, particularly the part where I dress like a priest and con middle-aged women into giving me loads of cash for a South American leper colony, keeping half for myself. But hey, you can understand that. You put on a stiff white collar, and anybody who's carrying around the smallest shred of guilt — meaning everybody — feels compelled to give you money, all of it tax-free. It's almost worth giving up sex, and it's definitely worth *saying* you'll give up sex."

The priests' faces became more than grim.

"Heretic," one said, almost growling.

"He should be burned at the stake," another said, and turned toward the Housemother. "We can do that, can't we?"

Mrs. Vonus nodded. "Keep in mind, however, that he won't die."

"As long as he hurts," the priest said.

Leonard stared at the Housemother. "But — When the Puritans put me in the pillory, you said —"

"You've made no progress since then," she said. "More serious measures are in order."

Every muscle in Leonard's body knotted with his outrage. "Hypocrite!" he screamed, and his voice shrieked from the walls with a sound like grinding metal. "You think you've fixed us so we can't say dirty words? Well, you forgot *hypocrite.* A hypocrite lies to the people she claims to be saving, and when she's caught in the lie, she says, 'That was then; this is now; you haven't been good enough.' "

Mrs. Vonus's smile disappeared. "You could have listened to me. You could have tried to understand why you have to change —"

"But NOOOOOOOOOOOOOOOO," John cried, bounding

up to stand beside Leonard. "You had to be an *individual*. You had to indulge your *self*."

Leonard couldn't tell whether John was being sarcastic or serious, but he chose to believe that the other comedian had found some courage.

"I know, I know," Leonard said melodramatically, closing his eyes and placing the back of his left wrist against his forehead. "How could I have been so unreasonable as to believe in the sanctity of anything so despicable as individual freedom?"

"REPENT!" fifty voices shouted.

Leonard opened his eyes and saw that the priests had been replaced by evangelical preachers in three-piece suits. They were all standing, waving heavy black Bibles and pointing at him.

"THE DAY OF JUDGMENT IS UPON YE!" they cried.

John touched Leonard's arm. "What's going on?" he whispered. He was still holding his microphone to his mouth, and the whisper hissed through the room like a gust of wind.

Leonard felt dizzy. He was afraid to see what the preachers would turn into next.

He lowered his microphone and spoke into John's ear. "She's pulling out all the stops," he said. "She wants to make an example of me."

"So why am I here?" John's whisper roared from the walls. "I've been good —"

"An example's useless without a 'beneficiary,' " Leonard said.

Mrs. Vonus, still seated, smiled up at the preacher standing next to her.

"Proceed," she said.

The preachers raised their Bibles higher and moved a step closer to Leonard and John.

"HE HATH APPOINTED A DAY, IN THE WHICH HE WILL JUDGE THE WORLD," the preachers roared.

"Holy sh — sh — What are they doing?" John said tremulously, his voice vibrating from the walls.

"I'm not sure," Leonard said, trying to squelch his fear, "but I think we're about to be bludgeoned with the Good Book."

"DEPART FROM ME, YE CURSED," the mass preacher-voice bellowed, "INTO EVERLASTING FIRE, PREPARED FOR THE DEVIL AND HIS FALLEN ANGELS."

John dropped his microphone and fell to his knees. "They're going to burn us!" he shrieked, and covered his face with his hands.

Leonard felt heat on his neck. He looked behind him and saw flames leaping in the fireplace.

"Goddamn," he said. He wished he had time to enjoy having said it.

He turned to face the preachers again, hoping to find a gap in the cordon.

The preachers had become blue-uniformed police officers. The Bibles had become billy clubs.

"YOU'RE UNDER ARREST, SCUM," they chanted. "YOU CAN'T SAY THAT IN A PUBLIC PLACE."

"I'm sorry, I'm sorry, I'm sorry," John was sobbing.

Leonard's teeth clenched. It was the cops or the fire.

He raised his microphone as if it were a blackjack.

"Come on!" he yelled. "This time I'm not gonna try to fight you with the Constitution! This time I'm giving back what I get, you bas — bas —"

"SCUM," the cops said.

John was crying hysterically.

The cops became judges in black robes; the billies became gavels.

"GUILTY," the judges said.

Leonard sucked in a breath that scorched his lungs.

"You *bastards!*" he shouted, and swung the microphone.

His head exploded in agony as the gavels rained down and transformed.

Now his attackers were lawyers; now priests; now cops; now Puritans; now nuns; now rabbis; now preachers; now SS troops; now judges.

After a while, Leonard didn't know whether he was being beaten with billy clubs, or Bibles, or whips, or rosaries, or briefcases, or gavels, or phylacteries. He didn't know whether the liquid on his tongue was sweat, saliva, blood, or wine.

19

It lasted until he hurt so much that he wished he could die again.

Then until he wished he had never died at all.

Then until he wished he had never been born.

Finally, when he had been beaten so long that he no longer knew what it was like not to be beaten, he wished he had never done anything against the Rules of the Home.

It stopped.

The priests, the judges, the rabbis, the cops . . . all were gone. Leonard's vision cleared, and he saw his hands pressed into the carpet, yellow and orange flickers dancing across the skin. The microphone lay a few inches beyond the fingers of his right hand. He smelled blood.

He stared at his hands and the microphone for a long time, trying to understand which was a part of him. He flexed his fingers, and the carpet fibers prickled his palms.

Gradually, he began to hear a sound that was unlike the sound of clubs striking flesh. Someone was crying.

He knew it wasn't him. He had gone beyond crying centuries ago.

"You may stand," a brittle voice said.

Slowly, Leonard pushed himself up until he was resting on his knees alone.

A small, elderly woman stood before him.

"I —" he began, and then coughed because he was unaccustomed to using his voice. "I remember you."

The woman nodded. "I am Mrs. Vonus."

The crying had not stopped. Leonard turned his head and saw a chubby man crouching next to the mantel, hiding his face against wooden cherubim.

"John?" Leonard said tentatively.

John twitched and turned away from the mantel. His face was tear-streaked. "They didn't kill you?" he asked tremulously.

This struck Leonard as funny, although he wasn't sure why. "No, they couldn't do that."

John blinked and then wiped his nose on his necktie. "I

guess not," he said, his voice half-muffled by the fabric.

Mrs. Vonus walked toward John, extending her right hand. "Come along. The remainder of Leonard's lesson will be private."

A nugget of panic pulsed in Leonard's chest. "Are they coming back?"

Mrs. Vonus helped John to his feet, then smiled at Leonard. "Not unless you want them to. Someone else is here to see you, though."

Satan, he thought. *Satan has come to throw me into the lake of fire.*

"No," Mrs. Vonus said, tugging on John's arm. "Not unless you want him to."

Leonard crawled to a chair and used it as a brace to help himself stand. By the time he was fully upright, Mrs. Vonus and John were going through the wide doorway.

"Don't leave me alone," Leonard said.

"I won't," the Housemother answered.

John looked back. "Sorry I let you down," he said weakly.

Then they were gone. Leonard tried to follow, but his legs wouldn't carry his weight. He collapsed into the chair.

He found himself facing the fireplace, where a small fire was burning. Standing in front of it was a slender woman wearing a cream-colored evening gown. Her face was hidden in shadow.

"Melody?" he said hesitantly. It was the only woman's first name that he could remember.

The woman walked toward him. "Who's that?" she asked. "One of your girlfriends?"

Her voice was like music with a sharp edge.

"No," he said, not knowing whether he was lying. "I don't . . . have any girlfriends."

"Better not," the woman said.

She sat in a chair beside him. He could see her clearly now — her smooth, fair skin; her incredibly long red hair; her penetrating blue eyes. Her expression was a combination of disdain and pity.

Leonard felt as though someone had stuck a knife in his throat.

"How have you been?" he said hoarsely.

"You cut out on me," she said.

He tried to swallow. "I didn't mean to."

"There were a lot of things you didn't mean to do," she said. "You did them anyway. You hurt me. You hurt everybody."

Leonard felt a small stirring of anger. "You hurt me too."

"We didn't wallow in it. We weren't so obsessed with truth that we forgot about caring."

His anger drowned in a wave of remorse.

"I never forgot," he said, almost whispering.

"You did," she said. "You forgot about everything except your tapes and transcripts, your affidavits and judgments. We wanted you to stop. But you kept after it until you killed yourself. Until you left us."

Leonard reached for her. He wanted to caress her hand, her arm, her cheek.

She was sitting right next to him, but his fingers found nothing but air. She was so near that he could smell her perfumed skin and hair, and she was much too far away to touch.

"I didn't do it on purpose," he said desperately, stretching for her. "They did it. They killed me."

The woman's eyes narrowed. "Who?"

"The lawyers, the judges, the priests, the councilmen, the cops —"

The woman shook her head. "If you had only tried a little, they would have left you alone."

"I had a right —"

"Which you exercised at our expense." The woman stood. "I didn't expect you to change entirely, not when I wasn't able to myself. But it wouldn't have hurt you to try."

She turned her back on him and walked toward the fireplace.

Leonard wanted to go after her, but he couldn't even stand.

"Don't," he pleaded. "I need to be with you."

The woman paused before the hearth. "It will have to be on the Hill," she said. "You'll have to change. Otherwise, this is goodbye."

She stooped and entered the fire, which flared and consumed her.

Leonard wanted to cry, but he still lacked the ability. Of all the things that had been taken from him, that was almost the worst.

Almost.

But he couldn't remember what else was missing. He couldn't remember ever having had anything to lose.

All he knew was that he was tired. He would do anything, anything at all, for just a little . . . peace.

He sat alone in the Parlor. The countenance of Calvin Coolidge half-smiled down on him, and Leonard imagined that it was conferring a blessing. A benediction.

20

In the days that followed, Leonard sometimes saw John in the theater, or at dinner, or sitting by the pond in the back yard. John always turned away as if afraid, but that was all right with Leonard. He knew that he and John weren't good for each other.

Everything else, though, was perfect. The season was always spring, and the trees and grass were always green. He accepted the Housemother's word as law, and he even began to understand the value of seeing *It's A Wonderful Life* over and over again.

He began to accumulate a long string of equals-signs on the Progress Board.

He said hello to the women behind the candy counter every day, but while an impure thought occasionally crossed his mind, he no longer considered attempting a seduction. The price, he knew, would be too high to pay.

Strangely, the brunette, Melody, was getting lines around her eyes that made her look sad. Leonard couldn't imagine why, but he tried to be especially friendly toward her. It didn't seem to make any difference, so he decided to pray for her.

He ate his meals silently and reverently. He sang the Doxology at housemeetings. He polished the woodwork in the foyer and Front Parlor. He dusted the glass cases that lined the long hallway. He threw bread to the geese and breathed deeply of the warm air. He was polite and respectful to his fellow comedians and to Mrs. Vonus. Occasionally, he was even allowed to escort the Housemother to dinner.

Once he saw a new arrival throw a roll at another resident, and he shuddered in revulsion. How could anyone be so ungrateful, wasteful, and rude?

Day followed day followed day, and at last the afternoon came when Leonard passed by the Progress Board on his way to the theater and saw a plus-sign in his most recent box.

He stopped and stared at it, unable for a moment to comprehend what it meant.

"It's a pleasant feeling, isn't it, Leonard?" Mrs. Vonus asked.

She had appeared beside him out of nowhere, but he didn't flinch. He was used to it.

"I don't know," he said. "I don't know what to feel."

"You should feel fulfilled," Mrs. Vonus said, "but not proud. Pride is the downfall of mankind, you know."

"Yes, ma'am," Leonard said.

The Housemother extended her right hand toward him and opened it. Instead of a balled-up handkerchief, a thick silver coin lay in her palm.

Leonard began to reach for it, then stopped himself. "I owe the Dessert Fund," he said. "I owe two dollars for every minus."

Mrs. Vonus smiled so broadly that Leonard saw for the first time that her teeth weren't all the same color. Some were a brilliant white, while others looked grayish.

"I may have neglected to tell you," the Housemother said, "that every plus received while paying off a debt to the Dessert Fund automatically becomes an equals sign." She nodded at the Progress Board. "All but the first few of your equals-signs actually started out as pluses. Your debt is paid, and this dollar is yours to keep."

She took his right hand into her left, pressed the coin into his palm, and closed his fingers over it.

Leonard gazed at the arc of silver that extended beyond his fingertips, then looked again at the Progress Board. The box at the end of his row contained the numeral 1.

"I have a long way to go," he said.

Mrs. Vonus patted the hand holding the coin. "You'll be

surprised at how quickly it will pass," she said. "Now that you've discovered the way of obedience and serenity, you'll be on the Hill in no time."

Leonard wondered if that could be true, then decided it must be. The Housemother had said so.

"You've learned well," Mrs. Vonus said, and waddled down the hall toward the foyer.

Before going on to the theater, Leonard looked at the total at the end of John's row and saw that his friend had two pluses. He briefly hoped he would see John at the movie so he could congratulate him, but then he decided he'd better ask the Housemother first to make sure that was proper.

At the candy counter, he said hello to the blonde and bought a box of Milk Duds from Melody, who still looked sad.

"Be happy," he told her. "You have a wonderful job in a wonderful place." He smiled. "It's a wonderful life. Or should I say afterlife?"

For some reason, she looked sadder than ever.

When he sat down in his usual seat and put a candy into his mouth, he found it so sweet that one was all he could eat. He was used to simpler fare — the beets, potatoes, beans, and bread that were the staples at dinner. It felt unnatural and sinful to eat chocolate and caramel.

He dropped the nearly-full box into the lobby's trash can after the movie.

That evening, he was served his first dessert — a slice of cherry pie with a scoop of vanilla ice cream on top. He couldn't eat it, but he didn't feel that he had lost anything.

The other residents at his table looked at him strangely.

The next day he received another silver dollar, and he asked Mrs. Vonus if he might give it to a less fortunate comedian. She told him that was a fine impulse, but that it would be impossible to act upon. If given to one who was undeserving, the coin would crumble into sand.

So Leonard began stacking his silver dollars on the floor of his room, building a shrine to the saint on the wall. He didn't know her name, but he could see that she was a great and righteous woman.

Day after day, he studied the rapturous look on her face.

Eventually, he decided that he knew just how she felt.

21

The little silver shrine was nothing more than two three-inch columns when Leonard stopped counting the coins and looking at the Progress Board. He was no longer so vain as to keep track of his status. Instead, he was content to spend his time praying for guidance.

The shrine consisted of ten five-inch columns arranged in a circle on the day that Mrs. Vonus appeared in his open doorway and asked him to escort her to the movie.

Leonard was surprised. In his memory, the Housemother had never gone to see *It's A Wonderful Life*. But he didn't question her; he extended his right elbow, and she slipped her left hand into the crook.

They walked downstairs at the head of a large group of residents. Leonard saw John, but he didn't speak to him. It would be rude to talk to the others while serving as the Housemother's escort.

When they were halfway down the hall to the theater, Mrs. Vonus stopped before one of the glass cases, and everyone stopped with her.

She took her left hand away from Leonard's arm and unballed the handkerchief that was in her right. Inside the handkerchief was a small key, with which she unlocked the case.

As Mrs. Vonus swung open the glass door, white light spilled out and blinded Leonard for a moment. When the Housemother closed the door again, though, he was able to see despite the green spots that swam in front of his eyes.

Mrs. Vonus held five golden medallions in her left hand, each on a loop of fine chain.

She turned to face the residents.

"Frederick, Theodore, Albert, John, and Leonard," she said. "Step forward."

Leonard didn't move, since he was already separated from the main group, but the others came up to stand with him. John stood immediately to his right.

"These will enable you to see the sign you must see," the Housemother said, "and to go where you must go."

She placed a medallion around each of their necks, beginning with Leonard. While she was giving the others their own medallions, Leonard took his between his right thumb and forefinger to examine it.

It was a gold coin with a hole near the edge for the chain. In the center of the coin was the face of a laughing clown. Leonard knew from the shape of the mouth that it was the same face that had been beaten smooth by the front door's knocker.

Forming an arc around the clown's face were block letters that said GOOD FOR ONE FREE RIDE.

"We'll continue now, Leonard," Mrs. Vonus said when she'd distributed the other four medallions.

He offered her his arm again, and they continued down the hall toward the theater.

22

When they reached the lobby, Mrs. Vonus told the medallion-winners to wait while the other residents went into the theater ahead of them.

Leonard smiled at the women behind the candy counter. The blonde smiled back, but Melody turned her face away.

After the main group of comedians had disappeared beyond the double doors, Mrs. Vonus lined up the five special men and stood in front of them, clearly pleased.

Leonard saw her teeth for the second time. They reminded him of piano keys.

A shadow seemed to flicker across the Housemother's face.

"Today you will be leaving us," she said. "I have every confidence that you will all do well on the Hill."

"Pardon me, ma'am," Leonard said. He hadn't known that he was going to speak, and the sound of his voice startled him. "Perhaps I shouldn't ask, but . . . what will happen to us on the Hill?"

The other medallion-winners — except John, who kept his eyes averted — looked at him as if he were foolish to ask such a question.

Mrs. Vonus pursed her lips and then said, "Good things, Leonard. Prayer. Contemplation. Fasting. Worship. All the things you have learned to do here at the Calvin Coolidge Home."

Leonard nodded and lowered his eyes. "Thank you, Housemother. Forgive me for asking."

"That's quite all right," Mrs. Vonus said with an odd strain in her voice.

Leonard looked up again and saw that Melody was bent over beside the cash register, hiding her face in her hands. Her body was trembling as if she were crying.

Why should she cry? he wondered. *Perhaps because she's not going up the Hill, too?*

He noticed that the blonde was standing well away from Melody and had her nose wrinkled in an expression of contempt.

"I must say farewell," Mrs. Vonus said. "Enjoy the movie. Then go where you must, and be obedient and humble."

Leonard shifted his gaze from the candy counter to the Housemother, and he thought he saw another shadow crossing her face.

"Aren't you going to watch the movie with us, Housemother?" he asked.

Mrs. Vonus sighed, then said, "I've seen it."

"Oh," Leonard said. "I'm sorry, Housemother. It's just that when you asked me to escort you to the movie, I thought that perhaps someone else would start the projector, and —"

"I understand," Mrs. Vonus said, interrupting him. "Go on, now. Go to your destiny."

Leonard nodded. "Yes, Housemother," he said, and turned to enter the theater.

As he pulled open the double doors, he thought he heard Melody sob. He didn't look back to see for certain.

But he wondered.

23

"Should auld ac-quain-tance bee for-got, a-and ne-ver brought to miiiind? Should auld ac-quain-tance be for-got, a-and daays of Auld Lang Syne?"

As *It's A Wonderful Life* ended with the triumphant song of a houseful of friends, Leonard felt moisture on his lower left eyelid. He reached up to rub it away, but as his thumb touched it, more came to replace it.

Tears.

How long had it been since he had shed actual tears?

More importantly, why was he shedding them now, when he should be happier than he had ever been before?

Maybe they were tears of joy.

As the music and credits faded away, he tried to examine his emotions and found that he had no idea what he was feeling. He had been content for so long that he'd forgotten what any other state of being was like.

It must be joy. How could it be anything else, when I'm going up the Hill?

The screen went white, and then the house lights came up. The unmedallioned residents began leaving.

Leonard waited. Mrs. Vonus had said that he and the other medallion-wearers would see a sign . . .

It was a few yards from the lower right corner of the screen, and it had never been there before:

A glowing red sign that said EXIT.

The last unmedallioned resident went through the double doors, leaving the privileged five alone. Leonard stood and shuffled to the aisle.

He couldn't feel his legs as he walked down the aisle and across to the slitted velvet curtain that hung below the sign. He couldn't even feel his thoughts. He was an automaton, doing what he had to do.

The others were ahead of him. John was immediately in front of him, and Leonard wanted to touch his friend's shoulder to get his attention. When he had done that, he would ask John what he was feeling, and whether he had cried at the end of the movie.

But Leonard's arms were as heavy as bars of lead, and he couldn't lift them.

The first three comedians went through the slitted curtain quickly, as if unable to contain their eagerness to reach the top of the Hill.

John paused at the curtain and seemed about to turn around, but then he went through also.

Leonard took a last look at the theater and wondered if he would miss Jimmy Stewart.

Then he stepped forward and found himself in the back yard, which was the same as it had always been except for the tulip-lined gravel path along which he and the others walked. Looking ahead, he saw that the path led from the northeast corner of the Home to a golden door set into the wall at the northern boundary of the grounds.

Leonard knew then that the path, the multicolored tulips, and the door in the wall had been there all along, as had the EXIT sign and the curtained doorway in the theater. But without the GOOD FOR ONE FREE RIDE medallion, he had been blind to them.

Pretty tricky, he thought, and then wondered if that was impious.

No matter. He had the medallion. The decision had been made. He was going to the top of the Hill, and Glory.

As he walked behind the others, he looked up at the pure blue of the sky and breathed in the delicious scents of spring. It was wonderful to be outdoors after being cooped up in the movie theater.

He lowered his gaze slightly and squinted at the half-hidden golden buildings that were his destination. He hoped the worship, obedience, and-so-on-and-so-forth in which he would participate there wouldn't prevent him from getting out into the sunshine occasionally.

A distant noise brought him out of his reverie.

He paused, listening, and the noise grew louder.

It was the sound of the red International pickup's engine.

"Do you hear that?" he said to John's back, and turned around to look at the road.

The truck was just pulling up beside the again-visible footbridge. The driver's side faced the Home, and Leonard could see Ol' Pete's profile.

"Hello!" he cried, waving his arms. "Mister Pete! I made it!"

Ol' Pete didn't seem to hear or see him.

Leonard took a deep breath, planning to shout as loud as he could, but let it out silently when he felt a touch on his arm.

He looked over his shoulder. John was right behind him, a troubled look in his eyes.

"Come on," John said nervously. "The others will leave us behind."

Leonard saw that the first three comedians had reached the wall and opened the door. He glimpsed a gleaming staircase beyond.

"Go ahead," he told John. "I'll catch up. I can open the door as long as I'm wearing my medallion."

John shook his head. "You don't know that. The Housemother sent us out as a group. There's no telling what might happen if we split up."

Leonard turned back toward the International. "I just want to see if I recognize the new man. If he's someone I know, I want to tell him not to be afraid, that he can make it to the Hill if he tries —"

The pickup's passenger door slammed, and Leonard felt a tension in his abdomen he didn't understand.

A slim, mustached black man walked around the front end of the truck, talking loudly and punctuating his words by slapping the hood.

" — kind of deal is this, motha — motha —" the black man said, and then pounded on the hood with both fists. "That rips it! You can mess with my clothes, you can mess with my name —"

The black man shook his left arm, and Leonard saw the wristband flash.

" — you can even mess with my memory, but when you mess with my *mind* so that I can't even talk like me, then you've ticked me! I want an explanation, and I want it *now*."

Leonard found himself grinning at the thought that Mrs. Vonus was going to have a tough time with this one.

That's terrible. I ought to be ashamed of myself.

" — get across the ditch when I'm good and ready, and that ain't gonna be until I get answers. Say what? Well, I'd better, man. I got your license number —"

Leonard laughed, and was shocked at himself.

What's funny about this? That man has no idea of the rewards of obedience, of the blessing of contentment . . .

The black man was halfway across the footbridge when Ol' Pete blared the International's horn.

The newcomer didn't flinch. Instead, he turned around with his arms akimbo.

"You think that's cool? How cool you think it'd be if I come back and beat your head on the gearshift, huh?"

The International's engine revved, and the pickup vanished. A small spray of dust swirled down the road.

Leonard couldn't see the black man's face, but he knew the newcomer was staring at the empty air.

John grasped Leonard's right arm with both hands and pulled hard. "They're through!" he cried, panic charging his voice. "They're going up the Hill! We're going to be left behind if we don't go *now!*"

Leonard stumbled backward.

The Hill. That's my goal.

Why? What's there that's so important?

"A few more seconds," he said, bracing his feet. "I want to see what he does . . ."

The black man turned around and, with incredible slowness, resumed crossing the footbridge.

"Motha —" the man said. "Motha —"

Come on, Leonard thought desperately, not knowing what it was that he was urging or why he wanted it. *Come on, come on, come on . . .*

The black man had reached the end of the bridge and was about to step onto the brick walk that led to the Home's front door.

"Motha —" the man said, hesitating.

Leonard wrenched forward, tearing his arm from John's grasp.

"*COME ON!*" he screamed.

"He can't hear you," John said, beginning to sob. "He's not like us; he doesn't have the coin . . ."

The stranger's right foot touched the brick walk.

"You've gotta come now," John said. "Please, please, you've gotta —"

"Mothafuck," the black man said.

Leonard felt himself teetering, as if standing on a wire over a canyon. He could actually see the wire and the empty air surrounding him.

The Hill. That's my goal . . .

He looked down at the jagged, multihued rocks of the canyon.

They were a lot more interesting than the slick golden mountain where the wire was anchored.

"Leonard" never did feel right . . .

He stepped into space, into another name.

"*Lenny!*" John cried.

The black man started up the walk, and Lenny turned to face his friend.

"I'll help you if you stay," he said. "I promise."

John, almost crying, shook his head and looked down at the gravel. "No, I . . . No. All I ever *wanted* was to be happy."

Lenny nodded slowly. "I hear you can get that up there. Happiness by the barrelful."

Without raising his eyes, John turned and walked toward the golden door.

Lenny watched until his friend stepped over the threshold. Then he turned and ran back down the tulip-lined path.

Yelling like Johnny Weismuller, he burst through the red velvet curtain, charged up the aisle, and straight-armed the double doors. They swung open with a *whooshing* sound, and Lenny leaped into the lobby, landing in front of the candy counter.

Melody and the blonde woman gaped at him. The blonde's mouth opened and closed repeatedly.

Lenny yanked the medallion off his neck, breaking the chain, and held it across the counter toward Melody.

"You can tie a knot in the chain," he said.

Melody held out her left hand, and Lenny dropped the

medallion into it. Then he closed her fingers over it and held on for a moment.

"What you do is your business," he said, looking into her eyes, which were a much darker brown than he'd ever realized before. "Personally, though, I hope you stick around. I still wanna take you on a picnic."

He saw the beginnings of a smile at the corners of her mouth.

Then he was running again, out of the lobby and down the long hallway.

As he shot by the Progress Board, he yanked the felt-tipped marker from its string. A blue knife of pain stabbed up his arm, but he didn't fall.

Aching, elated, he dashed to the foyer.

Mrs. Vonus was there, facing the front door.

"Hey, Daisy Duck!" Lenny yelled, sprinting into the Front Parlor. "Glad the new guy's not in yet — I've got something to show you!"

He bounded over a divan, then grabbed a chair and dropped it in front of the fireplace.

Looking back into the foyer, he saw Mrs. Vonus staring at him, her slack mouth giving her face a most unHousemother-like expression.

"Ah, you're confused, madame," Lenny said grandly. "Allow me to explain: Happiness and contentment are fine things for some, but for me they're just *boring*. So bring on the Puritans, because I've thought of a Thanksgiving bit that'll knock 'em on their asses."

He jumped onto the chair, uncapped the marker, and carefully drew an elegant mustache on Calvin Coolidge.

Thunder shook the blue-paisley walls.

The comedian glanced over his shoulder and grinned.

"Pardon me, Housemother," he said, "but don't you think you should answer the door?"

To the memory of Leonard Alfred Schneider.

THE SIN EATER
OF THE KAW

Pamela felt the derelict's eyes on her the moment that she entered the warmth of the Lawrence Public Library, and she couldn't help looking at him. He was sitting, shoulders slumped, on the padded bench against the foyer's limestone wall, cradling a lumpy plastic trash bag in his arms. He was wearing a dirty blue corduroy cap with torn ear flaps, a brown polyester jacket over a faded plaid shirt, green-and-white checked trousers, and crusted sneakers. Irises the color of the slush outside stared at her from a mottled, stubbled face that might have been forty or forty thousand years old.

She turned away, sorry that she had let herself look, and walked rapidly through the foyer toward the horseshoe-shaped circulation desk. As soon as she finished Donald's errands, she could go home to her apartment, change from secretarial clothing into a sweatsuit . . . and spend what was left of the evening waiting for his call.

She felt mild disgust at the thought. Twenty-seven years old, and she still found herself waiting for her boyfriend to telephone. On the other hand, she preferred waiting on a phone call to waiting for the bathroom. She almost hoped that Donald's final interview in Kansas City had gone badly, because if he was offered the job, he would probably ask her to move into his new place.

The thin woman inside the horseshoe didn't raise her eyes from her magazine until Pamela dropped Donald's borrowed books onto the desk. Frowning, the librarian said, "Nice weather for ducks, isn't it?"

Pamela loosened the wool scarf from around her face and neck. "Only if they're from Alaska. The temperature's going to keep dropping all night, so they might find their little webbed feet stuck in blocks of ice by morning."

The librarian looked at her as though she had just spoken in Russian. "I see," the thin woman said tersely, reaching for the books.

"I need to renew them all," Pamela said. It felt like the hundredth time she'd spoken the words. Donald kept library books month after month before reading them; if it weren't for her, he'd be up to his eyeballs in fines.

The librarian nodded and left the desk to check whether anyone had requested a recall of any of the books. Pamela took off her stocking cap and ruffled her short, dark hair, glad to be free of the itch for a few moments.

"Spare a dollar, ma'am?"

She heard the thick voice and smelled the deathlike stench of its accompanying breath in the same instant. Before she could react, a hand gripped her left forearm through the down padding of her coat.

"Just a dollar," the voice said. "I wanna get a cup of coffee at the Burger Shack. They make good coffee."

Pamela forced herself to turn toward the voice and saw the derelict from the foyer. He was short and stooped, and he smiled up at her with teeth that were like the ragged ends of chewed twigs.

"No," she said weakly, pulling away from him. His fingers left smudges on her blue nylon coat sleeve.

The derelict kept his hand extended and stepped closer. His other hand held the neck of his trash bag, which bumped against his knees. "I can earn it," he said.

Pamela, backing away, shook her head.

The librarian reappeared. "Out!" she snapped, pointing at the derelict. "This is the fourth time you've bothered a patron today! If I see you again, I'll call the police!"

The derelict's face crumpled, and his eyes dulled with disappointment. "I can *earn* it," he muttered, and then shuffled away in the direction of the foyer. Pamela didn't watch to see if he went outside, but stared at the desk's smooth veneer and tried to keep from shuddering.

"Did he assault you?" the librarian asked. "If he did, I'll

call the police anyway."

Pamela looked up. "No." Her voice still sounded weak.

"Well, if you're sure." The librarian picked up a date-due stamp and flipped open the first of Donald's books. "I don't know why those people come to Lawrence — we surely don't have facilities for them. Why don't they go to Kansas City where somebody could do something with them?" She paused as if waiting for an answer, but all Pamela could do was shrug.

The librarian sighed. "I'm renewing these," she said, stamping the first book, "but they're a week late. The total fine's $3.50." Pamela was sure that the books were only one day overdue, but she didn't argue.

"I surely hope February will be warmer than January has been," the librarian said as she stamped the last book. "There. You have a happy new year."

Pamela mumbled a thank-you as she scooped up the books, then hurried away. She felt an unaccountable guilt when she saw that the bench in the foyer was empty. Outside, a cold mist was falling, freezing as it hit the ground.

She left the books in her Renault in the library parking lot, then pulled her hat over her ears, wrapped her scarf around her mouth and nose, and walked up Vermont Street toward the post office. She was beginning to lose the physical tension that had knotted her muscles in the library, but she still felt uneasy. Part of the feeling was the result of the weather — the gray sky pressing down on her head; the bare trees lining the street; the wet, sanded sidewalk — but part of it was also due to the fact that she couldn't stop thinking about the derelict.

He had only wanted a dollar ... just one stupid dollar, and he would have stopped bothering her and wouldn't have had to leave the library until closing. She had spent three and a half times that to pay a nonexistent fine on four mysteries and a VCR movie catalog. So what if he would have used the money to get drunk? It was January in Kansas, which meant that a *lot* of people were using their money to get drunk.

She shivered as she reached the corner and waited for the light that would let her cross the street to the post office. The temperature was supposed to fall to eleven degrees Fahrenheit before morning. Slush would turn to hard crystal, streets would freeze slick enough to skate on, and if the mist continued much longer, tree branches would droop from the weight of tubular layers of ice. Down by the Kaw River, a quarter of a mile north of where she stood, a thin crust would replace the strip of scummy foam that usually separated the water from the mud and rocks of the riverbank.

As the light turned green and Pamela started to cross, her thoughts of the river followed it under the twin bridges of Vermont and Massachusetts Streets, which converged at the north bank. She had read in the paper that it was there that Lawrence's homeless people gathered to try to survive the winter nights. Occasionally, the bodies of vagrants were discovered on the rocks, abandoned, alone. Last year a corpse had been found with its throat cut open. Usually, though, the derelicts simply froze to death.

Would a dollar have made a difference for any of them? Pamela wondered. Would an hour in the Burger Shack, nursing coffee laced with wine, have meant one more day of life?

She slipped and almost fell stepping onto the curb, saving herself by grabbing the 15-MINUTE PARKING sign. As she pushed open one of the post office's double doors, she thought of how ironic it would have been to smash her skull on the sidewalk while worrying about whether a bum would die for lack of a dollar.

The post office seemed deserted, which didn't make her feel any better. The lobby was always gloomy, and the rectangular cave of brass-and-glass p.o. boxes was gloomier still. The cave's sputtering fluorescent lights glowed only at the ends of the tubes, and Pamela had to lean close to the rows of boxes to find Donald's. She didn't know why he had a box here anyway, since he never received anything that would be worth stealing from his East Lawrence apartment's mail drop. She removed her gloves and put them into a coat pocket so that she could grasp the box's tiny knob.

Before she could enter the combination, she heard a soft thumping noise behind her: the sound of the library derelict's trash bag hitting his knees. Her first thought was that she was being given a second chance to do something nice, but as she turned, it occurred to her that the derelict might see this as an opportunity to punish her for not doing it the first time. By the time that she was facing him again, she felt as though her heart had stopped dead.

He was ten feet away at the mouth of the cave. Even in the poor light, though, Pamela could see his slush-colored eyes peering at her — at first hopefully, and then, as he recognized her, with the same disappointment she had seen there after their earlier encounter. Mechanically, he turned and began to shuffle away again.

"Wait," Pamela heard herself say. Her voice sounded shrill despite the muffling effect of her scarf. When the derelict paused and looked back, she wished that she hadn't spoken. She felt chilled into immobility by his gaze and was only able to start fumbling with her purse when she realized that there was only one way to get rid of him now. Stray fibers from her scarf chafed her lips, creating a horrible itch that she couldn't take time to rub away. The junk in her purse had tangled so badly that she was afraid she would never find her wallet.

"That's okay, ma'am," the derelict said.

"No, no, wait," Pamela said immediately, and again wished that she hadn't.

Just as she finally grasped her wallet, she remembered that after buying lunch she'd had a ten-dollar bill and four ones left. Now that she'd paid Donald's fine, though, she only had the ten and two quarters. Fifty cents hardly seemed enough to give the derelict after making him wait, but —

She pulled out the ten and held it at arm's length.

The derelict came to her, his trash bag bumping before him, and plucked the bill from her hand. He did it so carefully, with such an obvious effort to keep his fingers from brushing hers, that Pamela felt her face flush with an uncomfortable mixture of shame and gratitude.

The derelict stared at the bill. "It's so much," he said, his voice low. "I hafta earn it."

Pamela's emotions shifted closer to horror as she realized that the money hadn't gotten rid of him after all. If she had given him the fifty cents, he would have taken it and left, but the ten-dollar bill had activated the remnants of his pride.

"No, please, that's all right," she said.

The derelict shook his head, the ear flaps of his cap bouncing as if made of flesh. "I always pay m'way," he said, putting the money into his jacket.

It was the most obvious lie Pamela had ever heard. "Well, I don't want to be paid," she said, "so please leave me alone." She had to suppress a wince at the sting of her own words, but at the same time she began to turn toward Donald's p.o. box. That movement would say that she was through with the derelict, that he was dismissed.

She wasn't able to complete it. The derelict's pale eyes still gazed at her, and she was afraid to turn her back on them.

"You don't think I can earn it," he said.

Pamela decided that she had to be free of him even if it meant being cruel. "As far as I'm concerned," she said, "the only way you can earn that money is to spend it on something besides liquor." She wondered if she had ever before said anything so trite.

The derelict nodded. "M'name's Griggs," he said. "D'you have anythin' t' eat?"

She couldn't believe it. She had just given him ten dollars and told him to get lost, and now he was introducing himself and asking for food.

"Anythin' at all," Griggs said, revealing his awful teeth. "A Lifesaver, or a piece o' gum."

Desperate, Pamela fumbled in her purse again and found a roll of breath mints with two left. She held it at arm's length as she had the ten-dollar bill, grasping it by a trailing ribbon of paper.

Griggs shook his head, making his ear flaps bounce again. "Not like that, ma'am. Unwrap one an' hold it a few seconds, like this." He made a fist.

Pamela was about to ask why, but stopped herself. She knew now that the derelict was crazy, so her only option was to humor him. As quickly as she could with her nervous fingers, she pulled a mint free of the wrapper and held it in her right fist. She put the remaining candy into her coat pocket.

Griggs nodded. "Good. Now, this ain't guaranteed to work, 'cause you're s'posed to be naked and have the food laid out on your skin —"

Oh God, he was a pervert who was going to leave her nude body in a cave of brass and glass . . .

" — and usually you're s'posed to've just died, but you don't want t' take off your clothes or die, so we'll do as best we can. Think of the worst thing you ever done."

Pamela, as confused as she was afraid, couldn't help asking, "What?"

Griggs chuckled. It was a wet, phlegmy sound. "Well, it don't have to be the very worst thing. A little piece o' peppermint won't hold anythin' big. Which ain't t' say that a lady like yourself could ever commit any big sin, ma'am."

"Sin?" Pamela hated the sound of her voice. The more she responded to him, the more likely it became that he would —

"Yes, ma'am," Griggs said, interrupting her thought. "You know, the bad things you've done that y'carry around for all eternity." He was looking at her intently, his pale eyes reflecting and amplifying the dim light. "Think of a sin you been carryin' around since you was little, an' squeeze it with your fist."

As Griggs talked, Pamela considered flinging the mint at his face and trying to dash past him . . . but then, as he finished, a memory flooded her, drowning all other thoughts.

She had been nine years old, taking swimming lessons at a community pool in Wichita. During the free-swim time at the end of the day's session, she had grown tired of the constant pestering of a younger girl named Sharon. Do this with me, Pammy; do that with me, Pammy; are you my friend, Pammy? Finally, when no instructors or lifeguards were looking, Pamela had dunked the bothersome child at the shallow end of the pool. Thrashing away, Sharon had run headfirst into the white cement rim and had come up screaming, her nose and mouth dripping crimson into the greenish water. Pamela had stood motionless, horrified, while two instructors had come to pull Sharon out. They had taken her to a hospital, and Pamela had spent the rest of the day huddled on her bed at home, waiting for punishment.

It had never come. Sharon had lost a baby tooth and some skin from her nose, but she had never told on Pamela. At first Pamela had been overjoyed, but later, after she had seen

Sharon's face ... She had tried to make it up to her, to be nice, but the younger girl had never again given her anything more than a sad look. Sharon and her family had moved away several months later, but Pamela had never forgotten or forgiven herself for what she had done to a child who had wanted nothing more than to be her friend.

" 'At's enough," Griggs said, touching her fist with one grimy finger. "I'll take it now."

Feeling dazed, Pamela watched as her hand opened like a flower to reveal the mint. The candy was sticky from the sweat of her palm, but Griggs plucked it up and popped it into his mouth without hesitating. It cracked between his rotten teeth like a sliver of shaved ice. The derelict's Adam's apple bobbed, and then he smiled.

"It ain't much," he said, "but it's payment, I reckon. Lord knows I've had worse." He touched the bill of his cap. "Evenin', ma'am." As he turned away, his trash bag rustled with a sound like dead leaves.

When he was gone, Pamela collected Donald's mail and chided herself for having been afraid. Griggs was an old man who needed a bath; nothing more. He would probably die within a year or two, poor guy.

But she had helped him, she decided as she left the cave and went out into the cold mist again. For a little while, his life would be better because of the money she had given him. It was the only reason she could think of to explain why she felt so good. She was scarcely able to keep from running or dancing across the icy street.

Pamela fell asleep on the couch with the television mumbling to her from across the living room. At first her dreams were full of paths that ended in empty space and streets paved with gelatin, but soon she found herself standing in the swimming pool in Wichita, the summer sun blazing so brightly off the white cement that she had to squint to see. The water was only ankle-deep, so she decided that she might as well get out — but then she saw that the pool was surrounded by hundreds of little girls in blue swimsuits, each one swinging her arms as if preparing to dive. But if they dove into ankle-deep water ...

One of them leaped, and Pamela ran splashing across the pool to catch her; but as she caught that child, another on the far side jumped. Pamela dropped the first child on its bottom so that she could run to catch the second, then dropped the second to catch the third, and then the third to catch the fourth. Soon she was dashing from one side to the other without rest, breaking stride only to dodge one of the growing number of crying children who sat in the shallow water. But even as the number of children in the pool increased, so too did the number waiting to jump. She would be here forever, trying desperately to save each child, but unable to hold any of the girls long enough to comfort them.

It went on and on until the bottom of the pool was crowded with wailing children up to their necks in water. Pamela could hardly move through them fast enough to catch each jumper, and she knew it wouldn't be long before she missed one. That child would crash headfirst into another, and then it would happen again and again as Pamela missed more and more, and the water would turn the color of rust.

As she struggled across to catch what must be the ten-thousandth child, the water level dropped with a terrific sucking noise. Griggs, covered with black slime, appeared in her path.

He grasped her arm as she tried to get past him. "My turn, ma'am," he said, smiling a rotten-toothed smile, and then looked down at a squalling child who had wrapped her arms around his filthy legs. He used his free hand to give the crying girl a peppermint stick from his trash bag.

Pamela pulled away and found herself sitting high above the pool in the lifeguard's chair. Below her, Griggs scampered to and fro, catching each jumper with ease and flinging peppermint sticks right and left. Each little girl who caught a candy cane stood up, made her way to the ladder, and disappeared. Gradually, the pool began to empty, and the number of children waiting to jump dwindled.

Pamela tried to call down to Griggs to thank him, but found her mouth full of peppermint stick. One red swirl liquified and dripped onto the shiny blue fabric of her swimsuit. It was the prettiest thing she had ever seen.

She awoke with the cool bite of peppermint still on her tongue, but as she opened her eyes she knew that she was tasting Donald's breath. His smooth-shaven oval face filled her vision, so close that it was out of focus. He was wearing his long, eggshell-colored winter coat, and the flickering light from the television made him look like a ghost.

"Greetings," he said, as though she were a space alien. It was what he always said. Pamela thought it was a stupid habit, but she had resigned herself to putting up with a few irritations for the sake of love.

She grunted sleepily, then muttered, "Never should've given you a key."

He kissed her forehead. "I would've rung the bell, but I thought you'd be in bed. I didn't want to wake you."

"That would've been a tragedy, all right," she said, yawning.

Donald turned off the television, then helped Pamela up from the couch and kept his arm around her while she stumbled into the bathroom. She considered telling him that she was capable of going to the john by herself, but thought better of it. She was glad he was here, and there was no point in saying anything that might start an argument.

Once they were in bed, he said, "I've got the job. Assistant head of marketing."

"Congratulations," she said, yawning again.

Later, after she was thoroughly awake as a result of their lovemaking, she asked him, "Do you believe in sin?"

Donald was almost asleep. "What?" he asked blearily.

Pamela propped herself up on an elbow. "I said, do you believe in sin?"

He rubbed his eyes. "You feeling guilty?"

"No," she said, tracing her left forefinger through his chest hair. She wondered if she was telling the truth.

"Hinting that we ought to get married?"

"*No.*" She felt his muscles tighten and realized that she shouldn't have responded so forcefully. "I mean, I was just thinking aloud. A guy I met today made me wonder whether I know what people mean when they talk about sin."

"What guy?" Donald sounded more awake now, and a little angry.

Pamela wished that she'd kept her mouth shut. "Just a bum at the library. He was babbling about everybody being guilty of sin, and it started me thinking, that's all."

Donald switched on the nightstand lamp. "What were you doing talking to a bum — especially to a Jesus-freak bum? That's the kind of schizoid who winds up committing mass murder."

Pamela let her head fall back to her pillow and closed her eyes against the light. "I wasn't talking to him. He came up asking for money and ranting about sin. I gave him some cash and he left. That's all."

"How much did you give him?"

"Don't worry about it. It didn't bankrupt me."

Donald exhaled sharply. "Considering what good ol' Kansas U. pays you, it wouldn't take much to make bankruptcy a real possibility. I mean, you're only netting . . ."

Pamela almost told him that her financial status was none of his business — although that might not be entirely true at this point — but she was determined not to argue tonight. At least he had driven back from the city to be with her when he could have spent another night in a hotel at his new company's expense. Besides, as long as they were both wide awake, there were better things to do than fight. She rolled on top of him and kissed him until he stopped trying to talk.

As they made love again, though, she couldn't help wondering whether using sex to avoid a conflict was a sin by Griggs's definition.

Much later, she lay staring up at nothing and wishing she were someone else. Donald came back from the bathroom and flopped onto the bed beside her, making the headboard thump against the wall. "I nearly passed out in the can," he said. "You drew all the blood away from my brain."

Pamela threw a wad of damp Kleenex onto the floor. "Don't jump on the bed, okay? If you put a hole in the wall, I'm the one who'll have to pay for it."

He turned over to switch off the lamp. "Sorry," he said as the light went out.

She wanted to say something to make things better, but decided not to try. She was sure she would only make them worse.

She hoped she wouldn't dream.

Pamela was jolted awake by the fast section of "Stairway to Heaven" blaring from the radio alarm on the nightstand. Reflexively, she swiped at the plastic cube and knocked it to the floor, where it continued to blare.

"Oh, sorry about that, babe," Donald's voice called from the bathroom.

Pamela sat up. "What's going on?" she yelled. Her tongue felt like a slab of corroded iron.

"Can't hear you over Led Zep. How come you keep the thing tuned to that moldy oldie stuff, anyway?"

She leaned over and yanked the radio's plug from its socket. Before blinking out, the orange numerals read 7:10. "Why'd you set the alarm?" she asked loudly. "It's Saturday, for Chrissake." She felt a headache coming on.

Donald appeared in the doorway dressed in last night's slacks and shirt, his shoes and socks in his hands. "I was afraid I might not be up in time otherwise."

"In time for what?" Pamela was trying not to sound whiny, but it wasn't easy.

"I've got lunch with my new bosses at noon," he said, "so I need to be at my place by eight if I want fresh clothes and a shave before I head for the city. If we were living together, I could've stayed in bed another hour."

Pamela gave up on trying to hold back her anger. "So if I don't like it, it's my own fault, right?"

Donald rolled his eyes. "I didn't say that, Pammy."

She felt as though she'd been given an electric shock. "Don't call me that! I don't let *anyone* call me that!"

"Okay, okay," he said, walking away into the living room.

Pamela got out of bed and followed him. "Why didn't you tell me you were going back today? Why'd you even bother to come over?"

Donald sat on the couch and pulled on his socks. "I told you first thing last night. You must've been too sleepy to remember. As for the second question, I came over because I wanted to see you. I meant to ask you to move to K.C. with me, but then we got busy with other things." He put on his shoes and stood, eyeing her. "It's too chilly to run around naked, Pam."

She was actually thankful for that, because it gave her an excuse to return to the bedroom without answering his implicit question. As she put on her pink flannel robe, she wondered whether Donald would be willing to leave Lawrence if *she* were the one with a job waiting elsewhere.

When she came into living room again, he was already at the door with his coat on and his books and mail on the floor beside him. "I really am sorry," he said. "I thought you heard me last night. I even asked about setting the alarm, and you mumbled something that sounded like yes."

"It's all right," she said, going to him. He hugged her, as always, too tightly; and his morning breath, as always, was awful. His coat was so bulky that she felt as though she were being held by an overstuffed chair. But it was better than not being held at all.

"Be careful if you go out today," he said in her ear. "The streets'll be slick."

"Same to you."

He released her, then picked up his books and mail and opened the door. An icy gust rushed in, making Pamela feel as though she were still naked. When she drew in a breath, the air became cold needles in her chest.

"Think about . . . moving to the city," Donald said as he stepped outside.

Pamela nodded and started to close the door.

Donald stopped it with his foot. "And stay away from bums, or start carrying mace. This town isn't as safe as it used to be, and Kansas City . . ." His voice trailed off as he turned and walked down the sidewalk toward the complex's parking lot.

Pamela shut and bolted the door, then ran back to the bedroom and jumped into bed, pulling the covers over her head until she stopped shivering. The door had been open less than thirty seconds, but she felt chilled to the bone.

She wondered how bad the wind had been under the Kaw's twin bridges during the night.

She had dressed in long underwear and jeans and was

even wearing a sweatshirt under her coat, but she was so cold that she thought she might as well have come out in her robe. The north wind cut at her eyes, nose, and cheeks like millions of tiny razors, and she could hardly feel her toes despite the fact that she was wearing two pairs of thick socks inside her boots. The Vermont Street bridge's pedestrian walkway wasn't enclosed, and the aluminum railing was only waist-high, so she felt as though she were walking on a wide cable strung between two peaks in the Himalayas.

She paused and faced west, as much to escape the sting of the wind for a moment as to gaze down at the Kaw. Forty feet below her, the gray river looked placid even though she could hear it rushing over the old eight-foot hydroelectric dam on the east side of the Massachusetts Street bridge. The rocky riverbank she had just passed over looked as if it should be populated with penguins.

Why was she doing this? she wondered as she turned, head bowed, to continue into the bitter wind. What possible reason could be compelling enough to make her leave her warm apartment for a walk along the coldest stretch of concrete in town? Even vehicular traffic seemed to be avoiding the bridges today.

As she reached the bridge's midpoint (How long was it, anyway? An eighth of a mile?), she paused again and had the perverse thought that it would be easy to lean against the fat aluminum rail, relax her upper body, and tumble over in a limp cartwheel. What would it be like to spin end-over-end and then hit that smooth grayness? Would the enveloping water feel frigid or warm in comparison to the freezing air?

Pamela put her gloved hands on the rail and leaned out slightly, then jerked back and continued walking at a faster pace than before. This was the first time she'd ever had thoughts that might be considered suicidal. Maybe the wind was freeze-drying her brain as well as her face.

The smart thing to do now would be to go back to the library for her car, then head home and thaw herself. An even smarter thing to do would have been to stay home in the first place . . . but she hadn't been able to stand that this afternoon. The apartment had felt empty and frustrating, so here she was, walking her muscles into constricted lumps over a river called the Kansas by everyone except the people of the state for which it was named. They and their river didn't make any more sense than she did.

She stumbled as she stepped off the bridge walkway onto the sidewalk on the north side of the Kaw, then stopped and wondered where to go next. Except for the river levee with its jogging path, there was nothing in North Lawrence but gas stations and sleazy bars. So why, she asked herself again, was she here in the first place?

She about-faced, but as she did so, she glimpsed a bundle of familiar clothing on the rocks below the levee. She tried to start back across the bridge without a second look, but then, cursing herself through clenched teeth, she turned north again and followed the sidewalk to its intersection with the levee path. As she stepped onto the path itself she could see that the bundle of clothing had a human being inside, and as she left the path to make her way down the slope, Griggs's mottled cheek came into view beside his cap's ear flap.

He was humped over as if frozen in a perpetual cringe against invisible blows, and Pamela felt a terrible certainty that she would discover he was dead. Then she would have to call the police, and her name would be printed in the newspaper under the headline KU SECRETARY ON INEXPLICABLE WALK FINDS DECEASED WINO/JESUS FREAK . . .

She stopped while still fifteen feet up the slope from the lump of castoff polyester that was Griggs. She didn't want to be the one to find him, to call the police, to have her name in the paper. She didn't want to know anything about what had happened to him, especially if what had happened was that he had gotten so drunk on her ten dollars that he had broken his neck.

Yet that was what she was here for, she realized at last; that was why she had walked across the bridge into a wind chill of ten below. When she'd left her apartment, she'd told herself that some exercise in the cold air might clear her mind and help her think about her problems with Donald — but on a deeper level she had known, even then, that what she was really planning to do was look for Griggs. And now that she had found him, she wanted an excuse to avoid going near him.

"Mister Griggs?" she called. If he would say that he was all right, or even if he would only move a little, she could leave him here with a clear conscience.

He didn't move. She had no choice but to continue down the slope. As she left the dead grass of the levee and stepped onto the fist-sized rocks of the riverbank, the sound of the water rushing over the dam downstream became an echoing roar. She was almost underneath the Vermont Street bridge now, and it and its twin amplified the noise. Even if Griggs made some small sound, she wouldn't be able to hear it.

She glanced eastward and saw three men huddled over a driftwood fire fifty feet away under the Massachusetts Street bridge. To her relief, they ignored her. She wondered why they had also ignored Griggs.

She hesitated a moment when she reached the derelict, then squatted and placed her hands on his shoulders, shaking him. He rocked back and forth without responding, looking like the discarded pile of clothing for which she had first mistaken him.

She shook him harder. Now that she had stopped walking, she was beginning to feel even colder than before. "Wake up!" she shouted over the river's roar. "This is no place to sleep, you stupid old man!" The words made her feel ridiculous, and she shook Griggs harder still in her frustration. Without meaning to, she lost her grip on his coat and shoved him onto his side. It was only as he fell that she saw he had been hunched over his trash bag, hugging it as if it would give him some warmth.

Griggs's eyes opened as he landed hard on the rocks, and he smiled. He had lost several teeth during the night, and his face was as pale as milk.

Pamela felt a sudden fury. "I thought you were *dead!*" she screamed.

Griggs's lips moved, but she couldn't hear whether he actually said anything. It didn't matter, though. If his fellow bums weren't going to help him, she wasn't going to leave him here. She stood and kicked the trash bag aside, then stooped and grasped the derelict's wrists.

"Come on," she said, pulling him to his feet. It was like lifting a scarecrow. "I'll take you to the Salvation Army . . . or something." The Salvation Army had a building somewhere in town, but she didn't know whether it was used to house vagrants.

That wasn't important right now, she decided as she picked up the trash bag with one hand and kept a grip on Griggs's arm with the other. Regardless of what she told either him or herself, she wasn't taking him to the Salvation Army. Not right away, at least.

The ascent to the street seemed to take hours, and Pamela felt completely numb long before they made it. She had to drag Griggs every step of the way, because he was either half-frozen or drunk and was unable to climb the slope as well as a two-year-old might. Adding to the burden was the trash bag, which weighed more than the derelict himself.

Finally, they stood on the sidewalk, resting with their backs to the wind. Pamela's breath formed thick clouds of steam, and she watched them dissipate so that she wouldn't have to look at Griggs. She could feel his eyes on her, though, and eventually had to meet their gaze.

He was still smiling. "I knew you'd come, ma'am," he said. His breath smelled like the candy she had given him the day before. She suspected that he had spent her money on peppermint schnapps.

She tugged on his arm, and they started across the bridge. Below them, the Kaw still appeared placid, its smooth gray skin masking the cold rush of water underneath.

It was while Griggs was in the bathroom taking a shower that Pamela, curled into a ball on the couch, began to have some feeling in her toes again. She also began to doubt her sanity. The derelict might be a murderer or a maniac . . . or *anything*.

The telephone on the end table rang, and she picked up the receiver automatically. It wasn't until she heard Donald's voice that it occurred to her that the hissing of the shower might be audible to him even though the bathroom door was closed.

"Greetings, and where've you been?" he said. "This is the

third time I've tried to call you this afternoon — evening, now. Your machine promised you'd get back to me, but it lied."

Pamela half-covered the mouthpiece with her free hand. "I was ... shopping," she said. "Didn't buy anything, though." A small voice insisted that she should tell him about the derelict, but a louder voice screamed that nothing she could do would be worse.

"Can you hear me okay?" he asked. "I can hardly make you out."

She moved her hand to cover still more of the mouthpiece. "Cold weather messes up the lines," she said.

"Yeah, I guess. Listen, babe, I just called to tell you I won't be making it back tonight or tomorrow. In fact, I probably won't get over to Lawrence again until Friday. I've got all kinds of prep work for my job, and when I'm not doing that I need to be apartment-hunting. I've got some viewing appointments tomorrow, and I thought you might want to look at the places with me."

Pamela almost forgot about Griggs. "You're looking at apartments on a Sunday?"

"Sure. What do you say?"

He sounded casual, but Pamela couldn't help thinking that he was pressuring her. "I haven't even said I'll move."

The line was silent for a few seconds. "Yeah, but you'll be over most weekends anyway, so I thought —"

"You're taking a lot for granted."

The pitch of Donald's voice went up sharply. "Jesus, I'm just asking for some help looking for an apartment. If you don't want to, just say —"

"I don't want to."

The silence was longer this time, and when Donald finally broke it, his voice was a forced monotone. "I know all this has you on edge. The job's important to me, but I shouldn't expect it to be important to you too. Tell you what — I'll call back Monday evening so we can talk. After you've thought about it more, I mean."

Pamela let out a breath that she hadn't realized she'd been holding. "Look, I just don't want to drive in this weather. I nearly wrecked going downtown today, and it's supposed to snow tonight." She hadn't heard a weather report all day.

"I understand. Let me give you my room number here just in case —"

The hiss of the shower stopped, and the apartment echoed with the noise of a rheumy, hacking cough.

"I've got to go," Pamela said abruptly.

"Hey, wait, just let me give you —"

"All right, all right, but hurry." She couldn't keep the panic out of her voice, and the only escape she could think of was another lie. "My dinner's boiling over."

He gave her the number hurriedly, and she pretended to write it down. By the time she hung up, she had already forgotten it.

"Got a beau, ma'am?" Griggs's voice croaked from the bathroom doorway.

Pamela turned to look at him. He was standing on the brown living room carpet, peering at her while holding a towel wrapped around his waist. His pale, stooped body was reed-thin except for a ludicrous pot belly, and his head, bald save for a few colorless wisps, was huge in comparison to his emaciated frame. He had shaved with one of her disposable razors, but had not done a good job. Still dripping wet, he was rapidly becoming encircled by a dark ring on the floor.

"Get back onto the tile, please," Pamela said.

He continued to peer at her without moving.

She gave up. "Yeah. I got a beau. So what?"

Griggs stepped backward onto the bathroom floor. "Won't he mind your takin' me in?"

"Not if I don't tell him," she said, standing and walking past the bathroom to her bedroom. "Stay in there and dry yourself while I scrounge up something for you to wear. We'll take your other things to the laundromat tomorrow. If you ask me, though, most of the stuff in your bag would be better off burned than washed."

"Lying to a loved one's a sin," she heard him say while she was rooting in her dresser's bottom drawer. Then she heard him hawk up phlegm and spit into the toilet. She didn't know which sound was worse.

*   *   *

Griggs ate with a reverence toward food that Pamela hadn't expected. She had imagined that he would wolf down rolls and chicken by the fistful, smearing his face with butter and grease. Instead, he ate slowly, using his hands but taking small bites and chewing with his mouth closed. At first she was amazed at how long he chewed each bite, but then realized that his few remaining teeth didn't leave him much choice.

"I'll pay you for all your kindness, ma'am," he said after they had eaten in silence for fifteen minutes. Pamela was startled by his voice and dropped her fork, which clattered on her plate like an alarm. "After yesterday," Griggs continued, "y'oughta know I can do it, too."

Pamela swallowed a chunk of broccoli and said, "I don't expect any money for this. I couldn't let you freeze." The truth, though, was that she didn't know why not.

Griggs wiped his mouth on the sleeve of the JAYHAWK BASKETBALL sweatshirt she had given him and then belched. She was almost relieved; she *wanted* him to behave like an ill-mannered bum. It was the only thing that made her feel superior to him.

"You know I ain't talkin' about money, ma'am," he said. "You know what I done with that little candy yesterday. I took away a sin so you wouldn't have to carry it around no more. I can do more o' that. I'm a sin-eater."

Pamela forced a smile, hoping that it didn't look as artificial as it felt. "I'm an atheist, Mister Griggs, and have been since I was eighteen. I couldn't be when I was a child because my parents wouldn't let me, but I am now, so I don't care to be told about sin, thank you."

Griggs laughed. It was a weird, barklike noise that gave Pamela gooseflesh. "If bein' a hey-thee-hiss means you don't love God, then I'm with you. God's a sonofabitch." He looked down at his plate. "Least He has been to me."

Pamela rubbed her arms to make the gooseflesh go away. "Love is irrelevant. I just don't believe."

"Same difference." Griggs pointed at the last dinner roll in the basket in the center of the table. "That'll do better'n the candy. You need to lie down and put it here on you —" He pulled up his sweatshirt and touched himself below his breast-bone and above his pot belly.

Pamela stood and took her plate and silverware to the sink. "I don't want to hear any more," she said. "I'm letting you sleep on the couch tonight because it's late and the Salvation Army might not have a place for you. But if you scare me, you'll be out in the cold again."

Griggs brought his own plate to the sink and handed it to her. "Ain't like I ain't used to it. Ma'am."

"I don't mean to threaten you. But this sin-eating busi-ness —"

"Is God's own truth," Griggs said, "or would be if there was such a thing. In your heart you know it, 'cause I freed you of somethin' that tasted like you hurtin' someone. I took it inside me an' gave you peace from it, an' that's the same as givin' you a corner o' heaven, or as takin' away a corner o' hell." He turned and left the kitchen, the sweatpants bagging at his ankles like bell-bottoms.

Pamela finished clearing the table, then rinsed the cook-ware and dishes and loaded them into the dishwasher. That done, she leaned against the counter and stared at the only thing left on the table: the roll in the basket. How much sin could it hold? she wondered. How was sin quantified, any-way? Liters or gallons? Mortals or venials?

She heard Griggs coughing in the living room. If she didn't believe him, then why had she brought him home? It couldn't be that she had done it out of the goodness of her heart — after all, she had seen plenty of other derelicts, and she had done nothing to help *them*.

"What the hell," she said aloud. No one would know. She picked up the roll and went into the living room, where Griggs was waiting.

"Lie on your back," he said, gesturing at the couch.

She hesitated. What if Griggs had only been biding his time to lull her into this moment?

"Those of us who ain't got homes got no home life neither," he said. "Lie down an' stop worryin'."

She sat on the couch but did not recline. "I don't know what you mean."

Griggs gingerly lowered himself to the floor, his joints cracking, and sat cross-legged. "A bum's crotch forgets its purpose. I can't do nothin' to you, and wouldn't if I could. An' if y'think I'm gonna clobber an' rob you, well, I'll just sit here, and you'll know if I move. Young healthy woman like you could snap my bones anyhow."

It was probably true. Clutching the roll with one damp hand, Pamela put her feet up and slowly reclined. By the time her head touched the cushion, her mouth was dry and her heart was pounding hard. It seemed to take forever for her fingers to pull up her shirt to expose her abdomen.

"What am I doing?" she whispered.

She placed the roll where Griggs had shown her and clasped it there with both hands. Then she stared up at the grainy, off-white ceiling, her muscles tense.

"You're tighter'n a sober banker," Griggs said. "Get relaxed, or you ain't gonna remember what you need to be free of."

"I can't help it," Pamela said, her jaws clenched.

Griggs coughed several times, and when he was through he said, "All right, ma'am. You fear what y'don't know, so just listen, and pretty soon that'll be solved." He coughed again.

Pamela raised her head. "I should take you to a doctor."

He motioned for her to lower her head again. "No damn doctors — and no Salvation Army, neither. You can kick me out whenever you want, but you ain't tellin' me where to go." He wiped his mouth on his sleeve again. "Now, then. Who is this Griggs, you're wonderin', and the wonderin' makes you scared. Well, Griggs is nothin' but the son of a Junction City whore and some Fort Riley private. He watched his mama die o' cancer — seems like it musta been, whatchacallit, lew-key-me-up — when he was seven, an' that was when he started learnin' 'bout sin-eatin' from a bum one of his mama's whore friends brought in. This particular whore friend claimed she was a witch, but everyone else said she was crazy.

"Anyway, Griggs saw his mama's body lyin' naked with bread and meat spread out on it as if she was a table, and he saw this scabby old bum the witch had brought take to eatin' the food. And the witch patted little Griggs and said,

"Don'tchew worry, child, 'cause the sin-eater is takin' away your mama's many sins so she can go to heaven."

Griggs's voice had a droning rhythm, and Pamela found herself entranced by both his words and the very sound of them. She began to relax, just as she had as a child during one of her father's infrequent bedtime stories.

"Soon after his mama went to heaven," the derelict went on, "Griggs was put in a foster home an' the witch was put in the State Hospital. Griggs got whipped by his new mama a lot, and she took the money what the state give her to take care of him and spent it on her own kids instead. So the older Griggs got, the more he took to runnin' away, and the more he took to runnin' away, the more time he spent with the bums who hung 'round the railroad bridge over the Kaw. There was almost as many bums as whores in Junction City in them days. Maybe still are.

"One o' the bums — and you'll prob'ly guess the turn the story takes here, ma'am — one of 'em was the scabby old bum what had eaten Griggs's mama's sins. Every time Griggs ran away from his foster home, this scabby old bum would take him aside an' tell him how in olden days, back in England and such, people knew about sin-eaters, and every town had its own. When someone died, they called in the sin-eater, and he took care o' the dead person's trip to Paradise. Trouble was, all that sin they ate stayed with the sin-eaters, doomin' 'em to hell, so nobody'd have nothin' to do with 'em except when somebody died. But the scabby old bum said it didn't matter if he was shunned, 'cause he had the power of defeatin' hell, of grantin' peace. And there ain't no greater power, he said."

Griggs paused. Pamela felt drowsy, and she let her hands slide away from the roll on her abdomen. She didn't want to sleep, though, so she asked, "What happened next?"

She felt a warm breeze on her cheek as Griggs's voice returned. "The scabby old bum died. Not right away, but like a piece o' fruit gettin' riper and riper until it molders an' withers. An' the dyin' sin-eater explained that all the sins inside him would take him to hell, meanin' that they'd stay with his soul and torment it forever, unless he found a new sin-eater to remove 'em as his soul left his body. That was how a sin-eater got started, he said — by eatin' the sins built up in *another* sin-eater. Matter o' fact, the scabby old bum claimed he was carryin' thirty-two generations of sin built up inside from all over the world, countin' all he'd inherited and all he'd eaten himself. To look at him, you'd've believed it, too.

"By now Griggs was fourteen an' with his second set o' foster parents, who weren't no better than the first. So one day he run away and didn't go back, and he an' the scabby old bum, who couldn't hardly walk, hitched a ride twenty miles east to Manhattan. They went down to the Kaw to camp, and that's where the scabby old sin-eater died 'bout a week later. Griggs dumped a can o' beans on him before he was cold and did what was necessary.

"That's pretty much the story, ma'am, 'cept that Griggs left the state for a time and bummed all over, even got to Bolivia once, eatin' sins and bein' shunned. After a while, though, he decided to come back to the Kaw, his only true home, and stick close to it. Oh, one more thing: In his travels, he found out that a few sins could be gotten rid of while a body was still alive an' kickin'. Not many folks take advantage o' that, though, seein' as how Griggs ain't too pretty to look at. Come to think of it, ma'am, you might be the subject o' some bad gossip if your neighbors seen you bring me in."

Pamela's eyelids were so heavy that all she could see was a fuzzy gray light. She could still feel her heartbeat, but it was slow now, thumping lazily. "The neighbors are jerks," she tried to say, and heard her voice as a distant murmur. This must be what being hypnotized was like, she thought, and noted with mild, sleepy surprise that the idea didn't frighten her.

"All right, now," Griggs said, his voice surrounding her like a warm bath. "You remember somethin', ma'am. Somethin' bad. You don't hafta be afraid, 'cause after this it ain't ever gonna bother you again . . ."

The derelict's voice faded, drifting away like bubbles in a sluggish river, as Pamela began to dream about a lie she had told her parents when she was seventeen.

She felt one quick pang of sorrow — *I should have told them the truth so they'd know I wasn't sorry I did it, so they'd know I didn't believe the same things they did anymore* — and then became filled with a euphoria that made her feel as though she were floating high above the earth, looking down and pitying the pain-racked masses below.

On Monday morning, Pamela saw her job with new eyes. Ordinarily, working in the university's financial aid office was neither boring nor exciting, and while she had never felt dissatisfied, she had never felt particularly fortunate, either. Today, though, it occurred to her for the first time that the forms she filed and the reports she typed represented people with hopes and dreams. She began to feel that what she did had importance, that it made a difference in the world outside the walls of the office.

She had Griggs to thank. Four times over the course of the weekend, he had freed her from successively greater sins, and each time she had felt as though something heavy had crumbled away from her like a great wall of ancient bricks.

The sin-eating seemed to have exhausted the old man, though; when she'd left for work, he had been sound asleep on the couch, his breathing a hollow rasp. She wanted to call to see how he was, but was afraid that he might think she was checking to be sure he hadn't run off with her small appliances. She didn't want him to think that, because she had come to trust him . . . and if that was a stupid thing to do, she was willing to live with the consequences.

Instead, she thought, she should call her doctor. Pamela didn't know much about derelicts and their diseases, but the phlegmy rattle of Griggs's breathing had to mean that something wasn't right. Even if she made an appointment for him, though, she didn't think he would keep it — and if she tried to force him, he might flee into the cold and become even sicker.

So maybe it was best to leave things as they were for now, because at least he could stay warm and eat decent meals as long as he stayed with her. Those factors alone were sure to improve his health, and sooner or later she would be able to persuade him that doctors weren't all bad.

Sooner or later . . . How long was she going to let him stay, anyway?

She didn't want to think about that, so she began working harder, typing and filing with an energy that made her office-mates tease her with speculations concerning the illegal drugs she must have used over the weekend. She teased them right back. She hardly ever did that, and they began to look at her as if seeing her for the first time. The rest of the morning went swiftly.

Her wonderful mood lasted until lunchtime, when she sat in the cafeteria with a clerk from the Chancellor's office who asked her when she was going to get around to making per-manent arrangements with Donald. That reminded her that he was going to call tonight and that she would have to think of something to say.

Her world compressed into dread. Despite the way Griggs had made her feel, she was still carrying walls that were bigger and heavier than the ones he had destroyed.

The afternoon was filled with typographical errors, im-properly filled-out forms, and a constantly ringing telephone that always turned out to be a wrong number. Pamela remem-bered the morning as if it had been a dream.

Griggs was lying on the couch when she returned home that evening. As she opened the door, she thought that he looked as if he hadn't moved since morning, but then she saw that he had put on his sneakers. He didn't react as she came in, though, and she felt a stab of fear at the thought that he might have died during the day. When she closed the door he awoke coughing, his body shuddering and twitching as he tried to rise to a sitting position.

"You look rotten," Pamela said, going to the couch to help him up. "If you don't see a doctor soon, you might have to be hauled there in an ambulance."

Griggs sat with his head between his knees until his cough-ing subsided, then looked up at Pamela and grinned. She counted only four teeth. He had lost two or three more during the day.

"'Course I look rotten," he said, his spine cracking as he sat up straighter. "Rotten at the core with sins both committed an' eaten, ma'am, purely rotten at the core. The worst of 'em sit down there an' eat outward, killin' you as they go. That's why a sin-eater can rid you of *all* your sin just as you die — 'cause it's there at the surface." He thumped a finger against his solar plexus.

Pamela sat beside him. "And yours is coming up, is that it?"

"As surely as bile, ma'am. As surely as bile."

He sounded completely matter-of-fact, which made her angry. The afternoon had brought her back down from the weekend's craziness, and she was no longer willing to believe that her joy had been anything more than a psychological escape from her troubles with Donald. She could see clearly again, and what she saw was that Griggs was dying.

"You're wrong," she said. "It's not sin doing this to you — it's pneumonia or emphysema. It's something that can be treated, and I don't mean by sin-eating."

Griggs's slush-colored eyes fixed on hers, holding her as they had at the post office. "It's the truly dark stuff that's down deep," he said. "The stuff we never really do, but just think about over an' over. But the only sins I can take from a livin' person are the ones floatin' near the surface. That's why you've gone back to feelin' like you always did, 'cause your core's the same. Y'see, the ones down there don't come up 'til death . . . an' if they ain't eaten then, they leave with the soul an' stay with it." His eyes shifted away and he chuckled, shaking his head. "I sound like a goddamn preacher repeatin' hisself. All I mean t' say's that I can take more o' your light sins if you want t' feel good again, but you're gonna be stuck with the other stuff for a while."

Pamela put her hand on his shoulder. His bones felt sharp through the sweatshirt. "Listen, I've tried your way, so now you try mine. Let me take you to my doctor tomorrow." She hesitated and decided to humor him. "If you're right and it's sins coming up, then there's nothing to be done. But if I'm right, if it's a disease, then maybe the doctor can take care of it. Then you could go on doing good, eating sins, for another ten or twenty years."

Griggs stood, shrugging off her hand. "Thank you for your kindness, ma'am. Time for me t' go."

Pamela was nonplussed. What had she said? "Why?"

Griggs shuffled across the room, stooped over in obvious pain, to where his laundered clothes were folded and stacked by the television. The corduroy cap sat atop the pile, looking like a blue igloo. "You're back out there where people wear suits, ma'am. You don't believe none of what's happened between us, so you want t' hand me over t' some needle-an'-pill pusher. Don't get me wrong, I ain't mad at you, but I ain't gonna do it, neither." He reached down, grunting with effort, and gathered up the clothes, holding them to his chest. "Besides, I don't want t' live another ten or twenty years, or even two. I've had a bellyful."

Pamela stood. "It's getting worse outside," she said. "My car radio said it'd be five below before midnight, with a north wind. You'd better stay. No doctors, I promise."

Griggs peered at her over the stack of polyester in his arms. "With all due respect, ma'am, I know better. I've tasted your soul. You don't want me here no more, an' if I stayed, you'd have me in a hospital the next time I so much as spit."

"That's not —" Pamela began, but stopped because she felt herself about to lie. She lied to her family, to her friends, and to Donald as frequently and easily as they probably lied to her, but she didn't want to lie to Griggs.

The derelict nodded. "See, you know it too. Now, if I can borrow your bathroom again, I'll put on some o' my own clothes. Then if you could spare a bag t' replace the one you threw away, I'll pack up an' go."

Pamela took a faltering step toward the kitchen. "I'll get the bag, but . . . keep the sweatsuit. Please." She couldn't imagine why it meant so much to her.

Griggs coughed into the pile of clothing. "Thank you kindly," he said. "These others is all dead men's clothes, from the last seven I helped to Paradise, and I ain't in no hurry to put 'em on."

Pamela went into the kitchen. She would not cry. She had done all she could, and that was that. She would not cry.

While she was tearing a trash bag from the roll under the sink, she heard the apartment door open, and the rush of cold air hit her almost simultaneously. Griggs was leaving without saying goodbye. She ripped the bag free and ran back into the living room.

But was not Griggs who stood in the doorway; it was Donald. He was staring at the derelict, who had put on his cap and was coughing again.

Pamela stopped. Donald stepped inside, turned toward her, and said, "Greetings." His voice sounded normal, but his eyes were angry. "Is this who I heard Saturday?"

She didn't answer. No matter what she said now, he would know that she had lied to him. And she, regardless of that, would feel persecuted.

Griggs, clutching his pile of clothes with one arm, came to her and pulled the fresh trash bag from her grasp. "I'll pack outside," he said. "You're losin' all your heat."

Donald didn't stand aside as Griggs went to the doorway. "Who are you?" he asked. Now his voice matched the look in his eyes.

Griggs grinned up at him. "I'm the son of a Junction City whore," he said. "Pleased t' meet you." Then he walked around Donald into the frigid evening.

Pamela wanted to go after him but didn't know what she would do when she caught him. Besides, Donald would follow, and she knew she wouldn't be able to stand that.

Donald closed the door, then removed his eggshell-colored coat and crossed the room to the couch. "Was he on this?" he asked. "I don't want to sit here if he was."

Pamela went to the couch and sat on it herself, as far away from Donald as possible. She wanted to be furious, but all she could manage was a dull sense of alienation. "He slept here," she said. "Two nights. I made him shower first. You don't have to worry about catching anything."

Donald remained standing, his coat slung over his arm like a shield. "What about you? Am I going to catch anything from you?"

She stared at his angry eyes. "What do you think?"

"I don't know what to think. After I called Saturday, I realized that I'd heard someone coughing. I thought about it all day yesterday, then called today to leave a message on your machine. I was going to tell you I was coming over tonight, but I got him instead. You know what he told me?"

Pamela was beginning to feel as though her blood were draining away, leaving her a husk. She couldn't even shake her head when Donald asked his question. All she could do was continue staring at his strange, smooth face, wondering who he was.

"He told me," Donald said, "that you were full of sin. He told me he'd *tasted* it. And then he told me that he was too old and couldn't take it all." Donald paused and looked at Pamela as if expecting her to protest. When she did nothing, he said, "I started to call the Lawrence cops because I thought he might have..." His voice quavered. "I was afraid he might have hurt you." He looked away and took a deep breath. "Then I made myself call your work number first. I hung up when you answered."

Donald dropped his coat on the floor and walked across the room to sit heavily on the carpet beside the television. He rubbed his eyes.

"I see," Pamela said. It seemed to her that her voice must be coming from a small box somewhere over her head. "You thought I slept with him."

Donald's hands dropped away from his face, and now his eyes reminded her of Griggs's when she had first refused to give him a dollar. "Of course not. But I didn't know what *he* would do, Pammy — no, you don't like to be called that. Sorry."

"So why did you hang up this afternoon?" she asked.

"I didn't have anything to say."

"But you came over here anyway so you could hit me with your righteous yuppie indignation." Pamela was surprised at the voice coming from the box. It was mean.

Donald shook his head. "I was still worried. I even skipped a meeting so I could be here when you came home. Then when I saw you, and him, all I could think about — all I'm *still* thinking about — is that I'm going to lose my job because you tried to make like Mother Teresa for a worthless bum."

"So you want me to say I'm sorry, is that it?"

Donald stood and went to the door. "I shouldn't have come. You don't want me here."

Pamela said nothing.

"Just tell me why you did it," Donald said. "Why'd you bother with a creep like that, anyway?"

Pamela thought of how good she had felt after Griggs had eaten the mint at the post office, and how wonderful she had felt that morning. "It gave me something to do so I wouldn't have to think about anything else."

"Like me, you mean."

Pamela didn't acknowledge that. She didn't have to. "I knew I was playing . . . Mother Teresa for the wrong reasons. That's why I didn't tell you. I felt stupid." She thought of Griggs's almost-toothless smile. "Funny, but I never really felt sorry for him. Not really."

Donald opened the door, and winter filled the apartment again. "Okay. I still don't get it, but you're all right and he's gone, so I'm going too. I'll be at my place here in town tonight if you . . ." He stepped outside without finishing the sentence.

Pamela stood and picked up his coat. "Don't forget this," she said, but the door had already closed.

Cute. Now he had an excuse to come back before leaving for the city in the morning.

She sat down again with the coat on her lap. As it warmed her, the thought came to her that Donald might have left it for another reason. Maybe he wanted to ease his conscience. After all, Griggs needed it more than he did.

She started to talk herself out of it, but decided not to listen. Then she went into the bedroom to take off her skirt and blouse and to put on clothes more suitable for a walk in the cold dusk.

Hours passed. First her car refused to start because she had forgotten to turn off the headlights when she'd come home. By the time she found a neighbor who would give her a jump-start, it was eight o'clock and she was starving. That in turn made her realize that Griggs had taken no food with him, so she drove to the Burger Shack and bought cheeseburgers and fries from the drive-through window. Then she had to drive to the library and walk from there, as she had on Saturday. It was almost nine when she began crossing the bridge, running from one white pool of artificial light to the next. The river below was so black that it looked like a bottomless pit, and when she reached the levee path she knew that she would have to get used to that kind of darkness quickly. There were no lights here.

As she left the path and began to make her way down the slope to the Kaw, she felt cold beyond anything she had even imagined on Saturday, cold beyond belief. Her right hand was knotted into a fist around the crumpled neck of the fast-food sack, and her left arm was crimped around the wadded bundle of Donald's coat. Despite her gloves, her fingers were numb. She was shivering so hard that she was afraid she would fall because her feet wouldn't touch ground where she wanted.

Soon she did fall, not because she was shivering, but because she hadn't been able to see the line where the dead grass gave way to rocks. She landed on her hip, holding the sack high, and knew she would have a bruise in the morning. She struggled up and then continued more slowly even though slowness made the cold sharper still.

The farther down the slope she went, the darker and colder it became. She could see some of the lights of downtown Lawrence above the river's south bank, but the broad, black stretch that separated her from them made them seem a world away. The town was a memory; she was somewhere else now. Except for the noise of the Kaw as it rushed over the dam, the only things she was aware of were the mingled smells of dead fish, rotten wood, and smoke.

Pamela was afraid that she was going beyond stupidity now. Why hadn't she at least brought a flashlight?

But this was the last time. Once she did this, she would never come here or even speak to a bum again . . .

The fire appeared as a sudden blaze of orange as she came down under the Vermont Street bridge. It was burning in the same place as two days before, on a flat spot under the Massachusetts Street bridge, and the same three men were squatting around it. Pamela paused for a long moment, gathering the courage to approach them and ask about Griggs.

Then she saw that on the cement slope above the fire, in the shadows where the dancing light hardly reached, an emaciated man with a pot belly lay on his back. He was naked.

One of the men at the fire shifted position, and Pamela saw that he was sitting on a lumpy trash bag and wearing a sweatshirt printed with the words JAYHAWK BASKETBALL.

Then she was running at the flames, hearing her own scream over the roar of the river. The three men looked up just as she reached them, and all she saw as she kicked were dull eyes just beginning to widen in surprise or fear. Her bootheel hit the man with the sweatshirt in the shoulder, knocking him over, and then her momentum carried her into the fire. She kicked furiously, scattering sparks and sticks and then clothes from the trash bag, and the three men fell over each other trying to run away to the east.

Pamela stopped kicking when they were out of range, and then she stood panting, glaring after them in the weak light given off by the scattered chunks of burning driftwood. The three of them were now beside the falls where the river went over the dam, looking at her through a cloud of mist. The man in the sweatshirt started back toward her.

"Get out of here or I'll kill you!" she screamed.

The man stopped and shouted, but all Pamela could make out was ". . . do nothin'!" Then he turned away, and he and his companions walked off downstream, huddling together for warmth. A moment later they were out of sight, swallowed by darkness.

Pamela was still clutching her paper bag and Donald's coat. She dropped the bag and snatched up a driftwood torch, then ran up onto the hard slope where Griggs lay.

He smiled at her. Even in the torch's poor light, she could see that he had no teeth left.

She laid the torch on the cement and knelt beside the derelict, covering him with Donald's coat and tucking it under his back and buttocks. Then she leaned down with her mouth next to his ear so that he could hear her over the noise of the falls. "I'm going to carry you," she said, trying to sound reassuring. "You'll be fine." Her lips brushed his earlobe, and it felt as cold as frozen meat.

As she slid her arms under him, he gripped her shoulder and whispered, "I ain't cold, ma'am." Even so close, she could barely make out the words.

"It's below zero," she said, "and those men stole your clothes."

Griggs's head wobbled back and forth. "I gave 'em to 'em, 'cause one of 'em said he'd take my place. He was lyin', though." The derelict's breathing was becoming more labored with each word.

Pamela shifted from a kneel to a squat. "Well, you have a good coat now," she said. "It'll keep you warm until we get to the hospital." She began to lift.

He struck her twice, in the nose and mouth, and the cold made the pain intense beyond the force of the blows. Recoiling, she pulled her arms out from under him and put her hands over her face. She was crying now, and didn't want to. It wasn't her fault that the stupid old bastard didn't want to live.

Her gloves stuck to her cheeks for an instant as she lowered her hands, because her tears were turning to ice almost as soon as she cried them. If she didn't stop, her eyelashes would freeze together. She could hardly see as it was, because the torch was dying along with the rest of the driftwood.

She leaned down to speak into Griggs's ear again. "I'm trying to help you, damn it." She hated that he was hearing her sob.

He began to whisper again, and she had to remove her hat and put her ear next to his mouth to hear him at all. His lips brushed her earlobe as hers had his. "I tol' you," he said. "No doctors. No Salvation Army. No nothin'."

Pamela steeled herself and put her arms under him again. She would be damned if she would let him die. "Think, Mister Griggs. If you were gone, what would people here do when they needed a sin-eater?"

His chuckle was a soft puff against her cold cheek. "They're gonna hafta take care o' their own sins now. I'm the last."

Pamela began to lift again, trying to do it gradually so that he wouldn't feel it until it was too late to fight her. "That's why you've got to stick around. You're the only one who can do it for them."

"No teeth. Can't chew."

"We'll get you some dentures." She lifted him from the cement, and he struck her in the face again, harder than before.

Almost blind from tears and pain, she let him down and pressed her cheek against his. As cold as she was, she could still feel his beard stubble scraping her skin. "At least let me take you home so you can die warm," she said miserably.

The wobble of Griggs's head was barely perceptible this time. "I got t' be by m'river," he breathed. "Yessir, stick close to your river, an' everything'll be fine."

Pamela pressed closer, holding him tight. His shallow breathing stopped briefly, and then he drew in a long, shuddering breath.

"Best chicken an' rolls I ever ate, ma'am," he murmured, and let out the breath. He didn't take another.

Pamela stayed there another minute and then pulled her arms out from under him, losing one of her gloves in the process. As she stood, she felt the ice of her tears crackle in his stubble.

She looked down at him for a few moments, barely able to see the dull gleam of his eyes, and finally stooped to pull Donald's coat away from him. Her bare fingers brushed his chest. There was a warm spot just below his breastbone.

She dropped the coat on the cement, then removed her other glove and walked back toward the river until she found the paper bag of cheeseburgers and fries. A smoldering stick had burned a black hole into it, but the food was undamaged. She took it back to Griggs.

The burgers were cold, but otherwise not bad. The fries were another matter. Fortunately, though, the boy at the drive-through window had thrown in a couple of packets of ketchup that made them tolerable. All in all, Pamela decided, she had eaten worse meals. When she had finished the last morsel, she remembered that she still had one mint left in her coat pocket. It cracked and crumbled in her mouth, tasting sharp and cool and perfect.

She cleaned up the excess grease and ketchup with a napkin, then retrieved her gloves and hat. She was starting to shiver again, and she didn't want to catch cold. As an afterthought, she put on Donald's coat over her own and stuffed the trash from her meal into one of its pockets. Then she searched among the scattered clothes from the trash bag until she found two shirts that, together, would cover Griggs's body.

After covering him, she left. There was no point in staying longer and getting even colder just to mutter some meaningless prayers. She had already said goodbye in the only way that meant anything to him.

Climbing the levee warmed her, and when she reached the bridge walkway she strode briskly, without hurrying, toward the haloed buildings of central Lawrence. After she retrieved her car, she would drive to the east side of town to see Donald. He might be in bed by now, but that didn't matter. He would have to get used to some changes if they were to live together.

She gazed down at the black Kaw and listened to it rush eastward. Maybe moving to Kansas City wouldn't be so bad. The confluence of the Kaw and the Missouri was practically downtown, and Donald would probably agree to an apartment nearby. There were a lot of sinners in that area.

Maybe they could even follow the Missouri to St. Louis, and from there the Mississippi could take them almost anywhere. After all, even the ocean currents carried water from her river. She would be able to see or smell it there, or to taste it in the spray.

Pamela looked up again and fixed her eyes on a single distant light. The dark knot of sin nestled still and warm in her belly, like a patient child waiting to be born.

THE HERO
OF THE NIGHT

Crispus usually dies so soon after awakening that he has no time for reflection, but this life is different. He awoke in this new place as dawn broke, and now, in the brightness of a spring day, he still lives.

As he walks to the university library, though, he sees the signs of what is coming and knows that this incarnation will end as the others have. Already he feels the first tug of his host's urge to meet the fusillade.

His host is a young white woman this time, a child only a little older than poor Sam Maverick was. Crispus wants to pray for her; but the Lord is punishing him, and he cannot expect to be heard.

Even so, as he enters the library he cannot help asking again: *Is it my fault that I was born with such pride and anger? Is it my fault that a thousand deaths have not quenched their flames?*

There is no response, so Crispus must search for an answer on his own. He flips through the card catalog until he finds a title with the phrase his host knows: *The Boston Massacre.*

The book stands on its shelf as if it has been waiting for him. The young woman's body trembles as Crispus takes the volume to an empty carrel — *all* the carrels are empty, he notices — to discover what history has to say about him.

His host is a rapid reader. Her intelligence will only make her loss all the worse for those who love her.

Crispus has her memories as well as his own, and knows her more thoroughly than she has known herself. He mourns for the beauty of who she is and for the beauty she might have become. He probes for her consciousness and cannot find it, so he hopes that the Lord has already taken her soul.

He does not want her to feel the bullets.

What Crispus finds in the book makes him clench his host's teeth. Incredibly, John Adams, lawyer of Boston, defended Crispus' killers against the charge of murder, saying:

> *"This Crispus Attucks appears to have undertaken to be the hero of the night; and to lead this army with banners, to form them in the first place in Dock Square, and march them up to King Street with their clubs. If this was not an unlawful assembly, there never was one . . .*
>
> *Now to have this reinforcement coming down under the command of a stout mulatto fellow, whose very looks were enough to terrify any person, what had not the soldiers then to fear? He had hardiness enough to fall in upon them, and with one hand took hold of a bayonet, and with the other knocked the man down. This was the behavior of Attucks, to whose mad proceedings in probability the dreadful carnage of that night was chiefly to be ascribed."*

Crispus slams the book shut, and the sound echoes through the deserted stacks.

What did his parentage or looks have to do with anything? Did the fact that his mother was black and his father Natick give the redcoats the right to shoot him?

To return for his thousand-and-first death, and to find himself accused of his own murder —

If you were here today, Mister John Adams, Crispus thinks, *I would split your lying tongue.*

He cannot recall every detail of every death . . . but of that first, he has no doubts.

He was born a slave in Framingham and ran away at the age of twenty-seven. His master advertised a reward, but Crispus avoided capture by hiring on with a vessel in Boston. He sailed from there to the West Indies, settling on New Providence, and continued to work on various whaling and trading ships.

Eventually, he realized that his old master must be dead and that no one would remember Crispus Attucks as being the property of another. So, two decades after leaving as a runaway slave, he returned to Boston as a free man.

But the city itself was no longer free, for the lobsterbacks had come to enforce the King's taxes and to harass free men and slaves alike.

Crispus could not hold his anger in check at the soldiers' bullying. Years before, he had struggled for his own freedom; now, he would struggle for Boston's. Or, at the very least, he would help give back to the lobsters some of what they had already given out.

He did *not* seduce his comrades of the fifth of March into following him. Each man joined the others of his own will.

The ropemaker, Sam Gray, was a prime example. As the mob approached King Street, Gray told Crispus that three days earlier a soldier had come to the ropewalk where Gray had been working and had demanded that he be hired.

"So you will work, will you?" Gray had asked him.

"I have said so, haven't I?" the soldier had snapped back.

"Then you may go clean my shithouse," Gray had said, turning back to his cable.

The furious redcoat had left then, but had returned with a gang of his fellows. The soldiers had started a fight, but the boys at the ropewalk had beaten them even though some of the lobsters had brandished cutlasses.

Crispus clapped Gray's back upon hearing the tale, and they went on together, shaking their staves above their heads.

Yes, Mister Adams, Crispus thinks, *some of us carried clubs that night. But the British carried muskets. Which weapon causes the more 'dreadful carnage'?*

"Come on, you bloody lobsters!" the crowd cried, throwing ice and stones. "Put down your guns, and we're your men!"

Crispus lunged forward through the darkness to grasp a musket barrel, and the soldier jerked the gun up, cutting Crispus' hand with the bayonet. Crispus stumbled back, staring down at his wounded palm —

And then two sharp pains speared into his chest with a heat so great that he was forced to his knees. His comrades panicked, and he was knocked onto his back. Young Sam Maverick staggered past with his mouth agape.

The pain rose up like a stormswell, hurting so much that Crispus could not even cry out. Then it engulfed him, and that was all.

That is the truth of that night, Mister Adams. If you still believe me to be the cause of it, then you may kiss my ass.

Crispus reopens the book and learns of the death of a man named James Caldwell, whom he did not know, and of the other victims who died later. As he reads, his anger fades and is replaced by a dull sadness.

If he was *not* wrong to do as he did in Boston, then why is he being punished? Why must he suffer death after death after death?

He lowers his host's head onto the book, pressing her cheek flat against the pages. One slender hand lies on the desktop as if already drained of life.

Crispus searches the young woman's mind and finds nothing there of evil. She does not deserve to die.

But neither did any of the others.

After falling to the cobblestones in King Street, Crispus awoke as a small boy. He did not have time to become awestricken at the miracle of his resurrection, though, for his second death came swiftly.

His host was shivering, so cold that he could hardly think, huddling with a cluster of women and children. They were mourning the defeat of their tribe by the longknives.

Crispus had been alive for less than a minute when a huge mass of strangely clothed soldiers on horseback charged into the camp with their swords drawn and their guns thundering. The air filled with smoke and screams. Crispus tried to run away through the snow, but even in his panic he knew that his frostbitten, wasted body could not escape.

He felt the vibration of the horse coming up fast behind him and tried to dodge, but his host's feet and legs were too cold. The horse ran him down, crushing his spine. The soldier rode on, leaving Crispus to suffer white spikes of agony, but another came soon after and put a bullet into his head.

Even with that wound, Crispus lived long enough to feel something worse than what he had felt in Boston. This time, his pain was steeped in despair.

The veins in the young woman's hand stand out in blue relief as Crispus knots the fingers into a fist. He hates being her, hates knowing that her mind will soon be dead and empty. A few of her memories will stay with him, but none of them will ever be hers again.

He closes her eyes and sees buildings of glass and steel so high that their tops seem to shrink to nothing. He sees winged ships carrying people into the sky and around the world. He sees men in thick white suits standing on the moon.

Yet as wondrous as these things are, they do not surprise him, for he has caught glimpses of their approach over the decades. They are simply part of the changing world, the world that he saw changing even during the forty-seven years of his first life.

He looks at his host's wristwatch and sees that he has lived for more than six hours. The Lord is giving him extra time to examine and repent of his sins.

But the longer he stays alive, the more deaths he remembers; and with each of these memories, he asks, *Why must there be such pain in the world?*

And why must I feel so much of it, over and over again?

It is so . . . lonely.

Crispus presses his host's face hard against the book as he remembers the death he experienced immediately before becoming her. Its sting is fresh.

He was a child for at least the hundredth time — a little girl who knew only hunger, mud, and fear. Her life up to the point that he became her had been nothing but misery, and he knew that it would get no better.

The wild-eyed soldiers who came into the village wore filthy clothing of green and brown. Crispus did not know how many there were, because as they arrived his host's mother picked up the child and held her tight. Crispus found himself covered with a conical grass hat, enclosed as though he were in a tent.

Shouting and shoving, the soldiers herded everyone into a ditch, and then the explosive rattling noises started. Crispus, responding to an imperative built into his host, began to weep.

The mother's body jerked, pushing him down.

"Bloody *lobsters!*" he tried to cry, but his host's mouth filled with mud.

Then came the pain, razor-keen but quick, and he awoke as a college student.

Crispus opens the fist as his host's head rises from the book. He is startled for an instant at the touch of her long hair on her cheek.

He wants to continue reading, but the young woman's death urge comes in full force now, overwhelming him. As she stands, he can hear the shouts and chants and threats beginning outside. He wishes the noises were as far away as they sound.

His host's thoughts flood in and mix with his. He sees her as she was yesterday, walking past a Guardsman who had a flower stuck in his rifle barrel.

Flowers are better than bullets.

They leave the library stacks. Crispus knows that his host is not planning to take part in the demonstration, and for a moment he clings to the useless hope that she will survive after all.

She blinks as she comes out into the sunshine. Crispus is a mere passenger now; he can do nothing more than watch as they move toward the mob, toward the Guardsmen, toward the guns.

It hurts a lot this time.

Crispus awakens with the knowledge that only eleven days have passed since his previous death. Never before has so little time elapsed between incarnations.

He is outside in the sun again, but the day is hotter, more humid. His host, a young black man, is sweating. The demonstration has already begun.

Brothers dying for nothing.

A voice bellows, sounding as though it has come from the sky, and orders them to disperse. The white cops move toward them.

The man beside Crispus throws a rock.

Then the familiar gunfire comes, and the rock-thrower falls. Crispus leans down to help, and his host's insides become an inferno.

He falls too, living just long enough to hear someone shout, "Goddamn *niggers!*"

Twenty-three more lives come in quick succession, some of them so brief that Crispus cannot even breathe before the bullets hit. He begins to long for a true death, for oblivion . . . for anything that will make it stop.

Then he awakens as a woman whose mind is so self-controlled and serene that he cannot help but share her calm. The blood of three races courses through her veins, and despite her sex, Crispus feels almost like himself.

The woman is alone in her one-room apartment, her golden fingers resting on the keyboard of a portable computer. Crispus has seen such machines in the minds of his most recent hosts, but this is the first time that he has been close to one.

The words on the flat blue monitor glow a soft amber, and Crispus reads what his host has just written:

> *That our government cannot comprehend the reasons for our anger should come as no surprise; thirty years ago, the official response to the uprisings of that era was much the same. For example, after armed "peace officers" killed two members of a protest rally, the President was heard to ask the head of the victims' college, "Look, what are we going to do to get more respect for the police from our young people?"*

Crispus remembers being told of similar questions from Governor Hutchinson in Boston: "What has happened to respect for the soldiers of the Crown? What are we to do about the young ruffians who roam the streets at night?"

Drawing on the skill of his host to operate the keyboard, Crispus writes, *Why do the people still allow Tories to hold positions of power? And why do these same Tories always blame dissent on the rebelliousness of the young? I was in my forty-eighth year when I challenged the red-coated bastards in King Street, and I am almost three hundred years old now. Yet despite all that God and man have done to me, I am ever angry, ever rebellious, ever*

He stops writing as he sees the face of his host reflected in the monitor. Her hair is long and dark; her mouth is firm and strong; her eyes are piercing and clear.

Crispus stands and walks to the narrow bed on the other side of the room. It is true that he is still angry, rebellious, and proud . . . but it is even more true that he has become sick of death.

He sits cross-legged on the mattress. A single translucent window in the west wall catches the last light of the day, warming the woman's skin as Crispus looks around at the room. The walls are covered with photographs, and the faces of girls and boys smile out everywhere. The woman works with children who have been hurt by their parents, teaching them that they are valuable, that they matter.

She lives simply. All of her clothes fit into a chipped four-drawer bureau. All of her cooking is done with a tiny microwave oven. Her bicycle, which leans against the foot of the bed, is her sole means of transportation. The room has no shelves, so her books are stacked against the walls, reaching up to the photographs like towers of words.

Crispus feels something like love for this woman. He wants her to live.

What would happen, he wonders, if he were to trap her so that she could not go out to meet her doom? Would she die anyway? If she survived, would Crispus survive as well? Could they live together, sharing one body, one brain?

Crispus decides to find out.

He probes the woman's mind for possible methods, hurrying for fear that the death-urge will come soon. It takes him less than a second to find something that might work.

He walks into the doorless, closet-sized bathroom and searches through the jumble of tools in the cabinet under the sink until he finds the spray can labeled INSTANT EPOXY. Then he returns to the main room, locks the hollow steel door, and sprays the doorknob and lock until they are encased in a thick, clear coat. The fumes give his host a headache.

As soon as he has finished with the door, he goes to the window and sprays its lock as well, emptying the can. The windowpane is made of stiff, heavy plastic, and he does not think his host could break it — but to make it tougher still, he fetches a roll of metallic tape from the bathroom and covers the pane with silver strips.

The light that had filled the room fades with each strip of tape, and by the time Crispus is finished, the only illumination in the apartment comes from the amber glow of the computer monitor.

Crispus drops the empty cardboard ring and crosses back to the door. The knob and lock will not budge.

But he is still not satisfied, for this host is strong and clever. He wants to immobilize her.

A chain with an electronic combination lock is wrapped around part of the bicycle frame, but the woman knows the combination. As Crispus racks her brain, though, he discovers that she keeps a metal box containing legal documents under the bed. The box is secured by an old-fashioned padlock whose key is hidden in the bureau's bottom drawer.

Once Crispus has opened the padlock, he slides the key out under the glued door and makes certain that his host cannot reach it. Then he goes into the bathroom and empties her bladder and bowels. When he comes out, he switches on the ceiling light and moves the computer table over to the bed. That done, he goes to the stacks of books and selects several volumes at random, tossing them onto the mattress.

Finally, he unwraps the chain from the bicycle frame. Then he sits on the edge of the bed and loops the chain around the woman's right ankle.

When he is certain that the chain cannot be slid off the bedframe and that it is pulled so tight that his host cannot work herself free, he slips the padlock through the end links and snaps it shut.

Then he waits.

One of the books on the bed is a thick paperback anthology on civil disobedience. For a moment, Crispus considers tossing it back to its stack against the wall; but then, assuring himself that the woman is safe no matter what he reads, he picks it up and turns to an essay on the Massacre.

He is surprised to find himself referred to as "the first martyr of the American Revolution," but what surprises him even more is an excerpt from the diary of John Adams, dated July 1773, that is in the form of a letter to Governor Hutchinson:

To Tho. Hutchinson/Sir:
  You will hear from Us with Astonishment.
  You ought to hear from Us with Horror. You are chargeable before God and Man, with our Blood.
  The Soldiers were but passive Instruments, were Machines, neither moral nor voluntary Agents in our Destruction more than the leaden Pelletts, with which we were wounded.
  You were a free Agent.
  You acted, coolly, deliberately, with all that premeditated Malice, not against Us in Particular but against the People in general, which in the Sight of the Law is an ingredient in the Composition of Murder.
  You will hear further from Us hereafter.

Adams has signed the letter *Chrispus Attucks.*

Crispus takes a tremulous breath. It is infinitely strange to know that these words came from the pen of the man who condemned him at the soldiers' trial. Their meaning, however, is clear: By 1773, John Adams blamed Governor Hutchinson, not the mulatto Attucks, for the Boston Massacre.

With that in mind, Crispus decides that he must forgive Adams for the lawyer's earlier remarks. But as he does so, he realizes that he must then also forgive the men who shot him on that cold March night.

The thought is troubling, for it suggests that he must in turn forgive everyone who has killed him in each of his incarnations.

He lies back on the mattress, painfully aware of the ankle chained to the bedpost, and covers the woman's eyes with one hand. Adams he can forgive, and perhaps even the soldiers at the Custom House . . .

The Soldiers were but passive Instruments . . .

You were a free Agent.

Is it so in every case? Crispus wonders. Is there always a Governor Hutchinson in a mansion somewhere, staying safe and pampered while his Machines commit his murders?

He thinks back over his many deaths and remembers seeing a horrible kind of lust in the eyes of some of his killers. Those men he can never forgive, even if it means that the Lord will punish him for all eternity. But he can also remember the faces of other killers — some who seemed tortured or frightened to the point of wildness, and some who seemed empty of all emotion, as if their blood had been drained and replaced with water.

Those frightened or empty ones, Crispus concludes, could not have been in possession of their own souls. Their souls, then, he will forgive.

The Hutchinsons of the world are another matter.

He damns their invisible faces.

Crispus is reading in the book again when he feels the first tremors of his host's urge to escape and die. Her ankle twists inside the tight loops of chain, chafing the skin so badly that he is afraid she will bleed.

Listen to me, he thinks fiercely. *If you leave this room tonight, you will not live to see the morning.*

The twisting and pulling weaken slightly, but in the woman's heart Crispus can still feel her desire to join her friends. He thinks again that he should not have selected this particular book . . . but he cannot stop reading yet, for he has found another passage about himself:

> A "Crispus Attucks Day" was first held in Boston in 1858. The primary speaker, Wendell Phillips, claimed that the shot heard round the world was not fired at Lexington. Rather, Phillips asserted, that shot was fired in Boston.
>
> "Who set the example of guns?" Phillips asked. "Who taught the British soldier that he might be defeated? Who first dared look into his eyes? The 5th of March, 1770, was the baptism of blood. I place, therefore, this Crispus Attucks in the foremost rank of the men that dared. When we talk of courage, he rises, with his dark face, in the clothes of the laborer, his head uncovered, his arm raised above him defying bayonets.

Crispus closes the book, wishing that he had done so earlier. He knows that he is no hero, no personification of courage. He is simply a man who was unwilling to take a blow without striking back.

His host's body quivers, then shakes violently, jerking at the chain.

Crispus flings the book across the room. Its words have made the woman's desire to sacrifice herself stronger than ever.

As he throws the book, he sees his bitter questions about Tories glowing in the computer screen. He turns away, afraid to face their bright rage.

Crispus picks up another book, an old volume of stories and essays about the future. This, he thinks, should provide some distraction. Dreams and fantasies are what he and his host need.

But the book is not what he expects, for most of the pieces are about war and injustice. His host's chained ankle begins to bleed.

He curses aloud and hears the woman's voice for the first time. Even in cursing, it is gentle.

Despite himself, Crispus continues reading, and his eyes light upon an essayist's list of "Commandments for Survival." The first of these Commandments says, NEVER THROW THINGS AT MEN WITH GUNS.

The woman struggles harder, and Crispus finds himself wanting to struggle with her.

A corollary to the Commandment says, NEVER STAND BESIDE SOMEONE WHO IS THROWING THINGS AT MEN WITH GUNS.

Crispus rips the page from the book and crumples it. Then he reaches for the computer keyboard and writes:

If armed men wrong you, whether of their own wills or at the bidding of another, then you must fight them. Though they have muskets and you have only stones and ice, I say throw what you have and Survival be damned. And if armed men wrong your friend instead, then I say stand beside your friend and throw stones and ice together.

Crispus hesitates, realizing that with every word, he slips closer toward defeat in the battle he has set out to fight today.

But he cannot stop himself. *If you do not do these things,* he writes, *then I say you are a coward and undeserving of Survival, or of the title of Free Man.*

"Or Free Woman," his host's voice says.

Crispus sits as if frozen for a long moment. Then, tentatively, he probes through the woman's mind and finds her, awake and alive.

"I throw words," she tells him. "The targets react as though the words were stones or ice, but I will not stop."

Crispus stares at his host's reflection in the monitor. *I do not even know what you are fighting for.*

She gives him a vision of fire, blood, and pain in a small, faraway country.

Crispus' anger flares. The name of the small country does not matter; what matters is that he has seen all this before, and that he hates it.

"Free me," his host says.

Crispus knows what will happen — and since the woman can see his thoughts, she knows too. She knows everything, and yet she wants to go. She wants to fight despite the fact that the fight will kill her.

Crispus decides that he does not have the right to save her.

As for himself . . .

He is a strong man, and can stand another painful transition into the future.

He has seen the colonies become a nation, and the nation become a mighty power. Perhaps, if he continues hurtling onward through the years, propelled by the burning sting of bullets, he will see something even greater come to pass.

Perhaps he isn't being punished after all. Perhaps he is being rewarded with the chance to see the day when Death is finally defeated.

He stretches his host's body out along the bed until her hands are able to grasp a bicycle spoke. It takes all of the woman's strength and costs her more blood, but the spoke breaks free from the rim.

Crispus unhooks the spoke from the wheel hub, then lowers his host to the floor and crawls to the door, dragging the bed behind him. After several minutes of trying, he is able to snag the padlock key with the spoke and to pull it back inside.

When the woman's leg is free of the chain, Crispus limps

into the bathroom and finds a screwdriver in the cabinet. The apartment door has three hinges, but he discovers that he only has to unfasten two before the door leans far enough to allow an escape.

Satisfied? Crispus asks. But his host has said all that is necessary, and remains silent.

Crispus takes a short, thick candle from the top of the bureau and lights it with a match. He begins to leave then, but stops with one foot outside the narrow passage.

He turns and walks back to the computer. There, in amber, are his last words, to which he adds two final sentences:

Though I die, I, Crispus Attucks, am a Free Man and have no need of your mourning or prayers. Mourn and pray instead for the Tories, for they will indeed hear further from me hereafter.

He hits the SAVE button and leaves the apartment.

In the moonless night, a flurry of snow creates white halos around the streetlamps. Crispus shields his small flame with his host's palm, and as he walks he sees hundreds of other flames converging at the foot of a dark hill at the edge of the city. There the flames become one tremendous dancing light, and the men and women inside that light begin singing an insistent song of protest.

Crispus feels outrage heating the winter air as he joins the crowd, and he knows he is home.

An inhuman voice shouts down from the top of the hill. "YOU ARE TRESPASSING ON GOVERNMENT PROPERTY. DISPERSE AT ONCE."

"*We* are the government!" the man beside Crispus cries, and the words ripple out from person to person until the chant shakes the earth.

Crispus grins. *Put down those muskets, you bloody lobsters, and we're your men and women.*

Then, feeling a joy that he has not felt for almost two and a half centuries, he links arms with his friends and ascends the hill, his fire defying the darkness ahead.

THE TERRITORY

Sam came awake and sat up choking. His chest was as tight as if wrapped in steel cables, and his heart was trying to hammer its way out. He gulped a breath and coughed. The air in the abandoned barn was thick with dust. There was just enough light for him to see the swirling motes.

A few feet away, the skinny form of Fletcher Taylor groaned and rose on one elbow. "What the hell's wrong?" he asked.

"Shut the hell up," the man on the other side of Taylor said.

"You go to hell," Taylor snapped.

"Go to hell yourself."

"Let me sleep, or I'll send you all to hell," another man said.

"The hell you will."

"The hell I won't."

Taylor shook a finger at Sam. "See all the hell you've raised?"

Sam put on the new slouch hat that Taylor had given him, pulled on his boots, and stood, picking up the leather saddlebags he'd been using as a pillow. "I'm sorry as hell," he said, and left the barn, trying not to kick more than four or five of the other men on his way out.

The light was better outside, but the sun had not yet risen. Sam closed his left nostril with a finger and blew through his right, then closed his right nostril and blew through his left, trying to clear his head of dust. The ground was dry. The thunderheads that had formed the night before had rolled by without dropping enough rain to fill a teacup. He could have slept outside, in clean air, and been fine. As it was, his head ached. This wasn't the first night he had spent in a barn or corn crib since leaving the river, but he still wasn't used to it. At three months shy of twenty-eight, he feared that he was already too old for this kind of life.

Most of the camp was still asleep, but a few men were

building fires and boiling chicory. One of them gestured to Sam to come on over, but Sam shook his head and pointed at the sycamore grove that served as the camp latrine. The other man nodded.

Sam went into the trees, and within twenty steps the smells of chicory and smoke were overwhelmed by the smell caused by two hundred men all doing their business in the same spot over the course of a week. It was even worse than usual this morning, because the leaders of other guerrilla bands had brought some of their own men into camp the day before. But at least Sam had the grove to himself for now.

When he had finished his business, he continued eastward through the grove until the stench faded and the trees thinned. Then he sat down with his back against the bole of a sycamore and opened one of his saddlebags. He removed his Colt Navy revolver and laid it on the ground beside him, then took out a pen, a bottle of ink, and the deerhide pouch that held his journal. He slid the notebook from the pouch and flipped pages until he reached a blank sheet, then opened the ink bottle, dipped his pen, and began to write.

> *Tuesday, August 11, 1863:*
>
> *I have had the same dream again, or I should say, another variation thereof. This time when I reached the dead man, I discovered that his face was that of my brother Henry. Then I awoke with the thought that it was my fault that Henry was on board the Pennsylvania when she blew, which in turn led to the thought that I was an idiot to ask a young and unsure physician to give him morphine.*
>
> *But I would have been on the Pennsylvania as well had it not been for the malice of a certain William Brown, perhaps the only man caught in that storm of metal, wood, and steam who received what he deserved. As for the morphine, Dr. Peyton himself instructed me to ask the night doctor to give Henry an eighth of a grain should he become restless. If the doctor administered too much, the fault was his, not mine.*
>
> *I see by my words that I have become hard. But five years have passed since that night in Memphis, and I have seen enough in those years that the hours I spent at Henry's deathbed do not seem so horrific now — or, at least, they do not seem so during my waking hours.*

A pistol shot rang out back at camp and was followed by the shouted curses of men angry at having been awakened. Someone had killed a rat or squirrel, and might soon wish that he'd let the creature live to gnaw another day. These once-gentle Missouri farmboys had become as mean as bobcats. They generally saved their bullets for Bluebellies, but didn't mind using their fists and boots on each other.

The dream seems more pertinent, Sam continued, on those nights when the man's face is that of Orion. Orion was as intolerable a scold as any embittered crone, and a Republican crone at that — but he was my brother, and it might have been in my power to save him.

Sam paused, rolling the pen between his fingers. He looked up from the paper and stared at the brightening eastern sky until his eyes stung. Then he dipped the pen and resumed writing.

It is as fresh and awful in my memory as if it had happened not two years ago, but two days ago.

I could have fought the Red Legs, as Orion and our companions tried to do. I had a Smith & Wesson seven-shooter. If I had used it, I would have either preserved Orion's life, or fallen beside him. Either result would have been honorable.

But I faltered. When the moment came, I chose to surrender, and handed over my pistol — which one of the Red Legs laughed at, saying he was glad I had not fired the weapon, for to be struck with a ball from its barrel might give one a nasty welt.

Then, as if to prove his point, he turned it on the driver, and on the conductor, and on Mr. Bemis, and on my brother.

As Orion lay dying, the Red Leg attempted to shoot me as well. But the pistol misfired, and I ran. Two of the Red Legs caught me and took my watch, but then let me go, saying that killing a Missourian the likes of me would not be so advantageous to their cause as letting me live.

I continued to run like the coward I had already proven myself to be.

Sam paused again. His hand was shaking, and he didn't think he would be able to read the jagged scrawl of what he had just written. But he would always know what the words said.

He rubbed his forehead with his wrist, then turned the notebook page and dipped his pen.

> *I could not have saved Henry. But Orion would be alive today, safe in Nevada Territory, had I been a man. And I would be there with him instead of here at Blue Springs; I would be thriving in the mountains of the West instead of sweltering in the chaos of Western Missouri.*
>
> *I have remained in Missouri to pay for my sin, but in two years have had no success in doing so. Perhaps now that I have come to Jackson County and fallen in with the Colonel's band, my luck will change.*
>
> *When this war began, I served with my own county's guerrilla band, the Marion Rangers, for three weeks. But there the actual need for bushwhacking was about as substantial as an owl's vocabulary. That was before I had crossed the state, entered Kansas, and encountered the Red Legs. That was before I had seen my brother shot down as if he were a straw target.*
>
> *I have not had a letter from Mother, Pamela, or Mollie in several weeks, although I have written to each of them as often as I can. I do not know whether this means that they have disowned me, or whether their letters are not reaching Independence. I intend to go up to investigate once this coming business is completed, assuming that it does not complete me in the process.*

Sam laid the journal on the ground and wiped his ink-stained fingers on the grass. Then he peered into the ink bottle and saw that it was almost empty. He decided not to buy more until he was sure he would live long enough to use it.

The sun had risen and was a steady heat on Sam's face. The day was going to be hot. Another shot rang out back at camp, and this time it was followed by yips and hollers. The boys were up and eager.

Sam slid his journal into its pouch, then returned it and the other items to the saddlebag. He stood, stretched, and walked back to Colonel Quantrill's camp.

As he emerged from the sycamores, Sam saw fifty or sixty of his fellow bushwhackers clustered before Quantrill's tent. The tent was open, and the gathered men, although keeping a respectful distance, were trying to see and hear what was going on inside. Fletcher Taylor was standing at the rear of the cluster, scratching his sparse beard.

"'Morning, Fletch," Sam said as he approached. "Sleep well?"

Taylor gave him a narrow-eyed glance. "Rotten, thanks to you."

"Well, you're welcome."

"Be quiet. I'm trying to hear."

"Hear what?"

"You know damn well what. The Colonel's planning a raid. Most of the boys are betting it'll be Kansas City, but my money's on Lawrence."

Sam nodded. "The story I hear is that the Colonel's wanted to teach Jim Lane and Lawrence a lesson ever since he lived there himself."

A man standing in front of Taylor turned to look at them. "I'd like to teach Jim Lane a lesson too," he said, "but I'm not crazy and neither's the Colonel. Lawrence is forty miles inside the border, and the Bluebellies are likely to be as thick as flies on a dead possum. It'd be like putting our pistols to our own heads."

"Maybe," Sam said.

The man raised an eyebrow. "What do you mean, maybe? You know something I don't?"

Sam shrugged and said nothing. Two nights before, in a dream, he had seen Colonel Quantrill surrounded by a halo of fire, riding into Lawrence before a band of shooting, shouting men. He had known the town was Lawrence because all of its inhabitants had looked like the caricatures he had seen of Senator Jim Lane and had worn red pants. Sam had learned to trust his dreams when they were as clear as that. Several days before the *Pennsylvania* had exploded, a dream had shown him Henry lying in a coffin; and before he and Orion had left St. Joseph, a dream had shown him Orion lying dead in the dust. But it wouldn't do to talk of his dreams with the other bushwhackers. Most of them seemed to think that Sam Clemens was odd enough as it was, hoarding perfectly good ass-wiping paper just so he could write on it.

"Well, you're wrong," the man said, taking Sam's shrug

as a statement. "Kansas City's got it coming just as bad, and there's places for a man to hide when he's done."

Taylor looked thoughtful. "I see your point," he said. "Calling on Senator Lane would be one thing, but coming home from the visit might be something else."

Sam stayed quiet. It didn't matter what the others thought now. They would mold bullets and make cartridges until they were told where to shoot them, and they'd be just as happy to shoot them in Lawrence as anywhere else — happier, since most of the jayhawkers and Red Legs who had robbed them, burned them out of their homes, killed their brothers, and humiliated their women had either hailed from Lawrence or pledged their allegiance to Jim Lane. And if Quantrill could pull several guerrilla bands together under his command, he would have enough men both to raid Lawrence and to whip the Federals on the way there and back.

Captain George Todd emerged from the tent and squinted in the sunlight. He was a tall, blond, square-jawed man whom some of the men worshipped even more than they did Quantrill. He was wearing a blue jacket he'd taken from a dead Union lieutenant.

"Hey, cap'n, where we going?" someone called out.

Todd gave the men a stern look. "I doubt we'll be going anywhere if you boys keep standing around like sick sheep when there's guns to be cleaned and bridles to be mended."

The men groaned, but began to disperse.

"Fletch Taylor!" Todd yelled. "Wherever you are, get your ass in here!" He turned and went back into the tent.

Sam nudged Taylor. "Now, what would a fine leader of men like George Todd be wanting with a lowdown thief like you?" he asked.

Taylor sneered. "Well, he told me to keep my eyes open for Yankee spies," he said, "so I reckon he'll be wanting me to give him your name." He started for the tent.

"I'm not worried!" Sam called after him. "He'll ask you to spell it, and you'll be stumped!"

Taylor entered the tent, and someone pulled the flaps closed. Sam stood looking at the tent for a moment longer, then struck off across camp in search of breakfast. Why Quantrill and the other guerrilla leaders were taking so long to form their plans, and why they were keeping the men in the dark, he couldn't imagine. There shouldn't be any great planning involved in striking a blow at Lawrence and the Red Legs: Ride in hard, attack the Red Legs' headquarters and the Union garrison like lightning, and then ride out again, pausing long enough to set fire to Jim Lane's house to pay him back for the dozens of Missouri houses he'd burned himself.

As for keeping the rank-and-file bushwhackers ignorant . . . well, there were about as many Yankee spies among Quantrill's band as there were fish in the sky. Sam had talked to over a hundred of these men, and all of them had lost property or family to abolitionist raiders of one stripe or another. Sam had even spoken with one man whose brother had been killed by John Brown in 1856, and who still longed for vengeance even though John Brown was now as dead as a rock.

Vengeance could be a long time coming, as Sam well knew. In the two years since Orion's murder, he had yet to kill a single Federal soldier, let alone one of the marauding Kansas Red Legs. It wasn't for lack of trying, though. He had fired countless shots at Bluebellies, but always at a distance or in the dark. He had never hit anything besides trees and the occasional horse.

Sam had a breakfast of fatty bacon with three young brothers who were from Ralls County south of Hannibal and who therefore considered him a kinsman. He ate their food, swapped a few East Missouri stories, and promised to pay them back with bacon of his own as soon as he had some. Then he shouldered his saddlebags again and walked to the camp's makeshift corral to see after his horse, Bixby.

Bixby was a swaybacked roan gelding who had been gelded too late and had a mean disposition as a result. The horse also seemed to think that he knew better than Sam when it came to picking a travel route, or when it came to deciding whether to travel at all. Despite those flaws, however, Sam had no plans to replace Bixby. He thought that he had the horse he deserved.

Sam tried to give Bixby a lump of hard brown sugar from one of his saddlebags, but Bixby ignored it and attempted to bite Sam's shoulder.

"Sometimes I think you forget," Sam said, slapping Bixby on the nose, "that I am the man who freed you from your bondage to an abolitionist."

Bixby snorted and stomped, then tried to bite Sam's shoulder again.

"Clemens!" a voice called.

Sam turned and saw that the voice belonged to one of the Ralls County boys who had fed him breakfast.

"The Colonel wants you at the tent!" the boy shouted.

Sam was astonished. Except for his friendship with Fletch Taylor, he was less than a nobody in the band. Not only was he a new arrival, but it was already obvious that he was the worst rider, the worst thief, and the worst shot. Maybe Taylor really had told Todd and Quantrill that he was a Yankee spy.

"Better come quick!" the boy yelled.

Sam waved. "I'll be right — God damn son of a bitch!"

Bixby had succeeded in biting him. Sam whirled and tried to slug the horse in the jaw with the saddlebags, but Bixby jerked his head up and danced away.

Sam rubbed his shoulder and glared at Bixby. "Save some for the Red Legs, why don't you," he said. Then he ducked under the corral rope and hurried to Quantrill's tent. He remembered to remove his hat before going inside.

William Clarke Quantrill leaned back, his left leg crossed over his right, in a polished oak chair behind a table consisting of three planks atop two sawhorses. He wore a white embroidered "guerrilla shirt," yellow breeches, and black cavalry boots. He gave a thin smile as Sam approached the table. Above his narrow upper lip, his mustache was a straight reddish-blond line. His eyelids drooped, but his blue-gray eyes probed Sam with a gaze as piercing as a bayonet. Sam stopped before the table and clenched his muscles so he wouldn't shudder. His own eyes, he had just realized, were of much the same color as Quantrill's.

"You've only been with us since June, Private Clemens," Quantrill said in a flat voice, "and yet it seems that you have distinguished yourself. Corporal Taylor tells me you saved his life a few weeks ago."

Sam looked at Fletch Taylor, who was standing at his left. Taylor appeared uncomfortable under Sam's gaze, so Sam looked past him at some of the other men in the tent. He recognized the guerrilla leaders Bill Gregg and Andy Blunt, but several of the others were strangers to him.

"Well, sir," Sam said to Quantrill, "I don't know that I did. My horse was being cantankerous and brought me in on an abolitionist's house about two hundred feet behind and to one side of Fletch and the other boys, so I happened to see a man hiding up a tree."

"He was aiming a rifle at Corporal Taylor, I understand," Quantrill said.

"Yes, sir, that's how it looked," Sam said. "So I hollered and took a shot at him."

"And that was his undoing."

Sam twisted the brim of his hat in his hands. "Actually, sir," he said, "I believe that I missed by fourteen or fifteen feet."

Quantrill uncrossed his legs and stood. "But you diverted the ambusher's attention. According to Corporal Taylor, the ambusher then fired four shots at you, one of which took your hat from your head, before he was brought down by a volley from your comrades. Meanwhile you remained steadfast, firing your own weapon without flinching, even though the entire focus of the enemy's fire was at yourself."

Sam licked his lips and said nothing. The truth was that he had been stiff with terror — except for his right hand, which had been cocking and firing the Colt, and his left foot, which had been kicking Bixby in the ribs in an effort to make the horse wheel and run. But Bixby, who seemed to be deaf as far as gunfire was concerned, had been biting a crabapple from a tree and had not cared to move. The horse's position had blocked the other bushwhackers' view of Sam's left foot.

Quantrill put his hands on the table and leaned forward. "That was a brave and noble act, Private Clemens," he said.

A stretch of silence followed until Sam realized that he was expected to say something. "Thank, thank you, Colonel," he stammered. It was well known that Quantrill liked being called "Colonel."

"You understand, of course," Quantrill said, "that in the guerrilla service we have no formal honors. However, as the best reward of service is service itself, I'm promoting you to corporal and ordering you to reconnoiter the enemy in the company of Corporal Taylor."

"And a nigger," someone on Sam's right said. The voice was low, ragged, and angry.

Sam turned toward the voice and saw the most fearsome man he had ever seen in his life. The man wore a Union officer's coat with the insignia torn off, and a low-crowned hat with the brim turned up. His brown hair was long and shaggy, and his beard was the color of dirt. His face was gaunt, and his eyes, small and dark, glowered. He wore a wide-buckled belt with two pistols jammed into it. A scalp hung from the belt on each side of the buckle.

George Todd, standing just behind this man, placed a hand on his shoulder. "I don't much like it either, Bill, but Quantrill's right. A nigger's the perfect spy."

The seated man shook Todd's hand away. "Perfect spy, my hairy ass. You can't trust a nigger any more than you can trust Abe Lincoln."

Quantrill looked at the man without blinking. "That concern is why I'm sending two white men as well — one that I trust, and one that he in turn trusts. Don't you agree that two white men can keep one nigger under control, Captain Anderson?"

Anderson met Quantrill's gaze with a glare. "I have three sisters in prison in Kansas City for the simple act of remaining true to their brother's cause," he said. "I do not believe they would care to hear that their brother agreed to send a nigger to fight in that same cause, particularly knowing the treachery of which that race is capable."

Quantrill smiled. "As for sending a nigger to fight, I'm doing no such thing just yet. I'm sending him as a spy and as a guarantee of safe conduct for two brave sons of Missouri. No Kansan is likely to assault white men traveling with a free nigger. As for treachery, well, I assure you that John Noland has proven his loyalty. He's killed six Yankee soldiers and delivered their weapons to me. I trust him as much as I would a good dog, and have no doubt that he will serve Corporals Taylor and Clemens as well as he has me." The Colonel looked about the tent. "Gentlemen, we've been jawing about this enterprise for twenty-four hours. I suggest that it's now time to stop jawing and begin action. If you never risk, you never gain. Are there any objections?"

No one spoke. Anderson spat into the dirt, but then looked at Quantrill and shook his head.

"Very well," said Quantrill. "Captains Anderson and Blunt will please gather your men and communicate with me by messenger when your forces are ready." He nodded to Taylor. "Corporal, you're to return no later than sundown next Monday. So you'd best be on your way."

Sam made a noise in his throat. "Sir? On our way where?"

Quantrill turned to Sam. "Kansas Territory," he said. "Corporal Taylor has the particulars. You're dismissed."

Sam didn't need to be told twice. He left the tent, picked up his saddlebags where he'd dropped them outside, and then ran into the sycamore grove.

Taylor caught up with him in the trees. "You should have saluted, Sam," he said. "It's important to show the Colonel proper respect."

Sam unbuttoned his pants. His head was beginning to ache again. "I have plenty of respect for the Colonel," he said. "I have plenty of respect for all of them. If they were to cut me open, I'd probably bleed respect. Now get away and let a man piss in peace."

Taylor sighed. "All right. Get your horse saddled as soon as you can. I'll find Noland and meet you north of the tent. You know Noland?"

"No. But since I've only seen one man of the Negro persuasion in camp, I assume that's him."

"You assume correctly." Taylor started to turn away, then looked back again. "By the way, we were right. We're going to Lawrence. You and I are to count the Bluebellies in the garrison, and —"

"I know what a spy does, Fletch," Sam said.

Taylor turned away. "Hurry up, then. We have some miles to cover." He left the grove.

Sam emptied his bladder and buttoned his pants, then leaned against a tree and retched until he brought up most of the bacon he'd had for breakfast.

"Kansas Territory," Quantrill had said. There had been no sarcasm in his voice. Kansas had been admitted to the Union over two and a half years before, but none of the bushwhackers ever referred to it as a state. In their opinion, its admission to the Union as a free state had been an illegal act forced upon its residents by fanatical jayhawkers. Sooner or later, though, those house-burning, slave-stealing jayhawkers would be crushed, and Kansas Territory would become what it was meant to be: a state governed by Southern men who knew what was right.

To that end, Colonel Quantrill would raid the abolitionist town of Lawrence, the home of Jim Lane and the Kansas Red Legs. And Sam Clemens was to go there first and come back to tell Quantrill how to go about the task.

Orion's ghost, he thought, had better appreciate it.

On Wednesday morning, six miles south of Lawrence on the Paola road, Fletch Taylor started chuckling. Sam, riding in the center, glanced first at him and then at John Noland. Noland didn't even seem to be aware of Sam or Taylor's existence, let alone Taylor's chuckling.

Noland was an enigma, both in his mere presence in Quantrill's band and in his deportment during the present journey. No matter what Sam or Taylor said or did, he continued to look straight ahead, shifting in his saddle only to spit tobacco juice into the road. Except for the color of his skin, though, Noland's appearance was like that of any other free man of the border region, right down to the slouch hat and the Colt stuck in his belt. He even rode with the same easy arrogance as Taylor. It was a skill Sam had never mastered.

Sam looked at Taylor again, squinting as he faced the sun. "What's so funny, Fletch?"

Taylor gestured at the winding track of the road. "No pickets," he said. "We ain't seen a Bluebelly since we came into Kansas. If the Colonel wanted to, the whole lot of us could waltz in and raise no more notice than a cottontail rabbit." He chuckled again. "Until we started shooting."

Sam nodded, but didn't laugh. It was true that they hadn't passed a single Federal picket, but that didn't mean Lawrence was going to be a waltz. The absence of pickets might only mean that the town had fortified itself so well that it didn't need them.

"You should carry your gun in your belt," Noland said. His voice was a rumble.

Sam was startled. Until now, Noland hadn't spoken at all.

"Are you addressing me?" Sam asked, turning back toward Noland. But he knew that must be the case. Both Noland and Taylor had their pistols in their belts, while Sam's was in one of his saddlebags.

Noland looked straight ahead. "That's right."

"I thought I should make sure," Sam said, "since you won't look me in the eye."

"Your eyes ain't pleasant to look at," Noland said.

Taylor chortled. "Whomp him, Sam. Make him say your eyes are the most beautiful jewels this side of a St. Louie whorehouse."

"It ain't a question of beauty," Noland said. "It's a question of skittishness. Mr. Clemens has skittish eyes. I prefer steady ones, like those of Colonel Quantrill. Or like your own, Mister Taylor."

Now Sam laughed. "It appears that you've bested me in the enticing eyeball category, Fletch. Perhaps we should switch places so you can ride next to John here."

Taylor scowled. "Ain't funny, Sam."

Sam knew when to stop joking with Fletch Taylor, so he replied to Noland instead. "My gun's fine where it is," he said. "Why should I put it in my belt and risk shooting myself in the leg?"

"If that's your worry, you can take out the caps," Noland said. "But it'll look better going into Lawrence if your gun's in the open. The county sheriff might be inspecting strangers, and he won't think nothing of it if your pistol's in your belt. But if he finds it in your bag, he'll think you're trying to hide it."

Sam didn't know whether Noland was right or not, but it wasn't worth arguing about. He took his pistol from his saddlebag, removed the caps, and tucked the weapon into his belt.

"Be sure to replace those caps when we come back this way with the Colonel," Taylor said. He sounded disgusted.

"I merely want to ensure that I don't shoot up the city of Lawrence prematurely," Sam said. But neither Taylor nor Noland laughed. Sam gave Bixby a pat on the neck, and Bixby looked back at him and snorted.

When the three bushwhackers were within a mile of Lawrence, they encountered two riders heading in the opposite direction. The two men, one old and one young, were dressed in high-collared shirts and black suits despite the August heat. They wore flat-brimmed black hats, and their pistols hung in black holsters at their sides. The younger man held a Bible with a black leather cover, reading aloud as he rode.

"Well, lookee here," Taylor whispered as the two approached. "I think we got ourselves a couple of abolitionist preachers on our hands."

Sam tensed. If there was one thing a bushwhacker hated more than an abolitionist, it was an abolitionist with a congregation. Taylor had particularly strong feelings in this regard, and Sam feared that his friend might forget that they were only in Kansas as spies for now.

"Good morning, friends," the elder preacher said, reining his horse to a stop. The younger man closed his Bible and stopped his horse as well. They blocked the road.

"Good morning to you as well," Taylor replied. He and Noland stopped their horses a few yards short of the preachers.

Sam tried to stop Bixby too, but Bixby ignored the reins and continued ahead, trying to squeeze between the horses blocking the way. The preachers moved their mounts closer together, forcing Bixby to halt, and the roan shook his head and gave an irritated *whuff*.

"I apologize, gentlemen," Sam said. "My horse sometimes forgets which of us was made in God's image."

The elder preacher frowned. "More discipline might be in order," he said, and then looked past Sam at Taylor. "Are you going into Lawrence?"

"That we are," said Taylor. His voice had taken on a gravelly tone that Sam recognized as trouble on the way. He glanced back and saw that Taylor's right hand was hovering near the butt of his pistol.

"I see that you are traveling with a colored companion," the younger preacher said. "Is he your servant?"

"No," Sam said before Taylor could reply. "My friend and I jayhawked him from Arkansas three years ago, and we've been trying to help him find his family ever since. Are there any colored folks named Smith in Lawrence?"

The elder preacher nodded. "A number, I believe." He twitched his reins, and his horse moved to the side of the road. "I would like to help you in your search, gentlemen, but my son and I are on our way to Baldwin to assist in a few overdue baptisms. Sometimes an older child resists immersion and must be held down."

"I have observed as much myself," Sam said as the elder preacher rode past.

The younger preacher nodded to Sam and thumped his Bible with his fingertips. "If you gentlemen will be in town through the Sabbath, I would like to invite you to attend worship at First Lawrence Methodist."

Taylor came up beside Sam. "I doubt we'll be in town that long, preacher," he said. "But we'll be sure to pay your church a visit the next time we pass through."

"I am glad to hear it," the young preacher said. "God bless you, gentlemen." He nudged his horse with his heels and set off after his father.

Taylor looked over his shoulder at the departing men. "You won't be so glad when it happens," he muttered.

Noland rode up. "'Jayhawked from Arkansas,'" he said. "That's a good one." He spurred his horse, which set off at a trot. Taylor's horse did likewise. Bixby, for once, took the cue and hurried to catch up.

"I'm sorry if my lie didn't meet with your approval," Sam said as Bixby drew alongside Noland's horse.

"I said it was a good one," Noland said. "I say what I mean."

"You may believe him on that score, Sam," Taylor said. "John's as honest a nigger as I've ever known."

Sam eyed Noland. "Well, then, tell me," he said. "Where

were you jayhawked from?"

"I was born a free man in Ohio," Noland said. "Same as Colonel Quantrill."

"I see," Sam said. "And how is it that a free man of your race rides with a free man like the Colonel?"

Noland turned to look at Sam for the first time. His eyes and face were like black stone.

"He pays me," Noland said.

Sam had no response to that. But Noland kept looking at him.

"So why do *you* ride with the Colonel?" Noland asked.

"Might as well ask Fletch the same question," Sam said.

"I know all about Mister Taylor," Noland said. "His house was burned, his property stolen. But I don't know shit about you."

Taylor gave Noland a look of warning. "Don't get uppity."

"It's all right, Fletch," Sam said. Fair was fair. He had asked Noland an impertinent question, so Noland had asked him one. "I was a steamboat pilot on the Mississippi, Mister Noland. I was a printer's devil before that, but I wanted to be on the river, so I made it so." He grimaced. "I was a cub for two years before I earned my license, and I was only able to follow the profession for another two years before the war started. I had to leave the river then, or be forced to pilot a Union boat. So here I am."

"How'd you come to be on this side of Missouri instead of that side?" Noland asked.

"I was going to Nevada Territory with my brother," Sam said, angry now at being prodded, "but the Red Legs killed him northwest of Atchison. I went back home after that, but eventually realized there was nothing useful I could do there. So I came back this way and fell in with one bunch of incompetents after another until I joined the Colonel." He glared at Noland. "*So here I am.*"

"So here you are," Noland said.

"That's about enough, John," Taylor said. He looked at Sam. "I didn't know you were a printer, Sam, but I'm glad to hear it. It'll make one of our tasks easier. Marshal Donaldson's posse tore up the Lawrence *Herald of Freedom*'s press and dumped the type in the Kansas River back in '56, but the

Lawrence *Journal's* sprung up like a weed to take its place. So when we raid Lawrence, the *Journal's* to be destroyed. But we'll need to know how well the office is armed, so I suggest that you go there and ask for employment. You'll be able to get a look at things without them wondering why. After you've done that, you can help me count Bluebellies, Red Legs, and Lawrence Home Guards, if we can find out who they are."

"What if the *Journal* wants to hire me?" Sam asked.

Taylor grinned. "Tell them you'll be back in a week or so." He looked across at Noland. "John, you're to fall in with the local niggers and see whether any of them have guns. You might also ask them about Jim Lane, since they love him so much. Find out where his fancy new house is, and how often he's there."

Noland was staring straight ahead again, but he nodded.

They were now skirting the base of a high, steep hill. Sam looked up the slope. "One of the boys at Blue Springs told me that the hill rising over Lawrence is called Mount Horeb," he said. "It must be named after the place where Moses saw the burning bush."

Taylor chuckled. "If Moses is still here, he'll see more burning before long, at closer range than he might like." He pointed toward the southeast, at another hill that was a few miles distant. "That might be a safer place for him to watch from. The Colonel says it'll be our last stop before the raid, so we can see what's what before it's too late to turn back." He spurred his horse, which galloped ahead. "Come on, boys! We've reached Lawrence!"

Noland spurred his horse as well, and he and Taylor vanished around the curve of the hill.

"Now that I think of it," Sam yelled after them, "he said Mount Oread, not Horeb. Moses doesn't have anything to do with it."

He kicked Bixby, but the horse only looked back at him and gave a low nicker. It was the saddest sound Sam had ever heard.

"Do you have a stomachache?" he asked.

Bixby looked forward again and plodded as if leading a funeral procession. Sam kicked the horse once more and then gave up. The sadness of Bixby's nicker had infected him, and he felt oppressed by the heat, by his companions, and by his very existence on the planet.

They followed the road around the hill, and then Lawrence lay before Sam like a toy city put together by a giant child. Its rows of stores and houses were too neat and perfect to be real. Small wagons rolled back and forth between them, and children dashed about like scurrying ants. Taylor and Noland were already among them.

Sam closed his eyes, but then opened them immediately, crying out before he could stop himself.

He had just seen the buildings, wagons, and children burst into flame.

Sam shook himself. Here he was having nightmares while wide awake. The ride had been too long, the sun too hot. It was time for a rest.

But maybe not for sleep.

Early Friday, Sam awoke in sweat-soaked sheets. He fought his way free, then sat up with his back against the wall. He had just spent his second night in Lawrence, and his second night in a real bed in almost three months. The dream had come to him on both nights, worse than ever. He was no more rested than if he had run up and down Mount Oread since sundown.

The dream always began the same way: He and the other Marion Rangers, fifteen men in all, were bedding down in a corn crib at Camp Ralls, fourteen miles south of Hannibal. They had to chase the rats away, but they had to do that every night. Then a Negro messenger came and told them that the enemy was nearby. They scoffed; they had heard that before.

But they grew tense and restless, and could not sleep. The sounds of their breathing were unsteady. Sam's heart began to beat faster.

Then they heard a horse approaching. Sam and the other Rangers went to the corn crib's front wall and peered out through a crack between the logs. In the dim moonlight, they saw the shadow of a man on a horse enter the camp. Sam was sure that he saw more men and horses behind that shadow. Camp Ralls was being attacked.

Sam picked up a rifle and pushed its muzzle between the logs. His skull was humming, his chest tight. His hands shook. The enemy had come and would kill him. The enemy had come and would kill him. The enemy had come and would —

Someone shouted, "Fire!"

And Sam pulled the trigger. The noise was as loud and the flash as bright as if a hundred guns had gone off at once.

The enemy fell from his saddle and lay on the ground. Then all was darkness, and silence. There was nothing but the smell of damp earth.

No more riders came. The fallen man was alone.

Sam and the others went out to the enemy. Sam turned the man onto his back, and the moonlight revealed that he was not wearing a uniform, and that his white shirt was soaked with blood. He was not the enemy. He was not even armed. And his face —

Was sometimes Henry's, and sometimes Orion's.

But just now, this Friday morning in Lawrence, it had been someone else's. It had been a face that Sam did not recognize. It had been the face of an innocent stranger, killed by Sam Clemens for no reason at all . . . no reason save that Sam was at war, and the man had gotten in the way.

Fletch Taylor, in the room's other bed, mumbled in his sleep. Sam could still smell the whiskey. One of Taylor's first acts of spying on Wednesday afternoon had been to hunt up a brothel, and he had been having a fine time ever since. He was counting Bluebellies too, but it had turned out that there weren't many Bluebellies to count.

Sam had visited the brothel with Taylor on Wednesday, but hadn't found the girls to his liking. So he'd spent most of his time since then trying to do his job. He had applied for work at the Lawrence *Journal*, as planned, and had been turned down, as he'd hoped — but had learned that the *Journal* was a two-man, one-boy operation, and that they didn't even dream of being attacked. A carbine hung on pegs on the wall in the pressroom, but it was kept unloaded to prevent the boy from shooting rabbits out the back door. The *Journal's* type would join the *Herald of Freedom's* at the bottom of the Kansas River with little difficulty.

From the purplish-gray color of the patch of eastern sky visible through the hotel room window, Sam guessed that it was about five A.M. He climbed out of bed and went to the window to look down at the wide, muddy strip of the town's main thoroughfare, Massachusetts Street. Lawrence was quiet. The buildings were closed up, and no one was outside. Even the Red Legs and Home Guards slept until six or six-thirty. If Colonel Quantrill timed his raid properly, he and his bushwhackers could ride into Lawrence while its citizens were still abed.

The Union garrison shouldn't be much trouble either, Sam thought as he looked north toward the river. The handful of troops stationed in Lawrence had moved their main camp to the north bank of the Kansas, and the only way for them to come back across into town was by ferry, a few at a time. Two small camps of Federal recruits — one for whites, the other for Negroes — were located south of the river, in town; but those recruits were green and poorly armed. The raiders could ignore them, or squash them like ladybugs if they were foolish enough to offer resistance.

Sam left the window, pulled the chamber pot from under his bed, and took a piss. Then he lit an oil lamp, poured water from a pitcher into a bowl, and stood before the mirror that hung beside the window. He took his razor and scraped the stubble from his throat, chin, cheeks, and sideburns, but left his thick reddish-brown mustache. He had grown fond of the mustache because it made him look meaner than he really was. The dirt that had been ground into his pores had made him look mean too, but that was gone now. He'd had a bath Wednesday evening, and was thinking of having another one today. Lawrence might be a den of abolitionist murderers, but at least it was a den of abolitionist murderers that could provide a few of the amenities of civilization.

When he had finished shaving, he combed his hair and dressed, then put out the lamp and left the room. Taylor was still snoring. Whiskey did wonders for helping a man catch up on his sleep.

Sam went downstairs and out to the street, opening and closing the door of the Whitney House as quietly as possible so as not to disturb the Stone family, who owned the place. Taylor had told Sam that Colonel Quantrill had stayed at the Whitney when he'd lived in Lawrence under the name of Charley Hart, and that Mr. Stone had befriended "Hart" and would therefore be treated with courtesy during the raid. So Sam was being careful not to do anything that might be interpreted as discourtesy. He wanted to stay on the Colonel's good side.

The wooden sidewalk creaked under Sam's boots as he walked toward the river. It was a sound that he hadn't noticed on Wednesday or Thursday, when he had shared the sidewalk with dozens of Lawrence citizens. Then, the predominant sounds had been of conversation and laughter, intermingled with the occasional neighing of a horse. But this early in the morning, Sam had Massachusetts Street to himself, save for two dogs that raced past with butcher-bones in their mouths. Sam took a cigar from his coat pocket, lit it with a match, and drew in a lungful of sweet smoke.

He had to admit that Lawrence was a nice-looking town. Most of the buildings were sturdy and clean, and the town was large and prosperous considering that it had been in existence less than ten years. Almost three thousand souls called Lawrence home, and not all of those souls, Sam was sure, were bad ones. Perhaps the raid would succeed in running off those who were, and the city would be improved as a result.

Sam paused before the Eldridge House hotel. The original Eldridge House, a veritable fortress of abolitionist fervor and free-state propaganda, had been destroyed by Marshal Donaldson in 1856, but it had been rebuilt into an even more formidable fortress in the service of the same things. It was a brick building four stories high, with iron grilles over the ground-floor windows. Quantrill might want to destroy the Eldridge House a second time, particularly since the Lawrence Home Guards would probably concentrate their resistance here, but Sam's advice would be to skip it. A mere fifteen or twenty men, armed with Sharps carbines and barricaded in the Eldridge House, would be able to kill a hundred bushwhackers in the street below.

"Hello!" a shrill voice called from across the street. "Good morning, Mister Sir!"

Sam looked across and saw a sandy-haired boy of ten or eleven waving at him. It took a moment before he recognized the boy as the printer's devil from the Lawrence *Journal*.

Sam took his cigar from his mouth. "Good morning yourself," he said without shouting.

The boy pointed at the Eldridge House. "Are you staying there, Mister Sir?" he yelled. "You must be rich!"

Sam shook his head. "Neither one. But if you keep squawking like a rusty steamboat whistle, I imagine you'll be meeting some of the inhabitants of the Eldridge House presently." He continued up the street.

The boy ran across and joined Sam on the sidewalk. Sam frowned at him and blew smoke at his face, but the boy only breathed it in and began chattering.

"I like the morning before the sun comes up, don't you?" the boy said. "Some days I wake up when it's still dark, and I ride my pa's mule out to the hills south of town, and I can look down over Lawrence when the sun rises. It makes me feel like the king of the world. Do you know what I mean, Mister Sir?"

"I'm sure I don't," Sam said.

The boy didn't seem to notice that Sam had spoken. "Say, if you aren't at the Eldridge, where are you at, Mister Sir? I'll bet you're at the Johnson House, is what I'll bet. But maybe not, because the Red Legs meet at the Johnson, and they don't like strangers. So I'll bet you're at the Whitney, then, aren't you, Mister Sir?"

"Yes," Sam said. "The Johnson was not much to my liking."

"The Red Legs seem to like it just fine."

Sam nodded. "I have made note of that." And indeed he had. If the Red Legs could be punished for their crimes, he would be able to sleep a little better. And if the specific Red Legs who had killed Orion could be found and strung up, he would sleep better than Adam before the Fall.

"Those Red Legs, they have a time," the boy said. "I just might be a Red Leg myself, when I'm old enough."

"I would advise against it," Sam said, gnawing on his cigar. "The profession has little future."

The boy kicked a rock off the sidewalk. "I guess not," he said. "They say they'll have burned out the secesh in another year, so there won't be nothing left to fight for, will there, Mister Sir?"

"Stop calling me 'Mister Sir,' " Sam said. "If you must speak to me at all, call me Mister Clemens." He saw no danger in using his real name. The self-satisfied citizens of Lawrence clearly didn't expect bushwhackers in their midst, and wouldn't know that he was one even if they did.

"I'm sorry, Mister Clemens," the boy said. "I listened to you talking to Mister Trask at the *Journal* yesterday, but I didn't hear your name. Would you like to know mine?"

"No," Sam said.

They had reached the northern end of Massachusetts Street and were now walking down a rutted slope toward the ferry landing. Before them, the Kansas River was dull brown in color and less than a hundred yards wide; hardly a river at all, in Sam's opinion. But it would be enough to protect Quantrill's raiders from the soldiers on the far bank, provided that the soldiers didn't realize the raiders were coming until it was too late. To assure himself of that, Sam wanted to see how active or inactive the Bluebellies were at this time of morning. If they were as slumberous as Lawrence's civilians, he would be able to report that there was little chance of any of them ferrying across in time to hinder the raid. There weren't many soldiers in the camp anyway. Taylor had counted only a hundred and twelve, and some of those weren't soldiers at all, but surveyors.

"How come you're heading down to the river, Mister Clemens?" the boy asked. "Are you going fishing?"

Sam stopped walking and glared down at the boy, taking his cigar from his mouth with a slow, deliberate motion. "Do you see a fishing pole in my hand, boy?" he asked, exhaling a bluish cloud.

The boy gazed up at the cigar, which had a two-inch length of ash trembling at its tip.

"No, sir," the boy said. "I see a cigar."

"Then it is reasonable to assume," Sam said, "that I have come to the river not to fish, but to smoke." He tapped the cigar, and the ash fell onto the boy's head.

The boy yelped and jumped away, slapping at his hair.

Sam replaced his cigar between his teeth and continued

down the slope.

"That wasn't nice!" the boy shouted after him.

"I'm not a nice man," Sam said. He didn't look back, so he didn't know if the boy heard him. But he reached the riverbank alone.

A thin fog hovered over the water and began to dissipate as the sun rose. The sunlight gave the tents on the far bank a pinkish tinge. The camp wasn't dead quiet, but there wasn't much activity either. At first, Sam saw only two fires and no more than five or six men up and about. As he watched, more men emerged from their tents, but military discipline was lacking. Apparently, these Bluebellies could get up whenever they pleased. That would be good news for the Colonel.

Sam threw the stub of his cigar into the river and heard it hiss. The sun was up now, and the soldiers began emerging from their tents with increasing frequency. From old habit, Sam reached for his pocket watch. But he still hadn't replaced the one that the Red Legs had stolen two years before.

He heard a scuffing sound behind him and looked over his shoulder. The boy from the *Journal* was close by again, twisting the toe of his shoe in the dirt.

"Say, boy," Sam said, "do you have a watch?"

The boy gave Sam a look of calculated contempt. "Of course I have a watch. Mister Trask gave me his old one. I got to get to the paper on time, don't I?"

"Well, tell me what time it is," Sam said.

"Why should I tell anything to someone who dumped a pound of burning tobacco on my head?"

Sam grinned. The boy was starting to remind him of the boys he had grown up with in Hannibal. "Maybe I'd give a cigar to someone who told me the time."

The boy's expression changed. "Really?"

"I said maybe."

The boy reached into a pocket and pulled out a battered timepiece. He peered at it and said, "This has six o'clock, but it loses thirty-five minutes a day and I ain't set it since yesterday noon. So it might be about half-past."

Sam took a cigar from his coat and tossed it to the boy. "Much obliged, boy."

The boy caught the cigar with his free hand, then replaced his watch in his pocket and gave Sam another look of contempt. "Stop calling me 'boy,'" he said. "If you must speak to me at all, call me Henry." The boy jammed the cigar into his mouth, turned, and strode up the slope to Massachusetts Street.

Sam turned back to the river. The fog was gone, and most of the soldiers were out of their tents. To be on the safe side, Sam decided, the raid would have to begin no later than five-thirty, and a detachment of bushwhackers would have to come to the river to train their guns on the ferry, just in case. He didn't think he would have any trouble persuading Colonel Quantrill to see the wisdom in that.

He started back up the slope, but paused where the boy from the *Journal* had stood.

"Henry," Sam murmured. "God damn."

Then he went up to the street and walked to the livery stable to check on Bixby. Bixby was in a foul mood and tried to bite him, so Sam knew that the horse was fine.

That evening, Sam was in his and Taylor's room at the Whitney House, writing down what he had learned so far, when he heard the *Journal* boy's voice outside. He went to the open window, looked down, and saw the boy astride a brown mule that was festooned with bundles of newspapers. The boy dropped one of the bundles at the Whitney's door, then looked up and saw Sam at the window.

The boy shook his finger at Sam. "That seegar was spoiled, Mister Clemens!" he shouted. "I was sick all afternoon, but Mister Trask made me work anyway!"

"Good," Sam said. "It builds character."

The boy gave Sam yet another contemptuous look, then kicked the mule and proceeded down the street.

As the boy left, four men wearing blue shirts and red leather leggings rode past going the other way. They all carried pistols in hip holsters, and one had a rifle slung across his back. They were unshaven and ugly, and they laughed and roared as they rode up Massachusetts Street. They would no doubt cross the river and make trouble for someone north of town tonight. Sam didn't recognize any of them, but that didn't matter. They were Kansas Red Legs, meaner and more murderous than even Jennison's Jayhawkers had been; and if they themselves hadn't killed Orion, they were acquainted with the men who had.

"Whoop it up, boys," Sam muttered as they rode away. "Whoop it up while you can."

He came away from the window and saw that Taylor was awake. Taylor had gotten up in the afternoon to meet with Noland, but then had gone back to bed.

"What's all the noise?" Taylor asked.

"Newspapers," Sam said. "I'll get one."

Taylor sneered. "Why? It's all abolitionist lies anyway."

But when Sam brought a copy of the *Journal* back upstairs and began reading, he found news. Horrifying, sickening news.

"Sons of bitches," he whispered.

"What is it?" Taylor asked. He was at the mirror, shaving, preparing for another night out in Lawrence's less-respectable quarter.

"A building in Kansas City collapsed yesterday," Sam said.

"Well, good."

Sam shook his head. "No, Fletch. It was the building on Grand Avenue where the Bluebellies were holding the women they suspected of aiding bushwhackers. The paper says four women were killed, and several others hurt."

Taylor stopped shaving. "That's where they were keeping Bloody Bill Anderson's sisters," he said. "Cole Younger and Johnny McCorkle had kin there too. Does the paper give names?"

"No. But of course it suggests that the collapse might have been caused by a charge set by guerrillas 'in a disastrous attempt to remove the ladies from Federal protection.' "

Taylor's upper lip curled back. "As if Southern men would endanger their women!" He shook his razor at the newspaper. "I'll tell you what, though. I was worrying that the Colonel might have trouble riling up some of the boys for this raid, especially since Noland has found out that Jim Lane's out of town. But this news will rile them like nobody's business. And if Bill Anderson's sisters have been hurt, you can bet that he and *his* boys will shit blue fire. God help any Unionists who cross their path." He dipped his razor in the bowl and turned back to the mirror. His eyes were bright. "Or mine, for that matter."

When Taylor had finished shaving, he asked if Sam would like to go out and have a time. Sam declined, and Taylor left without him.

Then Sam read the rest of the newspaper, most of which he found to be worthless. But he admired the typesetting. There were few mistakes, and most of the lines were evenly spaced and straight. He wondered how many of them the boy had set.

He put the newspaper aside and wrote in his journal until the evening light failed. Then he undressed and got into bed, but lay awake for so long that he almost decided to join Taylor after all. But he had no enthusiasm for the idea. Spy-work wasn't physically strenuous, but it took a lot out of him mentally.

When he finally fell asleep, he dreamed that he was a printer's devil for Orion again. This time, though, their newspaper was not the Hannibal *Journal*, but the Lawrence *Journal*.

He was setting type about a fire in which over a hundred and fifty people had been killed, when a man burst into the pressroom. The man was jug-eared, greasy-haired, narrow-faced, and beardless. His thick lips parted to reveal crooked, stained teeth. Sam had never seen him before.

The jug-eared man pulled a revolver from his belt and pointed it at Orion.

"Henry!" Orion shouted. "Run!"

Sam, his ink-smeared hands hanging useless at his sides, said, "But I'm Sam."

The jug-eared man shot Orion, who shriveled like a dying vine.

Then the stranger pointed his revolver at Sam.

Sam tried to turn and run, but his feet were stuck as if in thick mud.

The revolver fired with a sound like a cannon going off in a church, and the jug-eared man laughed.

Then Sam was floating near the ceiling, looking down at two bleeding bodies. Orion's face had become that of Josiah Trask, one of the editors of the Lawrence *Journal*. And Sam's face had become that of the boy, Henry, to whom he had given a cigar. The cigar was still in Henry's mouth.

Sam awoke crouched against the wall. He was dripping

with sweat.

Night had fallen, and Lawrence was quiet. Taylor had not yet returned to the room. Sam crept away from the wall and sat on the edge of the bed, shivering.

"Henry," he whispered. "God damn."

At noon on Wednesday, August 19, Sam and Taylor were sitting on a log in southern Jackson County near the village of Lone Jack, in the midst of their fellow bushwhackers. They and Noland had returned to the Blue Springs camp two days before, and Colonel Quantrill had received their report with satisfaction. Then, on Tuesday morning, Quantrill had ordered his guerrillas to move out without telling them their objective. In order to fool any Federal scouts or pickets that might spot them, the Colonel had marched the bushwhackers eastward for several miles before cutting back to the southwest. En route, the band had been joined by Bill Anderson with forty men and Andy Blunt with over a hundred, almost doubling the size of Quantrill's force.

The men all knew something big was at hand. And now, finally, the Colonel was going to tell them what. Sam thought it was about time.

Quantrill, flanked by George Todd and Bill Anderson, sat before the bushwhackers astride his one-eyed mare, Black Bess, and gave a screeching yell. Over three hundred voices responded, and a thrill ran up Sam's spine. The sound was both the most magnificent and most terrifying thing he had ever heard. If he were the enemy and heard that sound, he would be halfway to Colorado before the echo came back from the nearest hill.

The Colonel nodded in satisfaction. He was wearing a slouch hat with one side of the brim pinned up by a silver star, a loose gray guerrilla shirt with blue and silver embroidery, and gray trousers tucked into his cavalry boots. His belt bristled with four Colt pistols, and two more hung from holsters on either side of his saddle.

"Well, boys," Quantrill shouted, "I hope you ain't tired of riding just yet!"

He was answered by a loud, ragged chorus of "Hell, no!"

Quantrill laughed. "That's good," he cried, "because come nightfall, we're heading for Kansas Territory to see if we can pull its most rotten tooth: Lawrence!"

A moment of silence followed the announcement, and for that moment Sam wondered if the men had decided that the Colonel was out of his mind. But then the bushwhackers exploded into another shrieking cheer, and at least a hundred of them rose to their feet and fired pistols into the air.

Taylor clapped Sam on the shoulder. "Are these the best damn boys in Missouri, or ain't they!" he yelled.

"They're sure the loudest," Sam said.

Quantrill raised a hand, and the cheers subsided. "Save your ammunition," the Colonel shouted. "You've worked hard to make it or steal it, so don't waste it shooting at God. There are plenty of better targets where we're going!"

Another cheer rose up at that, but then Quantrill's expression changed from one of glee to one of cold, deadly intent. The bushwhackers fell silent.

"Boys," Quantrill said, no longer shouting, "there's more danger ahead than any of us have faced before. There could be Federals both behind and in front of us, coming and going. Now, we sent some men to spy on Lawrence, and they say the town's ripe to be taken — but there might be pickets on the way there. So we could have General Ewing's Bluebellies down on us from Kansas City, and some from Leavenworth as well. I doubt that we'll all make it back to Missouri alive." He straightened in his saddle, and it seemed to Sam that his metallic gaze fell on each bushwhacker in turn. "So if there's any man who doesn't want to go into the Territory with the rest of us, now's your chance to head for home. After we leave here tonight, there will be no turning back. Not for anyone."

Beside Quantrill, Bill Anderson drew a pistol. Anderson's hair was even wilder than it had been when Sam had seen him in Quantrill's tent the week before, and his eyes were so fierce that they didn't look human. "Anyone who *does* turn back after we've started," Anderson cried, "will wish to God he'd been taken by the Yankees before I'm through with him!"

Taylor leaned close to Sam and whispered, "I think Bloody Bill's heard about the building in Kansas City."

Sam thought so too. In the face of Bill Anderson he saw a hatred that had become so pure that if Anderson ever ran out of enemies against whom to direct his rage, he would have to invent more.

"But although we'll be going through hardships," Quantrill continued, "the result will be worth it. Lawrence is the hotbed of abolitionism in Kansas, and most of the property stolen from Missouri can be found there, ready and waiting to be taken back by Missourians. Even if Jim Lane ain't home, his house and his plunder are. We can work more justice in Lawrence than anywhere else in five hundred miles! So who's going with me?"

The shrill cheer rose up a fourth time, and all of the men not already standing came to their feet. Despite Quantrill's warning to save ammunition, more shots were fired into the air.

Quantrill and his captains wheeled their horses and rode to their tent, and Sam left Taylor and went to the tree where he had tied Bixby. There, after avoiding Bixby's attempts to bite him, he opened one of his saddlebags, took out his revolver, and replaced its caps.

When he looked up again, he saw John Noland leaning against the tree, regarding him with casual disdain.

"You ain't gonna shoot something, are you, Mister Clemens?" Noland asked.

"I'll do my best if it becomes necessary," Sam said.

Noland gave a sardonic grunt. "'If it becomes necessary,'" he repeated. "Why do you think we're goin' where we're goin'?"

"I should think that would be obvious," Sam said. "To retrieve that which belongs to Missouri, and to punish the jayhawkers and Red Legs who stole it."

"You'll know a jayhawker on sight, will you?" Noland asked.

"I'll know the Red Legs on sight, I'll tell you that."

Noland pushed away from the tree. "I reckon you will, if they sleep in their pants." He sauntered past Sam and tipped his hat. "Hooray for you, Mister Clemens. Hooray for us all."

"You don't sound too all-fired excited, Noland," Sam said.

Noland looked back with a grim smile. "You want to see me excited, Mister Clemens, you watch me get some of that free-soil money into my pocket. You watch me then." He tipped his hat again and walked away.

Sam watched him go. How, he wondered, could two men as different as Bill Anderson and John Noland be riding in the same guerrilla band on the same raid?

Then he looked down at the gun in his hand and remembered that he was riding with both of them.

Bixby nipped his arm. Sam jumped and cursed, then replaced his revolver in the saddlebag and gave Bixby a lump of sugar. The horse would soon need all the energy it could get.

At dusk, the Colonel had the bushwhackers mount up and proceed toward the southwest. Only thirteen men had left the raiders after Quantrill's announcement of the target, and only two of those had been members of Quantrill's own band. Sam marveled. Here were more than three hundred men going to what might be their deaths, just because one man had asked them to do so. True, each man had his own reasons for becoming a bushwhacker in the first place, but none of them would have dreamed of attempting a raid so far into Kansas if Quantrill had not offered to lead them in it.

In the middle of the night, the guerrillas happened upon a force of over a hundred Confederate recruits under the command of a Colonel John Holt. Holt and Quantrill conferred for an hour while the bushwhackers rested their horses, and when the guerrillas resumed their advance, Holt and his recruits joined them.

At daybreak on Thursday, August 20, Quantrill's raiders made camp beside the Grand River. They were only four miles from the border now, and this would be their final rest before the drive toward Lawrence. Late in the morning, fifty more men from Cass and Bates counties rode into the camp and offered their services. Quantrill accepted, and by Sam's count, the invasion force now consisted of almost five hundred men, each one mounted on a strong horse and armed with at least one pistol and as much ammunition as he could carry. A few of the men also had rifles, and many carried bundles of pitch-dipped torches.

If Federal troops did attack them, Sam thought, the Blue-bellies would get one hell of a fight for their trouble. They might also become confused about who was friend and who was foe, because almost two hundred of the bushwhackers were wearing parts of blue Union uniforms.

At mid-afternoon, Captain Todd rode among the dozing men and horses, shouting, "Saddle up, boys! Lawrence ain't gonna plunder itself, now, is it?"

The men responded with a ragged cheer. Sam got up, rolled his blanket, and then carried it and his saddle to the dead tree where Taylor's horse and Bixby were tied. He had spread his blanket in a shady spot and had tried to sleep, but had only managed to doze a little. Taylor, lying a few yards away, had started snoring at noon and hadn't stopped until Todd had ridden past.

"How you could sleep with what we've got ahead of us, I can't imagine," Sam said as Taylor came up to saddle his horse.

"I wasn't sleeping," Taylor said. "I was thinking over strategy."

"With help from the hive of bumblebees you swallowed, no doubt."

Taylor grinned. "We're gonna be fine, Sam," he said. "You know they ain't expecting us. So there's no need for a man to be afraid."

"No, I suppose not," Sam said. "Not unless a man has a brain."

Taylor frowned. "What's that supposed to mean?"

Sam took his Colt from his saddlebag and stuck it into his belt. "Nothing, Fletch. I just want to get there, get it done, and get back, is all."

"You and me and everybody else," Taylor said.

As Sam and Taylor mounted their horses, a cluster of eleven men rode past, yipping and laughing. They seemed eager to be at the head of the bushwhacker force as it entered Kansas.

The man leading the cluster was jug-eared, greasy-haired, narrow-faced, and beardless.

Sam's heart turned to ice. Slowly, he raised his arm and pointed at the cluster of men. "Who are they?" he asked. His throat was tight and dry.

"Some of Anderson's boys," Taylor said. "Full of piss and vinegar, ain't they?"

"Do you know the one in front?" Sam asked.

"Sure do," Taylor said. "I've even ridden with him a time or two. Name's Frank James. You can count on him in a fight, that's for sure." Taylor clicked his tongue, and his horse started after the cluster of Anderson's men.

Bixby followed Taylor's horse while Sam stared ahead at the man from his dream. The man who had entered the *Journal* pressroom, killed an unarmed man and boy, and then laughed.

At six o'clock, Quantrill's raiders crossed the border into Kansas.

Ahead, the Territory grew dark.

By eleven o'clock, when the raiders passed the town of Gardner, the moonless night was as black as Quantrill's horse. Gullies, creeks, and fences became obstacles, and some of the bushwhackers wanted to light torches to help them find their way. But Quantrill would not allow that. They were still over twenty miles from Lawrence, in open country, and could not afford to be spotted from a distance. Besides, the torches were supposed to be reserved for use in Lawrence itself.

Soon after midnight, Quantrill halted the bushwhackers near a farmhouse, and the word was passed back along the column for the men to keep quiet.

"What are we stopping here for?" Sam whispered. He and Taylor were riding near the middle of the column, and Sam couldn't see what was happening up front.

"Shush yourself," Taylor hissed.

A minute later, there was a yell from the farmhouse, and then laughter from some of the raiders.

The tall form of Captain Bill Gregg came riding back along the column. "All right, boys, we can travel on," he said. "We got ourselves a friendly Kansan to guide us!" He wheeled his horse and returned to the head of the column.

"Wonder what he means by that," Sam said.

Taylor chuckled. "What do you think?"

The bushwhackers started moving again and made rapid progress for a few miles, zigzagging around obstacles. Then Quantrill called another halt. The men began muttering, but fell silent as a pistol was fired.

Bixby jerked his head and shied away from the column. Sam had to fight to bring the horse back into place. "What in blazes is the matter with you?" he asked. Bixby had never been spooked by gunfire before. In fact, he had hardly noticed it. "It was just somebody's pistol going off by mistake!"

At that moment, Captain Gregg came riding by again. "No mistake about it," he said, pausing beside Sam and Taylor. "Our friendly Kansan claimed he didn't know which side of yonder hill we should go around. So the Colonel dispatched him to a hill of his own, and we're to wait until we have another friendly Kansan to guide us. There's a house ahead, and some of Anderson's boys are going to see who's home. We'll be on our way again before long." Gregg spurred his horse and continued back along the column to spread the word.

"Well, good for the Colonel," Taylor said. "Now that Kansan is as friendly to us as a Kansan can be."

Sam was stunned. When the raiders began moving again, they passed by the corpse. Bixby shied away from it and collided with Taylor's mount.

"Rein your goddamn horse, Sam!" Taylor snarled.

The dead man was wearing canvas trousers and was shirtless and barefoot. Even in the dark, Sam could see that his head was nothing but a mass of pulp.

It made no sense. This man wasn't a Red Leg or a Bluebelly. He might not even be an abolitionist. He was only a farmer. Colonel Quantrill had shot a farmer. Just because the man couldn't find his way in the dark.

Just because he was a Kansan.

Sam began to wonder if the preposterous stories he had read in abolitionist newspapers — the stories about Quantrill's raids on Aubry, Olathe, and Shawneetown — might have had some truth in them after all.

The column halted again after only a mile, and there was another gunshot. Then another farmhouse was raided, and the bushwhackers continued on their way. But soon they stopped once more, and a third shot was fired.

The process was repeated again and again. Each time, Sam and Bixby passed by a fresh corpse.

There were ten in all.

Sam felt dizzy and sick. This was supposed to be a raid to punish the Red Legs, destroy the newspaper, burn out Jim Lane, and recover stolen property. Some Kansans were to be killed, yes; but they were supposed to be Red Legs and Blue-bellies, not unarmed farmers taken from their wives and children in the night.

At the tenth corpse, Taylor maneuvered his horse past Sam and Bixby. "'Scuse me, Clemens," Taylor said. "My horse is starting to make water."

Taylor stopped the horse over the dead man and let it piss on the body. The bushwhackers who were close enough to see it laughed, and Sam tried to laugh as well. He didn't want them to see his horror. He was afraid of them all now. Even Taylor. Especially Taylor.

"Have your horses drink deep at the next crick, boys!" Taylor chortled. "There's plenty of men in Lawrence who need a bath as bad as this one!"

"Amen to that!" someone cried.

The shout was echoed up and down the line as Taylor rejoined the column next to Sam.

Captain Gregg came riding back once more. "I admire your sentiments, boys," he said, "but I suggest you save the noise until we reach our destination. Then you can holler all you want, and see if you can squeeze a few hollers from the so-called men of Lawrence as well!"

The bushwhackers laughed again, but then lowered their voices to whispers. To Sam, it sounded like the hissing of five hundred snakes.

He saw now that what was going to happen in Lawrence would resemble what he had imagined it would be only in the way that a volcano resembled a firefly. He had let his guilt over Orion's death and his hatred of the Red Legs blind him to what the men he was riding with had become. He wanted to turn Bixby out of the column and ride hard and fast back to Missouri, not stopping until he reached Hannibal.

But he knew that he couldn't. Anderson had told them all how deserters would be dealt with. Sam and Bixby wouldn't make it more than a hundred yards before a dozen men were after them. And there was no doubt of what would happen to

Sam when they caught him.

Besides, his and Taylor's report from their trip to Lawrence was part of what had convinced Quantrill that the raid was possible. That made Sam more responsible for what was about to happen than almost anyone else. To run away now would make him not only a coward, but a hypocrite.

Another farmhouse was raided at about three in the morning, and this time the entire column broke up and gathered around to watch. By the time Sam was close enough to see what was happening, the farmer was on his knees in his yard. Captain Todd was standing before him holding a pistol to his forehead and telling him the names of some of the men waiting for him in hell.

Quantrill, on Black Bess, came up beside Todd. "We're too close to Lawrence to fire a gun now, George," he said.

Sam could just make out Todd's expression. It was one of fury.

"Goddamn it, Bill," Todd said. "This man's name is Joe Stone. He's a stinking Missouri Unionist who ran off to Kansas to escape justice, and I'm going to kill him no matter what you say."

Stone, wearing only a nightshirt, was shuddering. Sam looked away from him and saw a woman crying in the doorway of the house. A child clung to the woman's knees, wailing. An oil lamp was burning inside, and its weak light framed the woman and child so that they seemed to be suspended inside a pale flame.

Quantrill stroked his stubbled face with a thumb and forefinger. "Well, George, I agree that traitors must die. But we're within six miles of Lawrence now, and a shot might warn the town."

Todd seemed about to retort, but then took his pistol away from Stone's head and replaced it in his belt. "All right," he said. "We'll keep it quiet." He strode to his horse and pulled his Sharps carbine from its scabbard. "Sam!" he called. "Get over here!"

Taylor nudged Sam in the ribs. "Go on," he said.

Sam, almost rigid with terror, began to dismount.

"I mean Sam Clifton," Todd said. "Where is he?"

Sam returned to his saddle as Clifton, a stranger who had

joined the guerrillas while the spies had been in Lawrence, dismounted and went to Todd.

Todd handed the rifle to Clifton. "Some of the boys tell me you've been asking a lot of questions, Mister Clifton," he said. "So let's see if you know what you're here for." He pointed at Stone. "Beat that traitor down to hell."

Clifton didn't hesitate. He took three quick steps and smashed the rifle butt into Stone's face. Stone fell over in the dirt, and his wife and child screamed. Then Clifton pounded Stone's skull.

Sam wanted to turn away, but he couldn't move. This was the most horrible thing he had ever seen, more horrible even than his brother Henry lying in his coffin or his brother Orion lying in the road. He watched it all. He couldn't stop himself.

Only when it was over, when Clifton had stopped pounding and Stone was nothing but a carcass, was Sam able to look away. Beside him, Taylor was grinning. Some of the others were grinning too. But there were also a few men who looked so sick that Sam thought they might fall from their horses.

Then he looked at Colonel Quantrill. Quantrill's eyes were unblinking, reflecting the weak light from the house. His lips were pulled back in a tight smile.

Todd took his rifle back from Clifton and replaced it in its scabbard without wiping it clean. Then he looked up at Quantrill with a defiant sneer.

"That suit you, Colonel?" he asked.

Quantrill nodded. "That suits me fine, Captain," he said. Then he faced the men. "Remember this, boys," he cried, "and serve the men of Lawrence the same! Kill! Kill, and you'll make no mistake! Now push on, or it'll be daylight before we get there!"

"You heard the man," Taylor said to Sam.

"That I did," Sam said. His voice was hoarse. He thought it might stay hoarse forever.

The raiders pushed on, leaving Mrs. Stone and her child to weep over the scrap of flesh in their yard.

As the column reformed, Sam found himself near its head, riding not far behind Gregg, Todd, Anderson, and Quantrill himself. It was as if God wanted to be sure that Sam had another good view when the next man died.

*   *   *

The eastern sky was turning from black to purplish-gray
as Quantrill's raiders reached the crest of the hill southeast of
Lawrence. Colonel Quantrill raised his right hand, and the
column halted.

Below them, less than two miles ahead, Lawrence lay as
silent as death.

Fletch Taylor cackled. "Look at 'em! Damn Yankees are
curled up with their thumbs in their mouths!"

Sam nodded, sick at heart.

Quantrill brought out a spyglass and trained it on the
sleeping town. "It looks ripe," he said. "But I can't see the river;
it's still too dark." He lowered the glass and turned to Captain
Gregg. "Bill, take five men and reconnoiter. The rest of us will
wait fifteen minutes and then follow. If you spot trouble, run
back and warn us."

Gregg gave Quantrill a salute, then pointed at each of the
five men closest to him. "James, Younger, McCorkle, Taylor,
and —" He was looking right at Sam.

Sam couldn't speak. His tongue was as cold and heavy as
clay. He stared at Frank James.

"Clemens," Taylor said.

"Right," Gregg said. "Clemens. Come on, boys." He
kicked his horse and started down the hillside.

"Let's get to it, Sam," Taylor said. He reached over and
swatted Bixby on the rump, and Bixby lurched forward.

Despite the steep slope and the trees that dotted it, Gregg
set a rapid pace. All Sam could do was hang on to Bixby's reins
and let the horse find its own way. He wished that Bixby
would stumble and that he would be thrown and break an arm
or leg. But Bixby was too agile for that. Sam would be in on
the Lawrence raid from beginning to end.

Halfway down the hill, Gregg stopped his horse, and
James, Younger, McCorkle, and Taylor did the same. Bixby
stopped on his own, almost throwing Sam against the pommel
of his saddle.

"What's wrong, Captain?" Taylor asked.

Gregg put a finger to his lips and then extended that finger
to point.

A few hundred feet farther down the hillside, a mule carrying a lone figure in a white shirt was making its way up through the trees. The mule and rider were just visible in the predawn light.

"What's someone doing out here this early?" Taylor whispered.

"Doesn't matter," Gregg whispered back. "If he sees us and we let him escape, we're as good as dead."

"But, but a shot would wake up the town, Captain," Sam stammered.

Gregg gave him a glance. "Then we won't fire a shot that can be heard in the town." He turned toward Frank James. "Go kill him, Frank. Use your knife, or put your pistol in his belly to muffle the noise. Or knock his brains out. I don't care, so long as you keep it quiet."

James drew his pistol, cocked it, and started his horse down the hill.

The figure on the mule came around a tree. He was alone and unarmed. Sam could see his face now. He was the printer's devil from the Lawrence *Journal*.

Henry.

Frank James plunged downward, his right arm outstretched, pointing the finger of Death at an innocent.

And in that instant, Sam saw everything that was to come, and the truth of everything that had been. He saw it all as clearly as any of his dreams:

The boy would be lying on his back on the ground. His white shirt would be soaked with blood. Sam would be down on his knees beside him, stroking his forehead, begging his forgiveness. He would want to give anything to undo what had been done. But it would be too late.

Henry would mumble about his family, about the loved ones who would never see him again. And then he would look up at Sam with reproachful eyes, and die.

Just as it had happened before.

Not when Sam's brother Henry had died. Henry had given him no reproachful look, and all he had said was "Thank you, Sam."

Not when Orion had died, either. Orion had said, "Get out

of here, Sam," and there had been no reproach in the words. Only concern. Only love.

Frank James plunged downward, his right arm outstretched, pointing the finger of Death at an innocent.

An innocent like the one Sam had killed.

It had been more than just a dream.

He had told himself that he wasn't the only one of the Marion Rangers who had fired. He never hit anything he aimed at anyway. But in his heart he had known that wasn't true this time. He had known that he was guilty of murder, and of the grief that an innocent, unarmed man's family had suffered because of it.

All of his guilt, all of his need to make amends —

It wasn't because of his dead brothers at all.

It was because he had killed a man who had done nothing to him.

Sam had tried to escape that truth by fleeing West with Orion. But then, when Orion had been murdered, he had tried instead to bury his guilt by embracing it and by telling himself that the war made killing honorable if it was done in a just cause. And vengeance, he had told himself, was such a cause.

But the family of the man he had killed might well have thought the same thing.

Frank James plunged downward, his right arm outstretched, pointing the finger of Death at an innocent.

And Sam couldn't stand it anymore.

He yelled like a madman, and then Bixby was charging down the hill, flashing past the trees with a speed no other horse in Quantrill's band could equal. When Bixby came alongside James's horse, Sam jerked the reins. Bixby slammed into James's horse and forced it into a tree. James was knocked from his saddle, and his pistol fired.

Henry's mule collapsed, and Henry tumbled to the ground.

Sam reined Bixby to a halt before the dying mule, leaped down, and dropped to his knees beside the boy.

Henry looked up at him with an expression of contempt. "Are you crazy or something?" he asked.

Sam grabbed him and hugged him.

Henry struggled to get away. "Mister Clemens? What in

the world are you doing?"

Sam looked up the slope and saw Frank James picking himself up. James's horse was standing nearby, shaking its head and whinnying.

Gregg, Taylor, McCorkle, and Younger were riding down with their pistols drawn.

Sam jumped up and swung Henry into Bixby's saddle. "Lean down close to me," he said.

"What for?" Henry asked. The boy looked dazed now. He was staring down at the dead mule.

"Just do it, and listen to what I say," Sam said. "I have to tell you something without those men hearing it."

Henry leaned down.

"Ride back to town as fast as you can," Sam said. "When you're close enough for people to hear, yell that Charley Hart's come back, that his new name is Billy Quantrill, and that he has five hundred men with him. And if you can't remember all that, just yell 'Quantrill!' Yell 'Quantrill!' over and over until you reach the Eldridge House, and then go inside and yell 'Quantrill!' at everyone there. If they don't believe you, just point at this horse and ask where the hell they think you got it. Now sit up!"

Henry sat up, and Sam slapped Bixby on the rump. Bixby turned back and tried to bite Sam's shoulder.

"Not now, you fleabag!" Sam yelled. He raised his hand to swat the horse again, but Bixby snorted and leaped over the dead mule before Sam could touch him. The roan charged down the hillside as fast as before, with Henry hanging on tight.

Sam took a deep breath and turned as he exhaled. Frank James was walking toward him with murder in his eyes, and the four men riding up behind James didn't look any happier. Sam put his hand on the Colt in his belt, but didn't think he could draw it. He feared that he was going to piss his pants. But he had to give Henry a good head start. And if that meant getting himself killed — well, that was just what it meant. Better him than a boy whose only crime was setting type for an abolitionist newspaper.

"You traitorous bastard," James said, raising his revolver to point at Sam's face.

Sam swallowed and found his voice. "Your barrel's full of dirt," he said.

James looked at his gun and saw that it was true.

Captain Gregg cocked his own pistol. "Mine, however, is clean," he said.

Sam raised his hands. "Don't shoot, Captain," he said. He was going to have to tell a whopper, and fast. "I apologize to Mister James, but I had to keep him from killing my messenger, didn't I? I would've said something sooner, but I didn't see who the boy was until James was already after him."

"Messenger?" Gregg said.

Sam looked up at Taylor, whose expression was one of mingled anger and disbelief. "Why don't you say something, Fletch? Didn't you recognize the boy?"

Taylor blinked. "What are you yapping about?"

Sam lowered his hands, put them on his hips, and tried to look disgusted. "Damn it, Fletch, that Missouri boy I met in Lawrence. The one whose father was killed by jayhawkers, and who was kidnapped to Kansas. I pointed him out to you Saturday morning, but I guess you'd gotten too drunk the night before to retain the information."

Gregg looked at Taylor. "You were drinking whiskey while you were supposed to be scouting the town, Corporal?"

Taylor became indignant. "Hell, no!"

"Then why don't you remember me pointing that boy out to you?" Sam asked.

"Well, I do," Taylor said uncertainly.

Sam knew he couldn't let up. "So why didn't you tell Captain Gregg that the boy promised to come here and warn us if any more Federals moved into Lawrence?"

Taylor's eyes looked panicky. "I didn't recognize the boy. It's dark."

"What's this about more Bluebellies in Lawrence?" Gregg asked.

"That's what the boy told me," Sam said. "Six hundred troops, four hundred of them cavalry, came down from Leavenworth on Tuesday. They're all camped on the south side of the river, too, he says."

Frank James had his pistol barrel clean now, and he pointed

the gun at Sam again. "So why'd you send him away?"

Sam was so deep into his story now that he almost forgot his fear. "Because he said the Bluebellies have started sending fifty cavalrymen out between five and six every morning to scout the plain between here and Mount Oread. I told him to go keep watch and to come back when he saw them."

Cole Younger, stern-faced and narrow-lipped, gestured at Sam with his revolver. "Why would you tell someone in Lawrence who you were and why you were there?"

"I already said why," Sam snapped. "Because he's a Missouri boy, and he hates the Yankees as much as you or me. Maybe more, because he didn't even have a chance to grow up before they took everything he had. And I didn't just walk up and take him into my confidence for no reason. Two Red Legs were dunking him in a horse trough until he was half drowned. When they left, I asked him why they'd done it, and he said it was because he'd called them murdering Yankee cowards. My opinion was that we could use a friend like that in Lawrence, and Fletch agreed."

John McCorkle, a round-faced man in a flat-brimmed hat, peered at Sam through narrowed eyelids. "So how'd the boy know where we'd be, and when?"

"He knew the where because we told him," Sam said. "The Colonel used to live in these parts, and he picked this hill for our overlook when he planned the raid. Ain't that so, Fletch?"

Taylor nodded.

"As for the when of it," Sam continued, "well, Fletch and I knew we'd be here before sunup either yesterday or today, so we told the boy to come out both days if there was anything we needed to hear about."

Younger looked at Taylor. "That true, Fletch? Or were you so drunk you don't remember?"

Taylor glared at him. "It's true, Cole. I just didn't tell you, is all. There's five hundred men on this raid, and I can't tell every one of you everything, can I?"

Younger started to retort, but he was interrupted by the sound of hundreds of hoofbeats from the slope above. Quantrill had heard James's gunshot and was bringing down the rest of his men.

Gregg replaced his pistol in its holster. "All right, then," he said, sounding weary. "Let's tell the Colonel what the boy said." He looked at Taylor. "You do it, Fletch. He knows you better than he does Clemens."

Taylor nodded, then shot Sam a look that could have melted steel.

There was a promise in that look, but Sam didn't care. Gregg had believed his story, and for now, at least, he was still alive.

And so was Henry.

Taylor told Colonel Quantrill that a Missouri boy had come to warn the raiders about six hundred new Bluebellies in Lawrence, all camped south of the river, and that a scouting party of fifty of the Federals was likely to spot the bushwhackers before they could enter the town. Quantrill listened without saying a word. He stared straight ahead, toward Lawrence, until Taylor was finished. Then he looked down at Sam, who was still standing before the dead mule.

Quantrill's eyes were like chips of ice, but Sam didn't look away. He was sure that if he flinched, the Colonel would see him for the lying traitor that he was.

A long moment later, Quantrill turned to Captain Todd. "What do you think, George?" he asked.

Todd looked as if he had eaten a bad persimmon. "You didn't see six hundred Federals through the glass, did you?"

"No," Quantrill said, "but I couldn't see the river. If they were camped close by its banks, they would have been invisible."

"Then let's go back up and take another look," Todd said.

Quantrill shook his head. "By the time the sun has risen enough for us to see the river, the people of Lawrence will have risen too. We must either press on now, or give it up."

"But if there are that many more troops down there," Gregg said, "we won't have a chance. I say we fall back to the border, send more spies to take another look at the town, and come back when we can be sure of victory."

Quantrill looked at the ground and spat. "Damn it all," he said, "but you're right. Even if there aren't that many troops, the town might've heard the pistol shot."

The men behind Quantrill murmured. Many looked angry or disappointed, but almost as many looked relieved.

Sam tried hard to look disappointed, but he wanted to shout for joy.

Then Bill Anderson shrieked, drew one of his pistols, and kicked his horse until it was nose to nose with Black Bess.

"We've come too far!" he screamed, pointing his pistol at the Colonel. "We've come too far and our people have suffered too much! This raid was your idea, and you talked me into committing my own men to the task! God damn you, Quantrill, you're going to see it through!"

Quantrill gave Anderson a cold stare. "We have received new intelligence," he said. "The situation has changed."

Anderson shook his head, his long hair flying wild under his hat. "Nothing has changed! Nothing! The Yankees have killed one of my sisters and crippled another, and I won't turn back until I've killed two hundred of them as payment! And if you try to desert me before that's done, the two-hundred-and-first man I kill will be named Billy Quantrill!"

Quantrill turned to Todd. "George, place Captain Anderson under arrest."

Todd drew his pistol. "I don't think I will," he said, moving his horse to stand beside Anderson's. "We've come to do a thing, so let's do it."

The murmurs among the men grew louder.

"What's wrong with you?" Gregg shouted at Todd and Anderson. "Colonel Quantrill is your commanding officer!"

Todd sneered. "No more of that 'Colonel' bullshit. Jefferson Davis wouldn't give this coward the time of day, much less a commission."

At that, Frank James, John McCorkle, and Cole Younger moved to stand with Anderson and Todd. Bill Gregg, Andy Blunt, and John Holt moved to stand with Quantrill. The murmurs among the bushwhackers became shouts and curses. A few men broke away and rode back up the hill.

Sam decided that he didn't care to see the outcome. He began edging backward, but came up against the dead mule.

Quantrill looked as calm as an undertaker. "All right, boys," he said. "I guess you're right. We've come this far, and we've whipped Yankee soldiers before." He pointed toward Lawrence. "Let's push on!"

"That's more like it," Anderson said, and he and his comrades turned their horses toward Lawrence.

As soon as they had turned, Quantrill pulled two of his pistols from his belt, cocked them, and shot Bill Anderson in the back. Anderson slumped, and his horse reared.

The hillside erupted into an inferno of muzzle flashes, explosions, and screams.

Sam dove over the mule and huddled against its back until he heard pistol balls thudding into its belly. Then he rolled away and scrambled down the hill on his hands and knees. When there were plenty of trees between him and the fighting, he got to his feet and ran. He fell several times before reaching the bottom of the hill, but didn't let that slow him.

The trees gave way to prairie grass and scrub brush at the base of the hill, and Sam ran straight for Lawrence. He couldn't see Henry and Bixby on the plain ahead, so he hoped they were already in town.

Thunder rumbled behind him, and he looked back just in time to see the neck of a horse and the heel of a boot. The boot struck him in the forehead and knocked him down. His hat went flying.

Sam lay on his back and stared up at the brightening sky. Then the silhouette of a horse's head appeared above him, and hot breath blasted his face.

"Get up and take your pistol from your belt," a voice said.

Sam turned over, rose to his knees, and looked up at the rider. It was Fletch Taylor. He had a Colt Navy revolver pointed at Sam's nose.

"You going to kill me, Fletch?" Sam asked.

"Not on your knees," Taylor said. "Stand up, take your pistol from your belt, and die the way a man should."

Sam gave a low, bitter chuckle. He was amazed to discover that he wasn't afraid.

"All men die alike, Fletch," he said. "Reluctantly."

Taylor kept his pistol pointed at Sam for another few seconds, then cursed and uncocked it. He looked toward the hill. "Listen to all the hell you've raised," he said.

The sounds of gunshots and screams were wafting out over the plain like smoke.

Taylor looked back at Sam. "You saved my life," he said, "so now I'm giving you yours. But if I ever see you again, I'll kill you."

Sam nodded. "Thank you, Fletch."

Taylor's lips curled back from his teeth. "Go to hell," he said. Then he spurred his horse and rode back toward the hill.

Sam watched Taylor go until he realized that the fighting on the hillside was spilling onto the plain. He stood, found his hat — the hat that Taylor had given him — and ran for Lawrence again.

When he reached Massachusetts Street, staggering, exhausted, he saw men in the windows of every building. Some wore blue uniforms, but most were civilians. Each man held either a revolver or a carbine. The sun was rising, and Lawrence was awake. One of the men came outside and pointed his rifle at Sam, but the boy named Henry appeared and stopped him. Then Henry grabbed Sam's arm and pulled him into the Whitney House.

Fifteen minutes later, Sam was watching from the window of a second-floor room when a magnificent black horse came galloping up Massachusetts Street. The horse's rider, wearing an embroidered gray shirt, gray pants, and black cavalry boots, had his arms tied behind his back and his feet tied to his stirrups. His head and shoulders had been daubed with pitch and set ablaze. He was screaming.

"It's Quantrill!" someone cried.

A volley of shots exploded from both sides of the street, and the horse and rider fell over dead.

Within seconds, a hundred Missouri guerrillas led by George Todd charged up the street. Fourteen of them were cut down in a hail of lead balls, and the rest turned and fled, with soldiers and citizens pursuing. A company of Negro Federal recruits led the chase and killed three more bushwhackers at the southern edge of town.

When the gunfire and shouting had ceased, a cluster of townspeople gathered around the carcass of the black horse and the charred, bloody corpse of its rider. The crowd parted to let two men in black suits and hats approach the bodies. Sam recognized them as the preachers that he, Taylor, and Noland had encountered the week before.

The elder preacher held a Bible over Quantrill's corpse. "Earth to earth," he intoned.

The younger preacher raised his Bible as well. "Ashes to ashes," he said.

In unison, they chanted, "And dust to dust."

Then they lowered their Bibles, drew their revolvers, and shot Quantrill a few more times for good measure.

"Amen," said the crowd.

Sam closed his curtains.

Senator Jim Lane had returned to Lawrence on Wednesday for a railroad meeting, and he sent for Sam at noon on Saturday, one day after the failed raid. Lane was thinner, younger, and had more hair than Sam had guessed from the caricatures, but his fine house on the western edge of town was all that Sam had supposed. It was packed with expensive furnishings, including two pianos in the parlor.

"How did you come to acquire two pianos, Senator?" Sam asked. He had not slept the night before and did not care if he sounded accusatory.

Lane smiled. "One was my mother's," he said. "The other belonged to a secessionist over in Jackson County who found that he no longer had a place to keep it." The Senator picked up a pen and wrote a few lines on a piece of paper, then folded the paper and pushed it across the table. "Kansas is grateful to you, Mister Clemens, and regrets the mistake of two years past when members of the Red-Legged Guards mistook your brother for a slaveholder. Had they known of his appointment as Secretary of Nevada Territory, I'm sure the tragedy would not have occurred."

"He told them," Sam said. "They didn't believe him."

Lane shrugged. "What's done is done, but justice will be served. General Ewing has ordered his troops to arrest all Red Legs they encounter. He believes that such men have been committing criminal acts in the name of liberty, and I must concur." He tapped the piece of paper. "I'm told that Governor

Nye of Nevada Territory is again in need of a Secretary. I cannot guarantee you the appointment, but this should smooth your way." He leaned forward. "Frankly, Mr. Clemens, I think your decision to continue to Nevada is a good one. There are those in this town who believe that the burning man was not Quantrill at all, and that you are here not as a friend, but as Quantrill's spy."

Sam stared at the piece of paper. "A ticket on the overland stage from St. Joseph is a hundred and fifty dollars," he said. "I have ten."

Lane stood and left the parlor for a few minutes. When he returned, he handed Sam three fifty-dollar bank notes and a bottle of whiskey.

"This was distilled from Kansas corn," the Senator said, tapping the bottle with a fingernail. "I thought you should have something by which to remember my state."

Sam tucked the money into a coat pocket and stood, holding the whiskey bottle by its neck. *My state*, Lane had said. What's done is done.

"Good day, Senator," Sam said. He started to turn away.

"Don't forget my letter of introduction," Lane said.

Sam picked up the piece of paper, tucked it into his pocket with the money, and left the house.

Henry was standing outside holding Bixby's reins, and twelve Bluebellies waited nearby. They had an extra horse with them.

"Mister Clemens," one of the soldiers called. "Our orders are to escort you to St. Joseph. We're to leave right away." He didn't sound happy about it. All of the Bluebellies in the escort were white, and Sam suspected that this was their punishment for failing to chase the bushwhackers with as much vigor as their Negro counterparts.

Sam nodded to the soldier, then looked down at Henry. "I suppose you want to keep the horse," he said.

"Well, *I* don't," Henry said. "He's mean, if you ask me. But my pa says he'll either have Bixby as payment for his mule, or he'll take it out of somebody's hide. And since you're running off, I reckon my hide will do him as well as any."

"A hiding would probably do you a considerable amount

of good," Sam said, "but since I no longer have a use for the animal, you may keep him and the saddle as well. I'll take the bags, however." He removed the saddlebags from the horse and put the bottle of whiskey into one of them. A few lumps of brown sugar lay at the bottom of that bag, so he fed one to Bixby. Bixby chewed and swallowed, then tried to bite Sam's hand. Sam gave the rest of the sugar to Henry and took his saddlebags to the soldiers' extra horse.

"Goodbye, Mister Clemens," Henry said, climbing onto Bixby. "I won't forget you."

Sam swung up onto his own mount. "Thank you, boy," he said, "but I shall be doing my best to forget *you*, as well as every other aspect of this infected pustule of a city."

Henry gave him a skeptical look. "Mister Clemens," he said, "I think you're a liar."

"I won't dispute that," Sam said. "I only wish I could make it pay."

The Bluebellies set off, and Sam's mount went with them. Sam looked back to give Henry and Bixby a wave, but they were already heading in the other direction and didn't see him.

On the way to the ferry, Sam and the soldiers passed by the Eldridge House, where eighteen bodies had been laid out on the sidewalk. They were already beginning to stink. A number of townspeople were still gathered here, and from what Sam could hear, they were curious about the dead black man, who had been one of the three raiders killed by the Negro recruits. Why on earth, they wondered, would a man of his race ride with Quantrill?

Sam started to say, "Because he was paid," but the words froze in his throat.

The last four bodies on the sidewalk were those of George Todd, Cole Younger, Frank James, and Fletcher Taylor.

Sam looked away and rode on.

He spent Saturday night camped beside the road with the soldiers and Sunday night in a hotel in St. Joseph, and did not sleep either night. At daybreak on Monday, he carried his saddlebags to the overland stage depot, paid his money, and boarded the coach. Two other passengers and several sacks of mail soon joined him, and the coach set off westward at eight o'clock.

As the coach passed the spot where Orion had been killed, Sam took out the whiskey that Lane had given him and began drinking. He offered some to his fellow passengers, but they each took one swallow and then refused more, saying that it was the vilest stuff they'd ever tasted. Sam agreed, but drank almost half the bottle anyway.

At the next station stop, he climbed atop the coach with his saddlebags while the horses were being changed. When the coach started moving again, Sam drank more whiskey and stared at the fields of green and gold. Soon, his head warm with sun and alcohol, it occurred to him that the corn and grass shifting in the breeze looked like ocean swells after a storm. He was reminded of a holiday he had spent near New Orleans, looking out at the Gulf of Mexico after piloting a steamboat down the Mississippi. He wondered if he would love anything in Nevada half as much.

The thought of Nevada reminded him of the letter that Jim Lane had written for him, so he took it out and read it:

> My dear Governor Nye:
> You will recall that your intended Secretary of two years past, Mr. Orion Clemens, was unfortunately killed before he could assume his duties. This letter will introduce his younger brother Samuel, who has provided service to his Nation and is a loyal Republican. I trust you shall do your utmost to secure for him any employment for which he might be suited.
> Yours most sincerely,
>
> James Lane, Senator
> The Great and Noble State of Kansas

Sam tore up the letter and let its pieces scatter in the wind. If Nevada held "any employment for which he might be suited," he would secure it without any assistance from a self-righteous, thieving son of a bitch like Jim Lane.

Nor would he drink any more of Lane's abominable whiskey. He leaned over the coach roof's thin iron rail and emptied the bottle onto the road. Then he opened one of his saddlebags, took out his Colt, and stood. He held the whiskey bottle in his left hand and the pistol in his right.

The coach conductor glanced back at him. "What are you doing, sir?" he asked.

Sam spread his arms. "I am saying fare-thee-well to the bloody state of Kansas," he cried, "and lighting out for the Territory!"

He looked out over the tall grass. It rippled in waves.

He missed the river.

He missed his brothers.

But killing men for the sake of a world that was gone wouldn't bring it back. It was time to make a new one.

"Half-less twain!" he cried.

Both the conductor and driver stared back at him.

"Quarter-less twain!" Sam shouted.

Then he brought his left arm back and whipped it forward, throwing the bottle out over the grass. As it reached the apex of its flight, he brought up his right arm, cocked the Colt with his thumb, and squeezed the trigger.

The bottle exploded into brilliant shards.

The coach lurched, and Sam sat down on the roof with a thump.

"Goddamn it!" the conductor yelled. "You spook these horses again, and I'll throw you off!"

Sam held the pistol by its barrel and offered it to the conductor. "Please accept this," he said, "with my apologies."

The conductor took it. "I'll give it back when you're sober."

"No," Sam said, "you won't."

Then he threw back his head and roared: "MAAARRRRK TWAIIINN!"

Two fathoms. Safe water.

He lay down with his hat over his face and fell asleep, and no dead men came to haunt his dreams.

For Sam Clemens, the war was over.

Acknowledgments

The author would like to thank Edward L. Ferman, publisher of *The Magazine of Fantasy and Science Fiction*, for reasons that will be obvious to anyone who reads the copyright page.

The author would also like to thank John and Kim Betancourt of The Wildside Press.

I am indebted to Howard Waldrop for his swell Waldroppian Introduction, Douglas Potter for his stunning illustrations, and Earl Cooley for heroic textfile conversions.

I am also indebted to my family and to far more friends than I can name for their encouragement and love. I hope you all know who you are.

Especially you, Barb.

       — Bradley Denton
        Austin, Texas
        October, 1991